THE COUNTERFEIT GIRL

a novel

Ryan McKaig

For Kelley and Jack

Now he has departed from this strange world a little ahead of me. That means nothing. People like us, who believe in physics, know that the distinction between past, present, and future is only a stubbornly persistent illusion.

Albert Einstein

For the last few months a man has been traveling about the city, known as the "Confidence Man." That is, he would go up to a perfect stranger in the street, and being a man of genteel appearance, would easily command an interview. Upon this interview he would say after some little conversation, "Have you confidence in me to trust me with your watch until tomorrow?" The stranger, at this novel request, supposing him to be some old acquaintance not at that moment recollected, allows him to take the watch, thus placing "confidence" in the honesty of the stranger, who walks off laughing and the other supposing it to be a joke allows him to do so.

The New York Herald
July 8, 1849

PART ONE

The Runaway

CHAPTER ONE

The preacher closed the book and folded his hands over it. "Receive now thy soul to heaven, O Lord," he said.

He put the book under his arm and walked out of the room, leaving the girl there alone with her mother. The hand of the mother resting in the hand of the child.

The last words hanging in the air and death having sealed the maternal lips, the girl sat there unable to breathe, the moment long in coming and now at last here. The person she loved most in the world now gone from her, departed, her spirit unmoored in the Sheol mist for all eternity.

The frozen image. Her mother's waxen and dead face. Gray and ridged and serene. The still lips. The black hair with streaks of gray.

The girl sat there for one long moment and then she folded her mother's hand over her heart and gently let go of it. She leaned forward in the chair and began sobbing into her hands. Tears came through the spaces between her fingers and fell in peppering drops on the floor.

She could feel the warmth from the last coursing of blood through the veins in her mother's hand. She felt the fading mortal heat against her fingers, against her face.

⚊⊰⊱⚊

Night fell in the rolling darkness beyond the light of the eaves and the old people walked the floorboards in casual bereavement. They talked about the departed and those who had preceded her. It was as though she had been dead for years.

They spoke of Daggett, the girl's great uncle, who lived in his car and had an orange cat named Cornbread who lived there with him. He died of a heart attack drinking a beer on the tailboard of a pickup truck, they said.

They remembered burying him in the woods after a long wandering procession with dirges playing. The men went the day before and dug the grave. They passed a bottle of Tennessee sour mash and a shovel and climbed in and out of the grave, sweating and grunting like apes. The next day they marched in a funeral parade through the woods.

They stood at the gravesite in the rain. They sang Amazing Grace and the preacher took off his hat and shook the rain from it. He read a simple eulogy and consecrated the ground as a ground fit to rest a man, entrusting it with his bones for a holy purpose.

They remembered her great aunt Punch, who wasted away with cancer and had her ashes scattered in the moonrise over Cherry Grove, where the ancient trawlers rode the sea plain like mechanical spiders lighting a trail through the black water. What an angel she was, somebody said.

The next few days brought a parade of mourners and more ceremonies of remembrance. They all wore black suits and gowns. The girl made her way into the church hall and saw her mother in the casket banked by bright flowers and she broke down at the sight of her mother lying there, so still and on display.

There was a picture of them there, next to the casket, all three of them together and smiling. She walked to the banks of flowers and folds of funeral cloth and stepped up on the tips of her toes to the coffin and saw the body of her mother lying on the yellow satin bed. It didn't look like any person she had ever known. The girl leaned over and kissed her mother goodbye and there was an otherwordly coldness to the kiss.

Poor little thing, someone said. Her mamma and daddy both now.

The house was filled with the smells of cooking and cigarette smoke. There was fried spot fish and steamed oysters and sweet cornbread baked in the pan. Baskets of buttermilk biscuits wrapped in cloth napkins to keep them warm and bubbling pots of Frogmore stew.

The aunts and uncles drank their cans of Budweiser and smoked their cigarettes. They stamped them out in the empty beer cans. They shook their heads and laughed and told stories about the old days.

Someone brought a square of plywood in from the garage and using a magic marker they diagrammed out the family history. Names and dates and places. Birthdates and death dates. They put it up over the hearth as a crude but collective family memorial to all those who had gone before them. Those who were born and those who had died. They all raised a drink to them and uncle Bunny proposed a toast.

The girl sat there transfixed at the sight of all the names. Her eyes ran down the board, ticking off faces in her mind's eye. The last name was her mother's name. When she closed her eyes, she could see her mother's face but the image kept changing. Sometimes she was young, sometimes she was old and sick, and sometimes she was alive and sometimes she was dead.

She read the names and said them to herself. It was important to say the names, her mother always said, because their names brought back memories of their stories and in turn acknowledged that their lives mattered and that other people loved them and remembered them. Saying their names was a prayer. That God might smile upon them and watch over them. That they all might someday gather again in reunion on the green meadows of Paradise.

The next morning, the girl stood alone under a raining sky and watched them lower her mother's coffin into the ground.

When the mourners left, she sat under a tree on the hill above and watched the backhoe cover up the hole. She watched them scrape the ground level and affix the tombstone. They clapped the mud out of their hands and left for the day laughing.

When she got home, she went upstairs and checked her mother's drawer where she kept the savings. She found the box and opened it and counted out the roll of twenties. There was three hundred sixty dollars in cash.

She packed her bags and when she was done, she waited for the darkness and when it came she sat there and watched the moon settle over the long empty fields and then she took out a pen and wrote down her mother's last words and closed them up in the purple notebook with all of her stories. The words were her warrant and her shibboleth.

She placed the notebook in a bag along with some clothes and then she left home forever.

CHAPTER TWO

She made it through town and put out her thumb and stood there in the blackness along the side of the road and waited for the world to come. Some cars passed at first and then none for awhile and not one of them stopped for her. She walked along the road with her bag slung over her back.

After a while a blue truck pulled over and a man wearing overalls and a John Deere baseball cap rolled down the window and leaned out to look at her. He waved her on in.

"Where you goin to, girl?" the man said.

"Florence," she said.

"What you goin there for?"

"I'm just catching a bus there. I'm really going to Charleston."

"Charlestown?"

"Yes sir."

"Well get on in here then. I'm headed by Florence. I can take you there."

She climbed up into the truck. The man smiled a hideous smile at her and nodded. He was chewing tobacco. He spat the juice out into the grass beside the road.

"You got family in Charlestown or somethin?"

She looked at the man and then looked back at the road again.

"My grandma," she said.

"Your grandmamma live there?"

"Yes sir. She's been sick. It's been awhile now. I'm going to see her. Maybe sit with her for awhile."

"Ever been there before?"

"No sir."

"You never been to see her before?"

"I been to see her before but not there. She used to live in Greenville. I used to go see her there. Like I said, it's been awhile."

He mashed the clutch and the gas and throttled the truck back onto the highway and slowly began to speed it up.

"So you ain't never been there?"

"No sir."

The man adjusted his hat. "Heck of a good town," he said. "They call it the holy city, on account of the churches and all."

"That's what I always heard," the girl said. "My mama always said it was like a city in a dream."

"It's nice there. It's real pretty. I've been there a couple of times and it's nice."

"I can't hardly wait."

The dark land whirled past. After awhile the man introduced himself.

"I'm Buddy, by the way," the man said. "Buddy Maynard. From Mobile, Alabama originally. Now I live in Hotlanta."

The girl nodded and smiled and looked away for a moment and then looked back up at him.

"I'm Lee Ann Pickler," she said.

⟞⟨⟞ ⟝⟩⟝

They drove on through the night. The man found an exit and pulled off the interstate. He bought her a Coca-Cola and some powdered donuts. They shared the donuts and the man drank his coffee and fiddled with the radio while the girl stared out at the interstate and the passing cars.

"What kind of music you like?" the man said.

"All kinds, I guess," she said.

"You don't mind old country music?"

"No sir. Not a bit."

"All right then," he said. He turned up the radio and she heard the familiar sounds of Emmylou Harris singing If I Needed You. She eased into the seat.

They pulled back onto the road and drove straight into the rising sun. Red streaks in the sky came reaching over the long horizon and the feathery tissues of morning clouds replaced the drowning stars. They reached Florence at breakfast time. The man stopped at a fast food restaurant and bought her a country ham biscuit and then dropped her off at the bus station.

"Thank you, mister," she said. "It sure was nice talking to you."

"You too," the man said. "Good luck to you." Then he turned the truck and slowly drove away.

She stood there. She looked out over the street and felt the heat of the morning air. The sun was beneath the trees but the air was choking. The heat rose from the ground and drove the insects to swarm in the grass.

She watched the trucks come rumbling down the street. They squealed their brakes in front of the shops. The men got out and began unloading the boxes.

The sound was the sound of a machine starting up. It was metal banging metal, things rolling in and out on carts and squeaking up and down loading ramps, doors opening and slamming shut. It was slow and clanking, the music of the world enlivening in the fire of the morning. The sun was rising over the treetops.

So this is Florence, she said.

CHAPTER THREE

She found the bus station and went inside and paid cash for a seat on the ten thirty bus to Charleston. She put some coins in the vending machines and bought a coke and some M&M's, then took a seat in one of the plastic chairs against the wall. She had a feeling of excitement that she could barely contain.

She suddenly felt exposed. She looked up and saw the eyes of two lecherous men greasing onto her from the opposite rows of benches. One man was maybe fifty five and the other closer to forty, she guessed. She saw them eyeing each other and then giggling to each other. After awhile they came over and sat down next to her, one on either side.

"What's a nice pretty young thing like you doin traveling all by your lonesome?" one of the men said.

She looked away.

"Just on my way to Charleston."

"Charlestown, huh? You from Charlestown?"

"No."

"Then why you goin there?"

"Cause I feel like it."

The older man wiped his nose and then looked around.

"Look, if you're a little short on cash, maybe me and Lester here could help you out a little bit."

She looked at the man, saw his eyes on her.

"I ain't short on cash."

"I'm just saying if you're looking to make a little extra. . . ."

"What are you getting at?" she said.

"You know, we'll help you out a little bit. If you help us out a little bit."

"Help you out?"

"Yeah."

"Help you out how?"

"Like. . . I don't know like what."

"What do you want?"

The man leaned forward.

"Look, it don't even have to be nothin dirty. You could just show us your underpants. Let us take a picture of you."

She looked at them and tasted the acid coming up from her stomach. She tried to compose herself.

"Go to hell," she said.

The older man's face changed.

"Now that's no kinda way to be, young lady. I'm tryin to help you here."

"Go to hell. Just go to hell."

A policeman appeared in the doorway and then wandered into the large hall. He saw the two men seated next to the young girl and saw her face wrinkled in anger. He saw her eyes meet his and then immediately she looked away. He became suspicious and walked over to the row of seats where the three of them were sitting.

"Ya'll know each other?" he said.

"Not before just now, but we sure do now," said the man. "I'm glad you're here officer."

The officer looked at the girl. She looked away again.

"This here little thing is selling her own self right here in this bus station."

"This true?" the policeman asked her.

She looked at him with astonishment.

"Damn sure true," the older man said. "Me and Lester here. We's just waiting on the ten thirty bus to Atlanta and this little thing come up and offer to give us each a blow job for twenty dollars."

"That right?" said the policeman.

"Ask Lester, he'll tell you," said the man.

"That's right," Lester said. "That's just what she done."

"They're lying," she said. "They're both fat lying perverts."

"Don't make sense that both of them would be lying," said the officer.

She looked away and crossed her arms and seethed.

"Think you better come with me, miss."

The officer took her out of the bus station in handcuffs. He drove her to the station and they booked her and processed her into the jail. A female officer put on a rubber glove and started to go through Lee Ann's pockets.

"Anything sharp in here I need to know about?" the officer said.

"What do you mean?"

"You got any needles or razor blades in here or anything. You better tell me before I stick my hand in there."

"No."

The officer emptied out the contents of her pockets and turned over the roll of twenties. She shook her head.

"Naw, you ain't been selling it, have you girl?" said the officer.

"That's money my mama saved up," Lee Ann said. "That's all the money she had."

The officer laughed. "That's a good one," she said. "You'll have to tell that one to the judge."

The officer put her up before a white background and told her to look into the eye of the camera.

"Hold this," he said, handing her a black plate with numbers and words on it. Lee Ann Pickler, it said.

Prostitution.

She steeled a defiant look into the black camera lens and held the numbers under her chin. A young cop with a fat face and a black mustache smiled at her from behind the camera.

"Say Conway Twitty," he said.

CHAPTER FOUR

S he stayed in jail for nine days eating baloney sandwiches on white bread and drinking little square boxes of milk. She met a real prostitute named Destinee and Destinee explained to her that jail was like being in kindergarten all over again. It was boring, but you got used to it, she said.

"When it comes to jail, there's only one thing you need to know," Destinee said. "Don't get nobody else to pay no attention to you."

"Why's that?" Lee Ann said.

"That's just the way the good Lord made it, I reckon."

She lay against the wall thinking about what she should do next. She did not know what actions to undertake. But she knew the name of the place in which she would undertake them. She saw it in her mind. It had been there for years. In her dreams. It was blasted on the wall of her imaginary memories. She had seen it a thousand times, but only in her mind and in some pictures. There were old mansions built on the brink of the sea with flags on their porches and a black sky full of stars and a moon dripping like a candle in the water.

Charleston.

It was cobblestone streets and soaring churches and Dixieland jazz playing on the sidewalk. Her mother used to talk about it all the time.

After nine days a guard came and turned a key unlocking the cell door and brought her out and they put her on a bus with other prisoners and drove her across a river to a redbrick courthouse standing in the center of two curving roads on a grassy meadow.

They parked in a garage under the courthouse and brought them up single file and loaded them into a holding cell and then brought them up in an elevator one by one as their cases were called.

When they brought her into the courtroom, the men from the bus station were nowhere to be seen. They appointed her a lawyer and she told the lawyer the story and then the lawyer talked to the D.A. and when he came back he told her the D.A. had agreed to dismiss the charges and let her go.

"Can I get my money back?" she asked the lawyer.

"Don't press your luck," he said.

When they released her, the same female officer who had processed her held the door open for her as she walked out.

"Good luck," said the officer.

Lee Ann kept walking, not looking back and not saying a word.

Yellow wires of lightning crossed in the distant skies but there was no thunder and no rain. Mist clogged the long empty fields. Out of town now, she walked and walked, a lonely girl on a road to nowhere. The grimy smell of creosote and chimney smoke teased at her in the breeze.

In the distance she saw a water tower shaped like a giant peach, leafed and ripe and enormous, the land rising up behind it and dark storm clouds gathering up on the edge of the world there.

The air cooled and the breeze lifted in the colonnades of the forest. She walked alone in the dark.

When the moon reached its peak, she left the road and walked up into the pine forest. She settled onto the leeward slope of a dark hill. She sat under the lights of a large billboard with a cartoon caricature. Sixty three miles, it said.

She watched the cars and trucks roll past below. She took out her purple notebook and tried to write something but the words would not come.

Eventually she got up and walked further into the woods in search of a place to sleep. She got down on her knees and scraped together a pallet of broomstraw and made a bed and climbed into it. A crooked pine tree was her headboard. She pulled the leaves around her and over her, piling them into a blanket to cover her. She used her bag as a pillow.

She closed her eyes and felt the darkness of the woods and assessed her place in them. The forest ticked and creaked around her. She listened to the singsong of Cicadas rattling their timbals high in the trees.

She remembered the way her mother used to tuck her in at night and the prayer they used to say and the way they used to say it. She remembered her room. The pink trim on white molding and the unicorns raring up and down the sides of a window. The egg-colored wainscoting. The darkness beyond the tree-shaded window and the long green fields below. The familiar barking of her dogs in the distance.

Now I lay me down to sleep. I pray the Lord my soul to keep. If I should die before I wake. I pray the Lord my soul to take. Amen.

Memories haunting her brain, she allowed the darkness to swallow her and she slept, a teenage orphan girl lying on the pine needled floor of the forest, defenseless and cold and alone in the night woods.

━◁┼▷━

She came awake to the screams of invisible birds. She opened her eyes and saw the forest in the mist. Dreams fast unspooling in her head.

She tried to hold onto the faces of the people in her dreams but was mostly unsuccessful, yet she retained the feelings they gave her. Inchoate thoughts haunted her brain. The ghosts were still there.

She remembered her mother's last words. She held them tightly against herself, saying them over and over. She was wet and freezing.

She wanted to feel sorry for herself but knew that the woods and the road were her home now and she decided she had better become accustomed to them if she was to live in them for very long and that, besides, it did her no good to feel sorry for herself when there was no one else left to feel sorry for her. Her life was a wasted act of pity.

She looked at her hands. They were covered in dirt and they looked so small. Worthless, she said. Worthless.

She looked around the forest. It was flooded with orange straw like the hair of dolls. Trees rose up like tombstones covered in green awning. The animals all hid from each other. One deer and several birds and small woodland creatures came out to look at her from a distance. They cocked their heads in suspicion of her. To hell with you all then, she said.

The forest was dark and directionless, a maze of black creek water and pine bracken. So what, she said. This was the place she was standing, and this place would now be her home until she could find a better home. The woods were a total mystery to her. She didn't know what was safe to eat or drink.

She finally decided that she would not make it there for long, and that there was no way to sustain her except to find a town and go into it to beg or steal.

She wandered through the forest and by suppertime she came upon the rise of a hill overlooking a small town. There were rows of two-story houses and a park with a baseball diamond.

She looked across the field to the tower of a church steeple reaching out over a long wall of blue glass. The sign of the cross lay in relief against the dark background. She took a seat on the hillside and watched the sky redden against the church and marveled at the stained glass glowing and coruscating in the dying sunlight.

A blood red horizon held up the falling sky. She listened to the bell's tolling, counted seven tolls, and waited. After awhile she stood up and dusted herself off and began to walk down the hill in the direction of the church.

CHAPTER FIVE

The priest pulled the chasuble over his head and took the ribbon stolewise from his neck. He unfastened the buttons on the prayer robe and removed it and hung the vestments on a wire coat hanger in the vestry closet and closed the door.

He then picked up a brass candle snuffer from the desk and went out into the church to suffocate the prayer candles.

He smothered the prayer candles one at a time. He watched the thin trails of smoke crook their way upward and die in the air. He turned off the lights above the altar and went to retrieve his keys and coat from the vestry. When he was halfway out the door he turned and looked once more into the nave of the church, seized as he was with the brief sensation that eyes had fixed onto his back.

Hiding in the shadows of the pews was a girl, perhaps in her late teens. She was skinny and pale and half her face was hidden in the darkness.

The priest stepped back into the doorway and allowed the door to shut behind him.

"Come on out of there," he said.

There was no movement.

"I said come out."

The girl stood up and watched the priest across the distance between them.

"What are you doing in here?" he said. "The church is closed, you know."

"I know it," the girl said. "I was just looking for someplace to sleep tonight. I wasn't going to mess nothin up."

The priest took a step toward the girl and she took a step back.

"Come here closer, so I can have a look at you," he said.

The girl didn't move.

"Come here. I'm not going to hurt you."

"I know."

"Come on."

She came forward and the priest looked her over. She was wearing wrinkled jeans tracked with dirt and mud caked shoes.

"You a runaway?"

The girl nodded.

"Where you from?"

"Someplace I'm never going back to."

"How long you been gone?"

"I don't know. A week maybe."

"How have you been living?"

"I had some money but that got taken from me. I've mostly been living here and there. I'm on my way to Charleston."

"What's in Charleston?"

"I don't know. A job maybe."

"But you don't have anything lined up?"

"I don't have anything lined up anywhere. Charleston is as good a place as any."

"How old are you?"

"I'll be eighteen in a week and a half."

"When was the last time you had something to eat?"

"I had a candy bar earlier."

The priest shook his head.

"Look at you," he said.

"If you let me stay just tonight, I'll be gone in the morning. Promise. I won't touch anything."

"We need to get you some help."

"I just need a place to stay, that's all. It's going to be cold out there tonight," she said.

"Why don't you go home?"

She shook her head.

"What's your name?" the priest said.

"Lee Ann," she said.

"Tell me about it then."

The priest took off his coat and folded it over his arm and took a seat on one of the pews. He patted the wooden plank with his hand. "Sit down," he said.

Lee Ann sat.

"What's so bad that you can't go back to it?"

"I can't," she said. "I just can't."

"Is it your family life?"

"I guess you could say that."

"Has someone abused you? You can talk to me about it. Anything you say is in strict confidence. It won't leave this room."

"No," she said. "Nothing like that."

"So it's something with your family then?"

"I guess you could say that."

"Family is struggle," said the priest. "Life is struggle. But the reward does not come from the struggle. The reward is the struggle. Running away won't change anything."

She shook her head.

The priest looked at her. "You think you're the first person to feel this way?" he said.

"No."

"I'll bet wherever it is you're from, there's a mother pacing back and forth in her kitchen worrying herself sick over her little girl."

"No there's not," she said.

The priest stopped.

"She's dead. That's how come I left. My daddy too. I didn't run away, mister. I escaped. I escaped from a place that didn't exist no more. Everything there is dead as far as I'm concerned. I just need to start over."

"You have no parents?"

"Nope."

"There's no one else you can stay with?"

"I got some aunts and uncles and some cousins."

"You can't stay with them?"

"No."

"Why not?"

"I just wanted to leave, mister. I don't know how else I can say it."

"And you have no one else?"

"No one to speak of."

"No brothers or sisters?"

"Nope."

The priest looked away into the darkness where the altar hid in shadows from the moonlight coming in through the stained glass windows. Then he looked at the ground.

"What made you come here?"

"I thought maybe you'd help me."

"Do you believe in salvation?" he said.

"What?"

"Salvation. Everlasting life through faith in Christ."

The girl nodded. "I was raised to," she said. "I'm sure hoping for it."

"Good," said the priest. "That's good."

"I was raised a Baptist."

"So you know about heaven?"

"Yes."

"And you know that if you have faith you'll see them again, don't you?"

The girl nodded again.

"You look awful depressed."

"I guess I am."

"God says: Blessed are the poor in spirit. For theirs is the kingdom of heaven."

She nodded weakly.

"God's plan is a long plan and an obscure plan," said the priest. "None of us will see it in its fullness. Not in this life anyway. All we are given is our one tiny part of it and the rest he keeps from us. And yes, there is much suffering.

"But I have studied and prayed and doubted just like you are doing. And I really believe this: God loves you. Believe it or not, he does."

She nodded. "I guess," she said.

"Look at the universe," he said. "Is there more evidence of chaos or design? Look at the ocean and the mountains and all the creatures in them and tell me if they are not the work of an artist. He is perfect in the details."

"Sometimes I don't think he even knows I'm alive," she said.

"He knows your name," said the priest. "He knows your name very well. He knows everything about you."

"Can I stay here?"

"Well you can stay the night, but only on one condition."

"What?"

"You must stay for mass in the morning and you must give me the chance to help you find a place to stay around here, temporarily at least. Maybe we could get you in school or help you find a job. There are no orphans in the community of Christ. I'll need time to call some of my parishioners. You can stay here until then."

"I stay for mass?"

"Yes. My oath and my faith require me to seek out charity for you in food and shelter and I am happy to do so. But what good would those things be if I neglected to attend to your soul as well?"

"I've never been to a Catholic mass before."

"Maybe you'll enjoy it."

"Maybe so."

"Just sit back and watch. There's no pressure. You won't share in the Eucharist but you can get in line and come up with everyone else and I'll give you a blessing instead."

"Okay."

"I'm not forcing anything on you, you understand? Man comes to God willingly or not at all. I'm not blackmailing you."

"Okay."

"So you promise then?"

"I promise."

"Do you understand the solemnity of a promise."

"Yes."

"A promise made in God's house?" The priest looked up at the ceiling and made the sign of the cross. The dim images of the saints in the glass stared down at them. Shadow reliefs on the wall showed the carrying of the cross, the crucifixion, the resurrection.

"I think so," she said.

"That's good enough, I suppose."

The girl nodded.

"So you mean it then?"

The girl nodded. "Yes," she said.

"Good."

"Okay then."

"I'll see you in the morning."

"See you then."

The girl waited for the priest to leave and then retrieved some robes from the coatrack and used them to lay a pallet on the floor.

She covered herself in a robe as a blanket and she slept in the warmth of the church. She had a feeling of safety, of peace, and the dreams passed on in the night and none stuck in her head but she awoke with a feeling of renewal and hope and therefore decided that she must have dreamed good dreams during the night.

In the morning the priest returned. He brought her two country ham biscuits and a bottle of milk to drink as he considered that she must be hungry and thirsty from such a long journey in which she had carried with her both grief and uncertainty. Faith is a kernel encircling the heart, he told himself.

When he got there the church was empty.

He set down the food and began looking around the church for the girl. He called out her name and opened the doors to the office and to the cellars and even opened the door to the outside and shouted her name but she was gone. He went into his office and went through his drawers and was relieved to find that nothing was taken. Everything was as it should be. The girl had vanished like the smoke from a prayer candle, a wisp floating before his eyes and vanishing forever.

He took a seat and wondered about the girl. There wasn't much you could say about her. She had mostly kept her word. She had not betrayed or deceived him in any manner save the breaking of her promise to allow his further attendance to her inmost wounds.

CHAPTER SIX

She was hungry now and broke in Santee. She found a Wal-Mart and went inside and thought about what she could steal.

She stood among the aisle of candy and various snacks looking out for anyone wearing a blue vest. She watched the people in the blue vests walking back and forth and when none of them were looking she stuffed a bag of peanut M&M's into her handbag along with a Dr. Pepper and squeezed the handbag tight. When she bypassed the register and walked back out into the parking lot, a swollen young man followed behind her. He was wearing jeans and a Clemson Tigers t-shirt.

"Excuse me, miss," he said.

Lee Ann turned around.

"What is it?" she said, smiling sweetly.

The man reached into his pocket and took out his badge. "You know what you done," he said.

He grabbed her around the arm gently and dragged her back toward the store.

"Come on with me," he said. "I seen you, girl."

Her brought her back to an office. She sat there with her knees trembling while he called the police and they waited for them to show up and then he handed her over to them.

"Don't you never come back," he said.

"They said don't never come back to Wal-Mart?" the officer said.

"Yeah."

"They call that the redneck death penalty, you know."

"I know."

"This your first offense?"

She nodded. Tears ran down her face.

"It ain't the end of the world you know?"

She nodded and cried.

"Look, you stay out of trouble from here on, this won't be nothin."

"I've never done anything like this before," she said.

"I can understand somebody stealing food because they're hungry. Anybody can make a mistake," he said. "But doing it again makes you just a criminal. Excuse or no excuse."

"I ain't never going to do it again."

"Well good then. You ain't got nothin to worry about."

"What's going to happen to me now?"

The man shrugged. "Probably nothin," he said. "They call your mama and daddy maybe."

She shook her head. "They won't have no luck with that."

"Where you from, girl?"

"Carthage."

"Where's that?"

"Up near Nichols."

"I never heard of Nichols."

"It's not too far from Dillon."

"What does your daddy do back there?"

"He don't do nothing. He's dead."

"I'm sorry to hear that."

"It's okay."

"What'd he used to do?"

"He ran the press for the newspaper and he farmed."

"How bout your mama."

"She's dead too. Died two weeks ago."

"Damn girl, I'm sorry."

She nodded and wiped her nose.

"You stayin with family now?"

"No sir."

"You got any place to go?"

"No sir."

The man shook his head in pity. "Damn girl," he said. "What are you going to do now?"

"I don't know," she said.

She looked out through the office window through the rows of retail trash. The stacks of peanut cans and DVDs and fishing rods, a glass encasement filled with shotguns and rifles against the back wall under a camouflage tent hanging from the high ceiling.

She wiped the tears from her eyes.

"I got an idea, but I don't know."

"Let's hear it," said the cop.

"It might sound funny to you. But I can do the work, I can. Swear to God."

"I believe you."

She wiped her eyes with her sleeve.

"I thought I might could get a job as a reporter," she said.

CHAPTER SEVEN

The magistrate placed her under a two hundred dollar cash bond and she stayed in jail for two weeks until her court date. There in her cell, she made a cross from string. She wove it in braids, using the knots to form the base and the crossbeam. She told herself stories. Over and over. Her lips silently moved and she would lie there and hold onto the cross, a weird ritual which alienated her from the others.

When they brought her to court, she met with her court appointed attorney and they spoke in a box, communicating through a telephone and looking at each other through plate glass.

"You can get out today if you want to plead guilty," the lawyer said.

"I can?"

"Yeah."

"I should do that then, huh?"

"Probably so. They got their witnesses here. Store security guy and the cop."

"What will that mean?"

"They'll put you on unsupervised probation. Hang thirty days over your head. Maybe forty five."

"Probation?"

"It's nothing. Don't screw up again and you got nothing to worry about."

"Okay."

"I'll have the sheriff bring you out. D.A. says she's ready to do it as soon as we can get them to bring you out."

She hung up the phone and banged on the door but no one came. She sat down again and waited and after awhile a deputy opened the door and brought her out into a large courtroom walled in cherry wood and trimmed with mahogany. The judge was a man with an enormous head as if made of granite with patches of white hair. The D.A. stated the charges.

"How does your client plead?" the judge said.

"Guilty, your honor," the lawyer said.

"Do you wish to be heard on sentencing?"

"Briefly, your honor."

"All right."

⇒⊹ ⊹⇐

"Your honor, my client as you can see is a young person. She comes from a good home and a good family. She lost her father several years ago in a farming accident and her mother just passed from cancer. This poor girl has been through an awful lot. Now that's no excuse to steal, and I'm not excusing what she done. But your honor, ours is a tribunal in which the courts of law and chancery are merged as one and it is to the latter that my comments are addressed.

"My client is a good person who made a mistake. She was broke and she was hungry and in trying to feed herself she broke the law. That is a fact, your honor, and I will not throw away my credibility or waste this court's time by contesting it. But I will simply ask, respectfully, that this honorable court see fit in its great wisdom to impose a punishment commensurate with the crime and its perpetrator. Anyone can make one mistake, your honor, and everyone deserves a second chance. We are all sinners and we are all capable of redemption. I would ask this court to give my client credit for time served, or in the alternative, place her on unsupervised probation and remit costs and attorney's fees, as she has no present means to pay them."

The judge looked at the girl for a long time then looked at the lawyer, then looked back at the girl.

"Are you in school?" the judge said.

"No sir," she said.

"Did you finish?"

"No sir."

"How far did you go before quitting?"

"Eleventh grade."

The judge just shook his head. "Do you work?" he said.

"No sir," she said. "Not yet. I was going to Charleston to find a job."

"So you're running away?"

"Yes sir. I guess so."

"How old are you?"

"I just turned eighteen the other day."

"Does the state wish to be heard?" he said.

"No, your honor," said the DA.

"Young lady, I have a daughter of my own," said the judge. "My hope for her is that she lives a good life, a life she'll be proud of. My hope is the same for you. I see young people such as yourself appearing before me all the time and it's happening a lot more now than it used to. Kids who have given up on themselves, given up on their lives. Don't you make that mistake. You hear me? I am moved by your attorney's thoughtful words and am inclined to grant you the mercy he requested. But if I see you again, it will be a different story. Madam clerk, on line 114, on a plea of guilty, enter a judgment of guilty and a sentence of time served. Strike the costs."

She smiled and the judge looked at her strangely and then she changed her expression for fear that he might change his mind and put her back in jail.

"You are free to go, young lady," said the judge. "Best of luck to you."

She had now been arrested twice. Once when she was innocent and once when she was guilty. Now she sat on the swing in an empty park looking up at the moon and the stars and wondering what might be up there. She thought about her mother and wondered if she was really up there with Jesus. If there really was a heaven. If it was real or a fairy tale.

She remembered her mother's last words and said them softly to herself over and over again. She could feel them on her lips and saying them to herself at once startled and comforted her. The feeling pulsed through her body like a gentle current of electricity. She liked it.

She got down on her knees and talked to Jesus and to her mother. She thought God's glory might be one vast and seamless web of interconnected goodness and memory and that both the past and the Creator could hear her and maybe the past could answer back and give comfort to her in the present since both rested entirely with Him.

Maybe the good souls stuck on the web and were preserved and the evil ones fell through the spaces between and disappeared forever. The mystery consumed her, it had always consumed her.

There had to be something. There had to be. She looked up into the sky and imagined the souls of all mankind burning brightly in the empyrean fires. She thought about life everlasting.

She begged God for one last exchange with her mother. She pled desperately. Please Jesus, she said. Please. Oh Please. Just answer me back, Mama. Just one time. Tell me you can hear me. Tell me I'll see you again.

She spoke to her mother in a mournful tone. I never felt so alone, she said. I just miss you all so much. I miss you, she said. I miss you. I miss you.

Her face became slicked with tears.

Nothing moved.

She got up off her knees.

I just love you so much Mama and I miss you. I miss you so much. I really really do, and I can't wait to see you again in heaven.

She sat back up on the swing and tried to feel happy somehow. All around her was neverending night. She was alone and the silhouettes of black empty woods rose like castle walls. She looked up at the sky and rocked back and forth on the swing. She looked up into the stars and stared at them intently and when she was done, she got down on her knees and said the prayer again.

CHAPTER EIGHT

She was broke and exhausted. She walked the blacktop hitch-hiking a ride to nowhere, the sun beating down on her. Toward evening she spotted a roadside motel in the town of Ravenel. It was a pink stucco job with rusted metal support columns holding up the second-floor walkway. She saw a maid in a blue uniform pushing a cart and knocking on doors. She walked over to her.

"Excuse me, ma'am," she said.

"Yes?" the woman said, turning and looking at her. The woman had a wrinkled face like an old paper bag.

"Do you know if they're hiring?"

The woman folded a towel and stacked it on the cart. "Don't know," she said. "You can check with Merle. He's the manager."

"Okay," Lee Ann said.

"Office is over there," the woman said.

"I'm Lee Ann Pickler," she said.

The woman didn't look up. "Nice to meet you," she said. "Good luck."

Merle was a small hairy man smoking a cigarette and drinking a large white mug of coffee. He had a copy of the local newspaper spread out before him. When Lee Ann Pickler's shadow crossed him, he stirred and folded the paper and looked up at the girl in front of him.

"Can I help you?" he said.

"Yes, sir," Lee Ann said. "I was wondering if you needed some more help around here."

The man looked puzzled. He tapped out his ashes into a green plastic ashtray.

"I'm just traveling through and I'm looking for some work," she said. "I thought maybe you needed somebody to turn down bed sheets."

The man just stared.

"I'm a really good worker," Lee Ann said.

"You staying around here?" the man said.

"No, sir. Not yet."

"You ain't a criminal, are you?"

"No."

"You ever been in jail?"

"No."

"Ever arrested for stealing anything?"

"No sir."

"You ain't lying to me are you?"

"No sir. I promise."

The man crushed his cigarette and rubbed his hands together and them blew into them as if heating them up.

"Tell you what," he said. "I'll give you a room and eighty bucks a week."

"Okay," Lee Ann said.

"But," he said. "You'll have to work every day but Sunday."

"Okay."

"I mean it now."

"I know. I mean, thank you and all."

Lee Ann trained her hands to turn over bed sheets and tighten them against the pillows. She pushed the cart and stacked and unstacked the piles of linen. Her life became measured by the creaking of the cart wheels and the hollow knocks on aluminum doors.

One night there was a boy bringing Cokes and nabs for the vending machine. Lee Ann Pickler watched him from the top of the motel stairs push the heavy cart up the ramp, his face puffing and reddening. She giggled and he looked up and saw her. She turned away in embarrassment.

"Hey there," the boy said. He was out of breath.

"Hey there, I'm Dusty," he said.

Lee Ann returned to the stairs.

"I wasn't laughing at you," she said.

"Yes you were."

"No, really. . ."

"Oh come on," the boy said. "I seen you laughing."

"So? I couldn't help it."

"So now you got to make it up to me."

"You have got to be kidding me," Lee Ann said.

The boy removed his baseball cap and ran his fingers through his hair. "No I ain't kidding," he said.

Lee Ann leaned against the wall and looked down at him.

"What do you propose?" she said.

"Go to the movies with me."

She began laughing.

"You're asking me out? I don't even know you."

"You know me. I said my name was Dusty. We know each other now."

"Okay."

She laughed harder now.

"I got a Camaro," he said. "A red one."

"You live around here?" she said.

"Right up the road," the boy said.

They looked at each other for what seemed like a long time.

"What do you say?"

"Pick me up at seven," she said. "Right here is fine."

She spent an hour petting her hair and getting it just right. She painted the lipstick onto her face and combed her delicate eyelashes. She felt a quickening in her stomach. She stepped out of the bathroom and looked at the clock on the bedside table. Then she went back to the mirror again.

CHAPTER NINE

Dusty picked her up in his red Camaro. He offered her a beer but she said no thanks.

"Suit yourself," he said.

He drank cans of beer as he drove. He threw the empty cans out the window onto the side of the road. When they reached the movie theater, Dusty pulled around the front and stopped at looked at Lee Ann with mischief in his eyes.

"You go up there and buy a ticket," he said, "and when you get inside go down to the exit and crack it open and I'll sneak in through the back door."

"What?" she said.

Dusty rolled his eyes.

"Oh come on," he said. "Everybody does that around here."

Lee Ann thought about it for a minute.

"Why don't we just go get some dinner or something," she said.

"No, come on. I really want to see this movie. I've been wanting to see it for months."

"Okay," she said.

Lee Ann purchased one ticket, then did as she was told and waited for the usher to walk out into the lobby and then opened the door for Dusty. During the movie he put his arm around her and snuggled against her shoulder. His breath smelled like stale beer.

The movie was an action movie about a cop whose daughter is kidnaped by a renegade band of Amish separatists. It featured men in white shirts and black vests with long mustacheless beards pirouetting in death ballet. Red splotches on crisp linen shirts. The orange muzzle fire of machine guns. Lee Ann closed her eyes and heard Dusty making snorting noises through his nose.

"That was something else now, won't it?" Dusty said after the show.

She looked down at her shoes. "Yeah. I guess," she said.

Afterwards, Dusty drove them to a secluded spot on a hill overlooking an alluvial meadow where the earth spread before them like the folds of a Chinese fan. Lee Ann looked down on the town. There were lights here and there for miles.

Dusty tried to put his arm around her again but she pushed him away.

"What's the matter with you?" he said.

"Stop it," she said. "Just stop it."

"Dammit girl."

Lee Ann looked into Dusty's eyes for a long time and then she reached for the door and opened it and stepped outside. Dusty got out and followed her around the side of the car.

She was walking toward the road's edge when he made it over to her. She pushed him away and he reached back and grabbed her by the arm and pulled her toward him and punched her in the face. She felt herself sitting in the wet grass, her ears ringing.

She heard the car door slam and the engine turn over. The tires spun and the car pulled away. She watched the taillights get smaller and smaller. They looked like a pair of sinister red eyes descending the hilltop and merging with the valley below.

She got up and felt the side of her face. It was tender and starting to swell. Well that just figures, she said.

She took off her shoes and spent the rest of the night walking barefoot through the swales of autumn dew. The grass was wet between her toes. She walked all the way back to the motel. She walked until sunrise. On the way she hummed a song and then began singing it out loud. It was a verse from Amazing Grace that no one sang in church except on Easter Sunday, when they sang the whole thing. It was her mother's favorite verse.

"When we've been there ten thousand years. Bright shining as the sun. We've no less days. To sing God's praise. Than when we first begun."

Looking in the motel mirror at the bruise closing her swollen left eye, she decided that the policeman was wrong. There was something wrong with turning down bed sheets night after night after night. There was something wrong with wanting nothing more than that.

Dreams mattered and they either came true or they died. She sat on the bed and thought of her life and where it had been and where it was going and might go. It was going nowhere.

She made some big decisions and then she made some promises to herself. The next day she found a library in town and took a seat before a computer screen. There she drafted a document that joined ambition and forgery and gave life to the dreams of a precocious but terrified little girl.

Dreams of a new world bright in its infancy. She sat there looking at the resume of the person she had always dreamed of being. It was the life of her fantasy and now she was willing to look at it there in black and white. She had tried living in the real world and that had not worked. Now she would try to live in her dreams.

The girl in the resume had graduated from high school and college and had excelled at both places. She graduated magna cum laude in journalism from Chapel Hill. She was a debutante and had won a scholarship to study at a university in Edinburgh, Scotland.

The girl just wanted a chance to prove herself as a reporter for a small town newspaper. She wanted to write features. To write about regular people, to celebrate their ordinary but meaningful little lives.

She was hardworking and idealistic and she didn't mind getting her hands dirty. She was an elite, pedigreed abstraction with long brown hair and the confidence to back it all up.

She had a past and now she would have a future as well. She would see to that herself. She was undeniable, she was the perfect girl. She was sweet, educated, and burning with ambition. Her name was Mary Dallas Page.

CHAPTER TEN

The newspaper editor cleared his throat and coughed into his fist. He spoke as if to no one in particular.

"I don't give a damn about no resume," he said. "My only question I got is this: can you do the job? That's it. That's all the hell I care about. Can you write? And can you report? That's the only thing I give a damn about."

He turned back to the desk and began looking back through the newspaper clips matted under sheets of plastic. He nodded his head. "You can write," he said. "I'll give you that."

"The ad in the paper said I didn't have to have no full-time experience. I'm a fast learner, I can promise you."

"It's this simple," he said. "Either you can dig in and find the stories or you can't. It's one or the other. It's pretty obvious either way. And I don't have time to teach you how or wait for you to get good at it."

"All I'm looking for's a chance," she said. "I'll prove it to you."

The editor looked down at the stack of clips and nodded his head. "Okay," he said. "I'll give you a month. See what you can do.

It won't take me that long though, you know. I'll know in a week or two, probably. I'll let you know if I know earlier. Don't misunderstand. I'm saying I'll pay you for a month, even if I don't keep you around that long. So if I was you, I'd keep sending out resumes."

⊷ ⊶

The stories under the sheet plastic were playful stories about people from Carthage, South Carolina, some of whom existed and some of whom did not. None of the stories had ever been published, but there they were in print, with pictures and cutlines. All laid out and formatted and very official-looking. They were perfect forgeries.

The stories were trophies from her afternoons playing with her father at the press. Clowning with the reporter and the editor and her father and going back forth from her father's press room to the newsroom.

Her father would come into the newsroom in his blue coveralls stained black as if he'd been swimming in a barrel of ink and say, Come on get out of there girl. Let them boys do their job.

She would sit on the desks and eat M&M's and laugh at them all and play her little games. The reporter and editor loved her so they allowed her to make up stories and they would edit them and format them just as they edited and formatted the real newspaper. Then her father would photograph the page, burn it onto a plate and print a special edition just for her. The Carthage News according to Lee Ann Pickler.

Her games became their own. She vacillated between playing reporter girl and watching the machine crank its red gears feeding out stack after stack of folded newsprint down an aluminum slide. Eventually she realized that it didn't look right to have all the stories by Lee Ann Pickler. So she took the name of her English teacher, Mary Dallas, and added to it her mother's maiden name

Page. The name sounded to her like an important name, like a rich woman's name.

Mary Dallas Page, it said. Staff Writer.

⊷⊶

Writing the fictional stories was easy for her because her brain had been programmed and trained for fiction from its most formative stages. When she was a child, her mother would come into her room at night and they would say their prayers and then her mother would kiss her on the head and say goodnight and try to turn off the lights.

But the little girl always wanted more and so her mother began to tell her stories. First she told her true ones. She told her about her parents and their parents, all the way back as far as she knew. She told the child about the way people used to live. Of barrel fires in red barns and secret kisses behind them. And when she ran out of true stories, she told made up ones. She quickly realized she enjoyed making them up. It was easy and the child was so hungry for them.

"Tell me a story, mommy," the little girl would say. "Please mommy please."

She always gave in. One night she told the child the tale of a faraway land and a peasant girl marched toward a marriage with the king's son, a man she did not love. Her secret lover, one of the king's knights, rose up and proclaimed his love for her and holding a blade to the neck of the prince he stole her away and the two lived as fugitives in the forest.

Although the king was furious, all in his kingdom held the two of them in the cradle of their collective arms and protected them and sheltered them from house to house. Eventually the king accepted that true love was more powerful than kings and he welcomed back into his order the once-condemned knight and restored him to his place of honor.

"How could they trust the king not to kill them?" said the child.

"They couldn't," the mother said. "They had to take a chance. They were lucky."

The mother looked into the eyes of the child, her face white against her brown hair and a hole where a tooth had been. The child's eyes, like polished glass, like a doll's eyes. The mother soothed her hair and looked into her eyes.

"You can't stop the darkness from coming," she told the little girl. "But don't be afraid of the darkness. The goodness is bigger and it will always win over the darkness."

"What was the knight's name, mommy?" the little girl asked over and over again.

The mother could think of only one name and it was a thoroughly ridiculous name and the thought of it made her laugh to herself and she almost laughed out loud but managed to suppress it. She knelt down by the child's bed and whispered the name to her as if imparting some ancient catechism, as if no one else should hear.

"Don Don Donkeyfish," she said.

From that night on a ritual. The sun setting in the pines and the mother coming to the child in her room and reading to her from the Bible and then looking into the enormous blue moons of the child's eyes and composing for her another chapter in the life and adventures of the child's favorite hero, Don Don Donkeyfish. Don Don Donkeyfish traveled through time and moved from land to land. He loved, lost, swam, murdered and saved whole villages from the clutches of warlords.

The child's imagination grew and she learned to retell herself the stories again and again. Details began to mean something to her and so did words. She would ask her mother to tell her the stories over and over again.

"That's not what happens," she would say in complaint. "Tell it again. Tell it right."

The stories began to live somewhere deep within her. At night, the child listened to the creaking of the floor boards as her mother walked from the room. She counted the steps. She felt the world closing in around her with the dying of the light from the hall. She lay there alone in the darkness with only her brain and its many reckonings to keep her company.

The mysteries of life and the limitlessness of her imagination carried her onward until the mortal earth became mixed and confused with the language of dreamland and then there was but one path wormholing its way through the universe. The little girl found that special and delicate place and she rested her head upon it and fell into the bottomless cavern of sleep.

CHAPTER ELEVEN

S he thought about the people in Carthage and wondered what they were doing now. Her high school class was probably graduating and getting ready to go to work on the farms or maybe go to junior college. She had never been one of them, even when she was among them, and she was not sad to leave them behind. Yet for some reason she missed them.

High school held nothing for her. There were no real friends. Only the girl who sat next to her in home room and talked to her sometimes, and the nerd boy she had a passing crush on. People paired up and then the pairs joined and whole groups of people came into alliance. She had walked alone among the nations of boys and girls.

She enjoyed science class and English class. Her mind grew in fascination at the delicate perfection of Avogadro's Number and the supple genius of constancy manifested in the Fibonacci Sequence. Nature proved itself in patterns time and time again and she found that fascinating. She had heard all the superstition in church and at home, but now suddenly she saw the Creator's stamp on all things and was amazed and nourished by it all.

She read Great Expectations and fell in love with Pip and Magwitch. She read Huck Finn and imagined riding on a riverboat in the dark, the hot night wind blowing in her face and the lights arranged like Chinese lanterns along the wide banks of the river. She read Romeo and Juliet and she cried. She read Moby Dick and tried to like it but couldn't understand why a man would want to kill a whale so badly or how a person could take enjoyment in reading about such a thing.

She set the book down and decided to write something for herself. She started writing funny little poems about other people in her class and she would giggle to herself as she looked in their direction and said the words to herself. When the English teacher called on her, she had nothing to offer and shyly acquitted herself of any knowledge though she might have and feigned ignorance.

She tried to mimic the others and hoped that they would love her for it but either they never loved her or they never showed it. She soon realized she was not a person among persons but a person outside of persons who was but a watcher of persons.

She decided that if she could not be like them or even mix with them, she would live outside of them and observe them and describe them for her own amusement. She discovered the immortality of language.

When she was fifteen, she completed her first short story and at a teacher's urging submitted it to her high school's annual literary contest. The story won first place and was published in the school newspaper. It went like this:

THE PRISONER OF GRISNAK
By Lee Ann Pickler

In the land of Shayla in the thirty third year of our Lord Grisnak lived a benevolent old king who had a wicked daughter named Malicia.

While the king negotiated treaties of peace with neighboring kingdoms, Malicia plotted to undo the accords and sow the seeds of war. She dreamed of poisoning her father the king and killing her younger brother and assuming the throne.

She would bring war to the west and conquer the neighboring kingdoms and seize all their treasures. She would be fierce and then, once she had secured her reign, she would be benevolent. She would bring to the peasants deposits of grain and demand only their continued obedience to the laws of her kingdom. She would become beloved and revered throughout the known world and feared beyond imagination by the lawless hordes of her kingdom's enemies who recoiled at the stories detailing her cruelties.

Grisnak intervened and had words with the king and the king listened for a time but then the advancement of time and the princess' indomitable nagging wore him down and eventually all her frightful dreams came true and were visited upon the land.

She conquered everything within sight and ruled with cold effect. She poisoned her father's goblet and he died on the courtyard floor. She pretended to cry but then was smiling and laughing at her coronation. She ordered the servants to feed her younger brother to the lampreys.

Her throne secured, she incubated in herself a sense and a fear that she would be betrayed and murdered by someone she loved or trusted. So she trusted no one. And she loved no one.

She slept with a dagger in each hand and awoke at anything that jumped in the night. She suspected them all. Jimodo, her most loyal servant, was plotting against her, she decided, and she spied on him for weeks and had others spy on him as well. Finally, and without any evidence of duplicity on his part, she had him crucified in the garden. She sat on a picnic table and bit into a peach as he hung there and cried out in suffering.

Her fits of madness made her the most feared and despised ruler in the land. She stated that her kingdom was hers and hers alone and that she was answerable to no one, not even to Grisnak.

Upon hearing this blasphemy, Grisnak summoned her to the mountaintop but she refused to go and told Grisnak that he had no right to interfere with the administration of her kingdom. Grisnak became furious and so he took from her her kingdom and every other possession of her being down to the animal skins she wore and he judged her there upon a stage before the entire world.

The faceless oracles scribbled the record onto their gray tablets and the queen stood there defiant and proud and shaking, naked upon her own stage, her life being taken from her piece by precious piece.

Eventually her countenance broke and she collapsed in sobs. Grisnak called on all around to behold her shattering and then he condemned her to a life bound naked and crucified in the wheat field. There, each night the crows would descend into the borderland and come for her and feast upon her bones. They pecked and ripped at her with their teeth. She closed her eyes and allowed the crows to consume her again and again.

The little girl cried out and awoke.

CHAPTER TWELVE

"Like I was saying, I'll probably know in a week or two."
The editor took another drink of coffee and squinted out toward the road where a drunk staggered past. "Anyway, like I was saying, a resume don't mean a damn thing to me. This job, you can either do it or you can't. You ain't in school no more. This is the real world now."

"I know," she said.

He looked at her. "Do you, now?" he said.

He looked at the girl in front of him. Just a damn kid. Another pony-tailed princess slumming to write hard news. A kid willing to go anywhere to report. That's what they told each other in J-school.

They believed it too, until they arrived in Sidney, Nebraska, or Havre, Montana, or Battle Mountain, Nevada, and realized they might as well be living in a yurt on the Mongolian steppe. And, just like that, they wanted the hell out. Wanted to do something where there was at least a chance that they might make some money.

It was impossible to keep the ones that were worth a damn and the rest, well, you couldn't get rid of them.

The good ones went on to places like Florence or Spartanburg, then maybe to Charleston or Savannah. Maybe once every ten years, somebody went all the way to Washington or Atlanta.

The bad ones stayed where they were and either learned enough to get by or you had to fire them. Most of them had no business for it. If you couldn't write it was all for shit anyway.

A few of them could put it together and make it sing. Most of them couldn't. Education didn't matter. You couldn't teach it. Experience didn't matter either. Lyricism was all that mattered. Lyricism and the nose for the story. You had to have the head for it and the ear.

This girl had lyricism, she had rhythm. He could see it in the bounce in her prose. It intrigued him. The little bit she had to show him. There were some awkward transitions, but the talent was there and besides, that's what editors were for. Her instincts were another matter and they would prove themselves out quickly enough or they wouldn't.

So what that she hadn't written for her college paper at Chapel Hill? He'd seen editors of college papers who couldn't write a suicide note. He had always hated them for some reason, even though he knew that what he should really feel was sorry for them because they were cursed with unattainable dreams and would always be cursed, no matter their pedigree or effort or connections, no matter how hard they tried. They were cursed to dream of success at something they weren't any good at. They were living proof that dreams didn't matter, talent did. If you didn't have the talent you might as well be holding a turd in your hand.

The editor finished his coffee. What the hell, he said. He hired her without checking her references and made her the new features writer. "Do stories about lemonade stands and shit like that," the editor said.

She was overwhelmed. She wanted so badly to call someone and share her joy with them but then realized that there was no one to call anymore. She would have to be happy for herself and that would have to be enough.

"This ain't Charleston," the editor said. "But Charleston is just down the road. Some of our stories get picked up there. So we expect you to be consistent and be good."

"I'll do my best," she said.

"Our staff meeting's at eight," said the editor. "Don't be late for that. Ever."

"I won't be."

"Good. You got a place to stay yet?"

"Not yet."

"We see the classifieds before anyone else, so we get first dibs. Go see for yourself. You probably want to get moving on that."

"Is there a motel or something before then?"

"What, like a joint that will let you go month to month?"

"Yeah."

The editor shrugged his shoulders. "Don't know. Maybe the Queen Anne over on Mason Street. Pink stucco type job. One of them Elvis looking signs out front."

"How do I get there?"

"I'll give you a lift if you want."

"Thank you."

"So when can you start?"

"How about tomorrow morning?"

"That's good enough."

<hr />

That night she lay awake staring at the ceiling and breathing the ammonia vapors from the bathroom and listening to the hum of the ice machine in the hallway. At the first crack of sunlight she got up and showered and dressed herself and walked down to the newspaper office.

When she got there, the editor was in his office listening to country music on the radio and drinking coffee. He was staring out into the road again. A fat man with streaks of black hair painted on the top of his head changed his computer screen again and again.

"That's Dan," said the editor. "He's our news editor."

"How you doin?" Dan said.

Lee Ann smiled. "Good," she said. "And you?"

"Just fine."

The editor pulled her back into his office and told her to take a seat and she did.

"You know anything about sculptures or anything?" the editor said.

"No," Lee Ann said.

The editor scratched his head.

"Me either," he said.

"Okay."

"Think you could learn about them?"

"Sure," Lee Ann said. "How come?"

"Fellow over in Merino carves these big sculptures out of trees. They look like something out of Dante's Inferno."

"Wow," she said.

"I want you to go over there and do a story on him."

"How do I find him?"

"You drive out to Merino and ask for Mr. Wisdom's shop. Mr. Wisdom is a rich man who makes carnival rides for a living. This sculptor, he works for Wisdom."

"Okay. But how do I get there?"

"Take county road number nine and head out toward. . ."

"But I don't have a car."

"Oh."

The editor looked at the ceiling and then looked back at her. "Take the pickup," he said. "We won't need it till they deliver the paper this afternoon. Just hurry back."

"Okay," she said.

CHAPTER THIRTEEN

S he found the truck out back. It was an orange F-150 with rust chipping away at the paint. She started the engine and put it in gear and felt the creaking chassis as it worked its way to life. She pulled out onto the road and felt the immediate rattling. The shocks were blown out causing the chassis to rattle.

She stopped at a filling station and put five gallons of gas in the truck. She bought a cold Pepsi and counted out the change for the gas station attendant.

"Where's the fellow who makes the carnival stuff and the trees?" she asked.

The man wiped grease off his hands with a rag and squinted into the sun.

"You in TV?" the man said.

"Not yet," Lee Ann said.

"What you want with him?"

"I want to see those tree sculptures."

"Them things is something else, now."

"That's what I've heard. I want to see them for myself and talk to him about them."

"Everybody thinks he's religious you know. Cause of the sculptures. But he ain't. He told me once he ain't."

"You know where I can find him?"

"Sure do."

"You mind telling me?"

"He works for Mr. Wisdom. Works over there making them carnival rides."

"How far is that from here?"

"Not more than a mile or two, I reckon."

The building had a large frame roofed in corrugated tin. The door was open and she walked in unannounced. She noticed that the factory smelled of cedar shavings.

The man stood with his back to her in the enormous cavern of his workshop. There were fair ride cars everywhere, some of them painted and alive and others whited and dead looking. There was a workbench covered in tools and a white sheet underneath. A giant tree sculpture of an angel pulling back her cloak to reveal frightened children at her feet stood in the center of the workspace.

The man stood on a scaffolding shelf carving away at the sculpture with a screwdriver to chip away on one side, narrowing the angel's figure and shaping it and giving it life. She stood back and watched him.

The man was an unassuming man. He was middle-aged and wore a blue mechanics suit and his long ringlets of chestnut hair covered his back. When he found a proper stopping point, he climbed down off the scaffold and looked down at Lee Ann. She was surprised at the thickness of his red beard. He looked at his shoes in embarrassment.

"I'm Brad Ray," he said. "Kindly nice of you to wait on me."

"It's nothing really," Lee Ann said.

"So you from the paper?"

"Yes," she said. "I'm Mary Dallas Page."

"Mary Dallas Page. Sounds like one of them Charleston debutante types."

She pretended to blush.

"I made my debut in Greensboro," she said. "That's up in North Carolina."

"What's that mean, make your debut?"

"That's where you come out into society. As a debutante."

"Oh. I see."

"It's a silly ritual really. But it was fun."

"I never remember knowing no debutante. I don't know if I ever even talked to one before. My wife was in the FFA. That's about it, I reckon."

He watched Lee Ann Pickler struggle to comprehend the thing before her.

"Why do you make them out of trees?" she said.

The sculptor shrugged.

"Michelangelo made them out of marble. Why not make them out of that?" she said.

"You see any marble around here?" he said.

"Nope."

"But you see trees, don't you?"

"Yessir."

The sculptor smiled and crossed his arms and took a seat on one of the fair rides. It was an orange duck wearing a Lone Ranger mask and gritting its teeth.

"Trees, marble, men and women. Each is just another piece of this earth," he said. "Another dead piece of this earth."

"Do they go bad?"

"What do you mean?"

"Do they stay like this or do they go bad?"

"Oh. They go bad usually. Dead trees are like dead folks. They decompose and rot. This looks like a studio," he said. "But it ain't. It's a graveyard."

Lee Ann shook her head.

"How can you do that?" she said. "To make something so beautiful and see it go to waste."

"Everything goes to waste," the sculptor said. "Don't nothing in this world endure. I love my children more than God loves me. But they will die too eventually. That breaks my heart to even think about but there ain't a thing me or anybody else can do a thing about it.

"Their bones will end up buried in the ground. And then they will be dust. And after enough time passes there will be no one on this earth who has any memory of them. And ultimately everything will be sucked into the sun and burned away to nothing. So what's any of it matter, if you look at it that way? Was it a mistake that any of us was born to begin with?"

"That's not the same."

"Isn't it?"

"No. I don't think so."

The sculptor stood and gestured, indicating the massive tree angel. "Michelangelo was a genius," he said. "He was a genius, a true spokesman for God. I'm a guy who makes fair rides and carves things out of trees and goes to rodeos on the weekends. I ain't nothing. But in death Michelangelo and I will be equals. Like I said, nothing endures. Not one thing."

"But his work endured. The Sistine Chapel is still there. David is still there."

"His work has endured, yes. Up until now. But that doesn't mean it will endure. You ever hear about the Colossus of Rhodes?"

"No."

"It was an enormous statue of a Greek sun god. It used to be a pretty big deal. Stood for fifty or sixty years, then it was destroyed by an earthquake. But the ruins laid there for another five hundred years.

"I made a tree sculpture for the library. It's an interpretation of a Peter Paul Rubens painting. I worked day and night on it for eight months. My hands bled. I couldn't close them because of all the splinters."

"My gosh."

"That work has endured. Going on four years now. That's all. Maybe tomorrow it won't endure no more. One good hurricane, that's all it takes. That's how things go when you're in the enduring game."

Lee Ann pointed to the sculpture. "What's this one about?" she said.

"I have an idea," the man said. "But I don't want to say just yet."

"Are you superstitious?"

"I guess so. A little bit."

"You have a name for it?"

"Yep."

"You mind telling me?"

"Exordium," the sculptor said.

"What's it mean?" she said.

The sculptor smiled. He twisted his hair into a pony tail and pulled it back behind his head. "You'll have to look it up," he said.

Merino's Michelangelo. That was the headline on her story. The picture on the front made the sculptor look like a madman with his greasy beard and long hair enameled in pomade. It was framed in an oaken light and the grooves and wrinkles gave relief to the shadows and the bright places in the cherry wood.

The sculptor read the story in the morning while drinking a large cup of coffee. He chewed on a powdered donut and then shook the white powdered sugar out of his beard. He folded the paper and stared out happily onto the world, then picked up his tools from his workbench and knelt before a plastic animal cast in mold and began carving a set of claws onto it. When Lee Ann got back to the office after lunch she had a message from the sculptor on her voice mail.

"You got talent," the sculptor said. "People with talent usually move on from here pretty quick. But it sure was nice knowing you while you was here."

CHAPTER FOURTEEN

She lay awake one night looking at the ceiling and thinking about the newspaper life. Spending time at a newspaper was all she had ever wanted to do. She almost felt dirty for taking their money for it.

She remembered her father and his routine. In the mornings he farmed their ruddy fields and in the afternoons he worked the press at the town newspaper. The paper was an eight page broadsheet filled with ads from the local grocery store mixed with a few local stories. The memories were pure magic to her, magic that such a place and time and people could have ever existed.

She remembered the soft news, the features, the pictures of kids eating ice cream, the stories about the local high school sports teams. She remembered following him to work at both places. She sat up behind him on the tractor and held onto him as he churned row after row in the hard black soil. And she would ride with him in the pickup to town, to the newspaper offices.

They would park in the back and walk in through the service door. She would follow him into the machine room and watch him load the plates and the ink onto the gears. When the machine cranked up and the bundles of papers began sliding down the chute, she would pull the first one out and marvel at the whiteness of it. Then she would watch the next one and the next, captivated by the process. The color began, coming on and brightening into focus, each edition more colorful than the last.

She remembered Christopher J. Ellers, the paper's news reporter. She could see him sitting there in his chair leaned back against the wall, his tie unfastened and hanging around his neck like a stethoscope, his brown fedora pushed forward on his head, snoring. She would come into the newsroom and sit up on his desk and he would sit there drinking his whiskey out of a coffee mug with a gamecock on it and say: What are you gettin into, girl?

One day Ellers gave her some advice. "Being a reporter is one easy thing, now. But don't you do it unless you can't do nothin else. You hear me?"

"But English is the only subject I like," she said.

"That's fine," Ellers said. "You can do something else though. You can be an English teacher or something. See, then at least you get your summers off."

"I don't want to be no English teacher. I just want to write."

"You can always write for yourself. I'm just saying, try that first. You can always be a reporter later. Anybody who can write can be a reporter. Even criminals. Just look at me. It don't take no special education. It's stupid how easy it is, really."

"Is it that easy?"

"It's easier than doing what your daddy does."

"Really?"

"Heck yes, girl. You see any lines or scars on my hands?"

"No."

"Well there you go."

"What do you do?"

"Just talk to people, tell their stories, try to find out what all's going on."

"It sounds like fun."

"It is fun."

"Then why shouldn't I do it?"

"It don't pay enough."

"But it's fun though?"

"Oh yeah, it's fun."

"Will you teach me?"

"Teach you what?"

"How to do it."

"If you want. It's pretty simple really."

"How so?"

"There's an old saying: You comfort the afflicted and afflict the comfortable."

"What does that mean?"

"It means you go to a good neighborhood and find something wrong with it. Then you go to a bad one and find something right with it."

"Okay."

"There is a certain crude art to straight news, even features. Any type of journalism, really. Journalism is all the same. There's the formula in every story. It's simple really. Once you get the hang of it, it's easy as a coloring book."

"I want to learn it."

"Well, all it is is putting words together. You think you can do that?"

"Yes I do."

"You're just telling stories. Think of your grandpa. Think of him telling stories on the back porch. That's how you do it. Leave the grammar and everything to the editors. Just get the pitch right. Then there's a formula you follow."

"What kind of formula?"

"Well first you need a catchy intro line. Something that teases the story and hooks in the reader. That's called your lede. Then you need what they call a nut graf," Ellers said.

"A nut graf?"

"It's a paragraph that puts the background of the story into a nutshell and forecasts what's coming. See? A nutshell paragraph. A nut graf, for short. That's why they call it that. You want the reader to know what's going on right away. Otherwise, he gets bored. It's like fishing. You got to get the hook in their mouth before you can pull them in. If you don't, you just end up drinking too much beer and falling asleep and getting sunburned."

Lee Ann looked confused.

"Nevermind about that."

"Okay."

"You see, it's like this. Lede. Nut graf. Body. Conclusion. That's all you need for a good story. But you gotta have all them things and in that order or else you ain't got nothing."

"The body, that's just mostly quotes, right?"

"Usually. It's a matter of organization, really. Especially if there's a controversy. Then it's real easy. You just find the crazies on both sides and just let them kill each other in print and you just get out of the way.

"And remember, it ain't got to be long neither. Twelve inches in print ain't nothing. Even twenty, hell, if it's a feature, there's no trouble filling it. The art of the thing is what to fill it with. After they wrap the text around the picture and cutline, you're lucky if you get more than eight or nine paragraphs. So there ain't much to it."

"The lede's the first sentence?"

"Yeah. That's your most important sentence. I had a teacher once. He said: If you're writing about a bear, bring on the bear. It's like that."

"And then the nut graf sums it up?"

"Yeah. The context and the background and everything."

"And then the body?"

"That's right. Just tell whatever's happening now and might happen next and do it through quotes if you can."

"Then the conclusion."

"Yep."

"What do I do there?"

"Tie it all together with something tight and leave them wanting more. That's the best I can tell you on that."

"Do you write all this down on paper or do you record it on tape?"

"Tape, usually. That way they can't say I misquoted them."

"That seems awful easy."

"Oh it is."

"Then why don't more folks do it?"

Ellers smiled. His crooked front tooth, yellow-tarred and sideways, winked at her when he smiled. He smiled at her like a playful big brother.

"I already told you," he said. "Cause they got sense enough not to."

CHAPTER FIFTEEN

"Got an assignment for you," the editor said. "You're going to fail at it but I'm going to give it to you anyway."

"Okay."

"You sure about that?"

"What is it?"

"You know who Beau Legare is?"

"Who?"

"Beau Legare."

"No."

"He's the greatest living southern writer. That's who he is."

"Okay."

"Do you know who William Faulkner is?"

"Yeah."

"Good."

"So you never read anything by Legare?"

"No."

"He's written about five or six books. He won the National Book Award for The Negroes of Whiskey Creek and the Pulitzer for The Colossus at Marshbanks."

"What's he write about."

"Weird shit. All pretentious and symbolic. Old South. All that guilt-ridden ghost shit. To be honest with you, I think his shit is unreadable. So I've never read any of it. But hey, I never read Moby Dick neither."

"Really?"

"Whales? What do I give a shit?"

"It's overrated."

"You read it?"

"Yes, in high school."

"Well, congratulations then."

"What do you want me to do?"

"I want you to try and get an interview with him."

"An interview?"

"Yeah, you know. One of your cute little feature pieces."

"Okay."

"You don't understand."

"Understand what?"

"He's going to say no."

"Why do you want to send me then?"

"Because what the hell. It's worth a shot. And when he says no, I want you to write a piece about what you two would have talked about if he hadn't said no. You know. An empty chair interview."

"Okay."

"Can you handle that, you think?"

"I think so."

"You probably need to read some of his books. Or at least skim through them. They're hard to get through, if you ask me."

"Okay."

"What are you waiting for?"

"Can I have twenty dollars to buy a couple of the books?"

"They got this new invention. It's called the library."

"When you want this by?"

"Next Wednesday."

"How do I find him?"

"He lives on an old plantation near Caw Caw. It's on Sheriff Roscoe Brown Road before you get into town. There's a long field running up to the house and the house is yellow with white columns."

"You been there?"

"I been by there."

"You ever seen him there?"

"I seen him out in the yard once."

"Why do you think he will he say no?"

"He don't do interviews. Not with anybody. When he won the Pulitzer, Oprah herself came to Ravenel and knocked on his door. But he wouldn't open it."

"I'd love to talk to Oprah."

"Yeah, well then you and Beau Legare disagree about something already. This is starting off great."

"What if I get him to talk?"

"You won't."

"But what if I do?"

"Then you lead the paper and we carry you around and pour champagne on you and dwarves throw confetti. What do you want from me?"

"That sounds nice."

"It is," he said. "That's why it won't happen."

CHAPTER SIXTEEN

The woods were composed of scrub oak and orange pine needles and there was an easy rolling way about them. The mansion stood on the crown of a bank, a swirl of marshland descending the hill on the outer rim.

Yellow cord grass and silvering troughs of black water stood out in the sunlight and minor disturbances moved in the narrow streams. Birds chirped in the trees.

The mansion was at the end of a long road with oak trees lining the road like a colonnade. Spanish moss hung from their giant branches. The house was an old plantation house with paint chipped from its sides and curling away and weeds growing high giving it a haunted look and making her wonder whether the inside was likewise so beset with decay.

She stopped on the road in the curve of the hill. She popped the hood on the truck and stood in front of the engine and waved her hand back and forth as if fanning away smoke. Then she put her palm over her eyes like a visor and looked at the long road up to the house. She thought about it and went over it all again in her head.

She had her tape recorder in her purse and she had practiced her story a million times in her head, saying the words over and over again. It felt so natural and rehearsed even though now it was for real.

She knocked on the door. Nothing. She tried to peer through the window but the white cloth blocked out the rooms inside. There was nothing to see.

She walked around the side of the house and saw the river running through the backyard. She walked to the backyard and saw a man standing and looking at the river. He was a man about six feet tall, slender build, he was wearing linen pants and a straw hat and his hands were in his pockets. The sleeves on his shirt were rolled up and the suspenders put a black crisscross down his back. Puffs of smoke rolled off his face.

The man turned and saw the girl.

"I'm Mary Dallas Page," she called out to him, trying to sound sweet.

"My car broke down up the road."

She pointed down the hill to the orange truck, its hood propped up.

"I was wondering if I could use your telephone to call my daddy."

The man looked at her curiously then took another drag on the cigarette. He tapped off the ash and gave a slow nod.

"Alright," he said. He gestured toward the house. "Reckon we ought to go on in."

The man led her into the house through the back door. He had a sad, courtly way about him and his eyes never met hers directly. It was dark inside and there were piles of books and newspapers everywhere and although there were numerous works of art preserved in frames, none of them were placed on the walls. They were all stacked on the floor at their appointed places as if he had just moved in and intended to put them up but had not yet gotten around to it.

"Phone's in the kitchen," the man said.

"I'm Mary Dallas Page," she said again.

"You said that already. It's a pleasure to meet you, Miss Mary Dallas Page. The phone's in the kitchen."

"Yes sir."

Lee Ann went into the kitchen and found the phone and pretended to have a conversation with her daddy. When she came into the living room the man had taken a seat in a red leather chair and was drinking a glass of whiskey.

"Thanks for letting me use your phone," she said.

"Don't mention it," the man said.

Lee Ann hesitated and then said, "My daddy says he can't come get me till mama comes back from the store with the car, so it might be an hour or more. Should I stay here or wait down at the road?"

"You can do either one," the man said.

"You mind if I stay here?"

"No ma'am, I don't mind."

"Thank you."

"You want a Co-Cola or something?"

"Yessir, that'd be great."

The man got up and walked into the kitchen. She heard a refrigerator door opening and closing and then the crack of a can top. She reached into her purse and pressed the record button.

The man came out and handed her the Coke and she took it and said thank you. When the man sat back down he crossed his legs elegantly. He was wearing an expensive pair of wine-colored ostrich boots. Her eyes fixed on the beaded quills that looked like rows of measles.

"Thank you, mister. Say mister, you never told me your name."

The man looked at the ground then looked up again.

"Clint Raggle," he said.

Lee Ann smiled at him.

"That's not really your name, is it?"

The man gave a playful smile. "What's wrong with my name?" he said.

"You're that writer aren't you?"

The man pretended to look puzzled.

"What writer would that be?"

She leaned forward.

"Beau Legare," she said.

"An unfortunate accident really," he said. "I was supposed to be named Alexander the Great but they got it all mixed up at the hospital."

"You're famous."

"I don't know who you're talking about. I'm a person in this world and Clint Raggle's my name."

"No it's not. You're a famous writer."

"Perhaps I used to scribble clusters of gibberish from time to time. So what?"

"Oh my God," she said. "Oh my God. It is you. I knew it. I knew it."

"It's nothing, really," he said. "A curse of laziness."

"I really doubt that."

"When you hide away from doing manual labor your entire life, you have to do something else. What I do is drink Tennessee sipping whiskey and listen to Mozart until I get tired enough to lay down on the couch and go to sleep. It don't take me too long in the summertime. And now you've caught me at it."

"It's really an honor," she said.

"Really? After what I just told you? I'm afraid that's a little pathetic, my dear."

"It's just. . . . You're one of my favorite writers. We read The Negroes of Whiskey Creek in English class. It was so beautiful the way you described the struggle of the sharecroppers and the way you made the broken crankshaft on the well a symbol of hope. It was so very beautiful and it touched me. It made me cry, the ending. It really did."

"I'm glad you liked it."

"It was so great, really."

"Thank you."

"Tell me though. . . ." She leaned forward and sat the purse down on the table between them. "Tell me, why did you take on the gentry the way you did?"

"The gentry?"

"Yes."

"Really. Those bow tie wearing devils? I went easy on them."

"Are you serious? I thought you were brutal. Reading that book made me hate them."

"If I said what I really think about them they'd tar and feather me and ride me out of town on a rail."

"What do you really think about them?"

Legare shrugged. "I grew up around those devils. I was born to be one of those devils but I couldn't quite do it. I always felt like a child looking in at them from outside a window. Like a boy at the fudge shop on Market Street watching fudge get made and then wanting some and instead watching everybody else eating it and realizing that he can never be one of them. But now I'm all grown up and I don't eat fudge anymore. I have diabetes now. Besides, I saw how they did everything and it was very ugly. I don't have no use for any man who's born into this world with an assigned lofty place right from the get-go. Inherited nobility don't impress me. They always made me sick ever since I learned to think for myself."

"Is that just the southern gentry or rich people everywhere?"

"In the South, gentry don't have to be rich. History or heritage or legacy or whatever the hell you want to call it. My granddaddy had more horses than your granddaddy and therefore I am better than you. That sort of thing. I feel the same way about the Queen of England. But the southern gentry is pretty bad. It's that same crowd that started the damn war. Bunch of hotheads that couldn't stand to suffer a man like Abraham Lincoln. No group of sons of bitches in all human history ever deserved the ass whipping they got worse than the South Carolina planter class. Now instead of starting wars they wear canary yellow pants and bow ties and sell commercial real estate. And this is supposed to be some improvement?"

"So you don't call it the war of northern aggression? I've heard that a lot, you know?"

Legare looked up.

"What could be more stupid or more vain?" he said.

"It's romantic though, is it not?"

"Romanticism is a wonderful thing," said Beau Legare. "But it is also a stupid thing. It is not even a true thing, but a false one. There is a thing called the physical world and its demands hit you right in the face. Romanticism is a thing belonging to the lovers and the mystics."

"That's a cold sounding thing to say."

"If your head and your heart disagree about something, your head is probably right. Nine times out of ten."

"That's interesting that you mention Lincoln."

"Lincoln was the greatest man ever lived."

"Do you really think so?"

Legare nodded. "Yes ma'am I do. It was like having Churchill and Shakespeare in one man. And one of his finest acts was sending General William Tecumseh Sherman to tear through this godforsaken belovery and burn everything to the goddamn ground."

"Wow," Lee Ann said. "I've never heard anybody talk like that before."

Amazing, she said to herself. Amazing. Just amazing.

"Everybody thinks Sherman raped Georgia but that just ain't so. He went easy on Georgia. Hell, he just taught them some manners. Did they teach you that in history class? He practically handed out hard tack in North Carolina. But South Carolina? Well he burned her to the stinking ground on account of her starting the whole thing. And that was the right thing to do. The only injustice is that Charleston herself was spared the caterwauling and the fires. Sometimes, getting your ass kicked is the only way to learn a lesson."

"So the old time Charlestonians, you don't feel like you're a part of them anymore."

"I don't feel like I'm a part of nothing no more. Except for me. I am very much a part of that, whatever that is. Like the man said: I ain't much, but I'm all I ever think about."

"Is that why you never give interviews?"

"No, I don't give interviews because I don't like talking to reporters."

"Why not?"

"What do I need some stranger digging around this haunted house I call my head? Everything in there is available at the bookstore for eleven ninety five. I mean it. I don't know a thing that ain't written on some page in some bookstore. Reporters are just looking for a shortcut."

"Have you ever been married?"

Legare gave a solemn nod. "A time or three, yes ma'am."

"You want to give a gal some advice?"

"Not really."

"Why not?"

"Would you take shooting advice from a man who shot his own pecker off three times?"

"No."

"It's not something I particularly like to talk about."

"Well what would you rather talk about?"

"I don't know."

"What do you think about the Middle East?"

"Same thing everybody else does."

"And what is that?"

"Glad I don't live there."

"Anything else?"

"Yes."

"What?"

"How long have you been lying to people to get interviews?"

She froze. The look in her eyes gave it away.

He looked down at the purse.

"That thing's miked up, ain't it?"

She looked down. He shook his head sadly.

"I'm sorry, I'm so sorry," she said.

The old man just sat back in the chair and crossed his arms. He looked very tired.

"I've seen them deliver the paper too, you know. I'd know that orange pickup anywhere."

"Please forgive me. . . . This isn't me. I promise this isn't me," she said.

"Well you and me are the only ones here."

"Please," she said.

"Miss, why don't you just go get in your newspaper truck and go on back. I don't like having my privacy invaded. This has been sort of fun, don't get me wrong, but I'm tired of it now and I'd appreciate going back to being by myself."

"Please," she said. Her eyes started to mist up.

"My name is not Mary Dallas Page. That's not even my real name. It's a lie. Everything about me is a lie. That's all I am."

"I don't need to know your life story. Please just go."

"Please. . . just please." Her voice was breaking as she spoke to him.

She stammered and sobbed and then composed herself.

"Please," she said. "Please at least hear me out."

She cried for awhile and then composed herself enough to talk to him. She told him about her loneliness and desperation, as if he were her priest and psychiatrist.

She told him everything. She told him about her mother's final days and the emptiness that followed. She told him about running away, about the men in the bus station and the police taking all her money. She told him about sleeping in the woods and getting punched in the face on her first date, and she told him about her plan to crash life's party by lying about who she was and where she came from.

While she was talking he reached into his shirt pocket and took out a handkerchief and handed it to the girl and she dabbed her eyes with it.

"You've already lied to get in here. A bunch of times. Why should I believe any of this now?" he said.

"You shouldn't," she said. "You shouldn't. I'm a liar. You're right. I'm a liar. I'm a liar. You're right about that and I wouldn't believe a word out of me either."

"So what's your real name then?"

"Lee Ann Pickler," she said.

He sat up and studied the girl. His lips began to curl upward into what almost looked like a smile.

"Nobody would make up a name like that," he said.

"And you never went to Chapel Hill? You just told them that to get the job at the paper?"

She nodded and cried.

"Serves them right," he said. "It shows you what a college degree is worth, don't it?"

"I guess so."

"If it makes you feel any better, I don't have one either. I spent two years at Ole Miss but I never learned a thing. Except how to mix whiskey with Co-Cola."

"I thought they'd catch me," she said. "I'm amazed they haven't got me yet."

"Darlin, if you can write like the birds sing, they'll never catch you. And if you can't, the fanciest school in the world couldn't teach you how anyway. It's a God given thing really. It's like being born left-handed. You are either born with lyricism and pitch or you are not."

"I've been able to write since I was a little girl. It's all I was ever good at."

He looked at the girl for a long time and then smiled whimsically. "Me too," he said.

CHAPTER SEVENTEEN

"Tell me about your mama and daddy," he said.

She told him. About the rows of tobacco and the goldenness of the ripe leaves and the way the sun struck them in the fields. About the accident with the machine. About finding her daddy lying there on the ground with both his arms missing and the sun shining down on him and his eyes and mouth open as if he died laughing at a joke. About Mama and the way it used to be.

"Sounds like they loved you."

"They did."

"That's more than most people get."

"I guess so. I was lucky, I guess. Wish I was lucky for longer, that's all."

"So you didn't leave home to leave home."

"No."

"You left home looking for a home."

"Yes."

"My family," he said, taking a drink of whiskey. "They always thought I was a bum."

"They must be proud of you now."

"Why?"

"Because you're famous."

"Who knows. Let me tell you. My daddy never liked anything I ever wrote. Never respected what I did. Thought I was a bum. My mama never even read anything I ever wrote. I'd give it to her and she would pretend to be interested but later I would find it laying around the house in one big unread pile. My work was my life, it was me, and they most assuredly did not love it."

"Millions of people read your books and they love them."

"To be candid, that does help things out a bit. Pays for my whiskey anyway. Pays for me to stand out in the backyard and stare at the river and think about things."

Lee Ann nodded.

"So what are you going to do with the interview?"

She opened the purse and took out the recorder and ejected the tape. She tried to hand it to him but he wouldn't take it.

"Put that thing away," he said.

"Please, I want you to have it," she said.

"No, you keep it."

"Please, I wouldn't feel right."

"No, keep it and use it."

"I promise you I won't."

"No," he said. "I want you to."

"For where you come from, you done alright so far. But here's where maybe I can help you."

"Okay."

"You did good. You dummied up a resume, faked a journalism degree, even had some fake clips. That's all jim dandy. But maybe I can help you take it even further."

"How's that?"

"Why lie small when you can lie big? You take the same risk in committing your heart to a lie, whether the stakes are high or low."

"You think so?"

"What do you reckon built this mansion?"

She didn't know. "Lies?" she said.

"No, African slaves."

"Oh."

"You think they gave a damn about whether some words were true or not?"

"Probably not."

"No."

"It must have been hard for them."

"I'm sure it was."

"I wonder what they would think about the way things are now."

"Don't matter what they would think. They didn't live now. They lived then and then they were still chaining up the Negro and putting his naked body on the auctioneer's block. They chalked his feet and hung a sign around his neck and checked his teeth and sold him like an animal. Can you imagine? But that's the world they lived in. You couldn't lie your way out of being a slave. My point is that power is a reality."

"I guess."

"Luck can be mean, but it isn't always. Luck, sometimes, is our only hope in this world. I'm more convinced of that every day, it seems like. You hope you're born in the right time, into the right conditions. You hope for some magic along the way."

"I guess so."

"But that don't mean you can't push back and try to subvert it. Your mind is the variable in your own life. It alone can rework the equation and sometimes even overrule the great author of destiny and I think even he is proud and amused by this fact.

"You can lie. You can build a life on lies. If you're careful and smart you can live in one perfect and brazen lie. This country, it don't just reward liars, it actually loves them. It worships them and makes them into stars."

"How do I do that?"

"How do you do what?"

"What you just said."

He laughed.

"How do I do it?" she said.

"You're only limited by your imagination."

"How do I put it into action?"

"There is a thing called a big con and a thing called a small con," he said.

"Okay."

"Both are forms of lies and both play to human nature. All you need in a mark is a man who doesn't mind cutting a corner to get something he doesn't deserve to have."

"What's the difference in them?"

"The scope."

"How so?"

"The small con is a short term sleight of hand game. Shoplifting. Pickpocketing. Things like that. Twenty bucks here, fifty bucks there. Small time fraud. What you're doing right now. You can't make much money in the small con game and the whole routine is a grind. It's easy and the turnaround is pretty quick, but it's a one-way ticket to Nowheresville."

"So why do it then?"

"I didn't say you should."

"What was the other one?"

"The big con."

"What is that exactly?"

"It's more elaborate. It's like theater. Like a symphony of deception. You need partners sometimes. The stakes are higher. It's a lot harder too. The marks are more sophisticated. But the payoff can be tremendous."

"What do you do?"

"You play a role."

"Play a role?"

"Yes. You become an actress playing a role. Victor Lustig once passed himself off as a French count and sold a man the Eiffel Tower by pretending he was a corrupt bureaucrat looking for a bribe. He convinced the man that the city was going to sell the tower for scrap and told him that he could rig the bid process to ensure that the man got the bid. He got the man's money and got the man to bribe him to take the money."

"That man must have been really stupid."

"No. He was a smart man, a successful man, a rich man. He knew how the process worked and Lustig knew he knew how it worked. That was the genius of it. It was just that the man was vain and had a little larceny in his heart. That's all it takes. That's why call it the confidence game."

"Why confidence?"

"Confidence is the very magic of the act. Your confidence in your own lie is what gives others confidence in it. Confidence makes the lie become real. The player's firmness of certainty in the venture is what drives it. The deception is absolute and bottomless. None of this should be news to you, Miss Mary Dallas Page. On some level, you had to know this a long time ago. You even acted on it, even if you didn't know what you were acting on."

"What do you mean?"

"You can lie about any damn thing in this world and not get caught if you do it with enough confidence."

"Do you think so?"

"It takes a lot of nerve but you can do it."

"Confidence?"

"Yes. Think about it. You can be stupid and blazing with confidence and you will succeed because your confidence in yourself will fool others. And you can be brilliant and lack confidence and you will sit in some office cubicle and slave away under trays of florescent lights and have a sad life. Have the people in your life fared any different?"

She sat there turning it all over in her mind. "But how do I get started?" she said.

"You start by bringing them the first, last and only interview ever conducted with the reclusive and mysterious Beau Legare."

"But, that's all true. I really did interview you."

"No. You tried to trick me."

"So now I can interview you for real?"

"No."

"What then?"

"You be my accomplice in a con game. Or rather, let me be yours."

"What does that mean?"

"You have already placed yourself into the game. I had nothing to do with that. But I can help you win, now that you're here."

"What do you mean by here?"

"What do you think I've been doing all these years? Writing is the biggest damn hustle there is."

"So what do we do?"

"We make it up."

"Okay. But I'm already doing that."

"It's time you traded up. If you're going to be a fake, you might as well be a beautiful and successful fake. Why be a weed when you can be a diamond?"

"Okay."

"We'll write it together. You don't know much about newspapers or publicity, do you?"

"Not really."

"You'll learn. There's nothing to it but human psychology, and if you weren't already fluent in that, you'd have been discovered by now."

"Okay."

"This is going to be fun. We're going to really mess with your readers and mine and make monkeys out of all of them. It'll be our little secret. We'll be partners in crime. Okay?"

"Okay."

"Tomorrow you will deliver to your editor the life story of Beau Legare, and I promise you it will be one spectacular and epic tale. And he will love it and love you for bringing it to him."

"What should I say?"

Legare got up and poured more whiskey into his tumbler. He thought about it some.

"I don't know," he said. "What do you think?"

"I don't know," she said. "It's your life. Or they'll think it is anyway."

"Yeah, but if you're going to learn how to do this you need to learn how to do it yourself. I can give you some pointers but you'll ultimately be on your own. There will be more stories beyond Beau Legare. And either you can write or you can't. I can't teach you that. You'll see.

"But here is something to remember: the world loves stories. And it does not care if they are true or not. All that matters is whether the story is good. A brazen enough lie may estop and supplant the truth. Every politician knows that. Now so do you.

So you and me, let's get our cynical and conspiratorial minds together. We two writers, we two fugitives from the normative habits of men. We two fabulists. You and I. Let's cook us up a good story for all the marks and the rubes. Let's see if we can trick them."

CHAPTER EIGHTEEN

THE RECLUSIVE PIRATE KILLING POET OF POSSUM CREEK
By Mary Dallas Page
Staff Writer

POSSUM CREEK, S.C. – With his one good eye, Beau Legare spies something stirring in the waters behind his home. He crawls forward on his stomach, inch by terrifying inch, the squirrel gun leading the way, its bore level on the interlopers and sighted from a hill overlooking the creek, the flintlock readied and then curiously the instrument set aside.

He takes up his binoculars and glasses the interlopers through his one good eye. A black patch obscures the other one.

"That's my land them folks is on," he says. "Technically." He speaks in a nasally Charleston brogue. It is the Geechee voice of a fugitive from his birth clan, the exiled son of Holy City gentry. In the wilds surrounding his rice plantation, located just outside Ravenel near the small town of Possum Creek, Legare gets to set the order of things.

"My land, my rules," he says. "I coulda killed them two sons of bitches if I'd a felt like it. Killed them both and put tags on their toes saying it was me killed them. Claimed their heads in replevin and mounted them to oak fixtures in my living room." He issues the pronouncement from on high like a Roman emperor announcing a pardon. "And won't nothing they could do to me."

Confronted with evidence that the state of South Carolina actually owns the creek, Legare becomes defensive.

"The potentates in Columbia may claim to own all navigable waters in this here state, but does that make any sense? Who can own navigable water anyway? You can't own it. Nobody can own it. All you can do is splash around in it. Show me a property line in there anywhere that I can't kick over with a paddle."

Later, across an old oak table made from a tree cut down by William Tecumseh Sherman, Legare for the first time opens up about his life and work. Like his National Book Award-winning novel "The Negroes of Whiskey Creek," his is a sad and mournful tale of a man's paranoia and repeated bouts of madness and his being driven to the edge of the earth by his fellow men but remaining determined to not tumble into what Legare calls "Lucifer's big ass varmint hole."

Today, Legare is known to millions as a reclusive genius who speaks to the world only through his novels. In addition to winning the prestigious National Book Award for "Whiskey Creek," he also received the Pulitzer Prize for "The Colossus of Marshbanks." His other novels are "Lamplight on Water," "Carl F. Pfatchner You're a Lucky Boy," and "Jesus the Pickpocket."

"Absolute shit," he says of both prizes. "I put every damn penny they gave me up my nose."

As to his novels, Legare is only slightly more reflective. "I wouldn't say it's a passion, per se," he says. "It's more like stuff I made up when I couldn't sleep and there was nothing good on TV.

Or maybe I was high on a mixture of Xanax and grain alcohol. Who knows really? It could be anything."

Tall, rumpled yet elegant, Beau Legare (pronounced Leh-gree) is dressed in a seersucker suit, bow tie, and fedora. He has changed out of his camouflage fatigues and duck hat and put away the squirrel gun, although Legare insists on keeping a loaded handgun on the table at all times when he speaks.

"It's not so much that I'm paranoid. It's just that you never know when somebody might try and kill you," he says.

He lost an eye years ago in an unfortunate accident with his cat, a creature he had named Copernicus, after the famous scientist.

"He looked like Copernicus. He had that pointy little face. That's why I named him that. He wasn't good at science or anything," he says. "He didn't really have any special talents at all, to tell you the truth. And he died a coward."

Legare won't talk about it except to say that Copernicus was killed in the same altercation that cost him his eye and that Copernicus had it coming. The remaining eye searches like a light through a milky film as he thinks of the right words to say.

"My family cut me off when I was a boy," he says, lifting a bolt of hot coffee to his jaw. "Left me at the train station with nothing but a can of beans tied up with a stick and kerchief. People never believe me when I tell them that, but that's the God's honest truth. I swear it is."

His eyes mist up as he tells the story and he looks away, the blue veins in his face quickening with pain.

"Faulkner said the past is prologue. Or that it ain't even the past. Or something. But it ain't. It's something else and I don't know what that thing is. I wake up in the middle of the night screaming because I can't figure out how it works. I look around at the world and I think: Who to love? Who not to love?"

Hanging on a wall behind him is a framed picture of Jaclyn Smith.

"I shook her hand once," he says proudly.

Asked why he has until now refused to speak publicly about his life and work, Legare stated, "I don't know. Some days I feel like taking down my guns and shooting the people who come into my yard. Today for some reason I didn't. Today was more of a talking day."

There have been rumors for years that Hollywood would adapt "The Negroes of Whiskey Creek" for the big screen and that Denzel Washington would star. One report had Spike Lee set to direct.

"I'm glad that fell through. I think Spike Lee is too short to direct that movie anyway," he says. "That movie is really about more normal size people. It's not about midgets."

Legare won't divulge what he's working on next, but indicates that we should expect a "sprawling" generational epic set between the Russo-Japanese War and the Crimean War and telling a love story about a Russian doctor in Dothan, Alabama and an idiot man child named Mongo.

"The two of them may or may not go on a cross country killing spree," Legare says. "I haven't decided yet."

Legare says that people can read into his books whatever they want, but that ultimately the reader's opinion is subordinate to his own.

"It's my book, ain't it? If they want it to be different they can write their own goddamn book. Once they've paid for the thing their relationship with me is over [as] far as I'm concerned. After that, they can shit on it for all I care."

Besides, he says, people "[have] never done anything for me. To hell with them."

He has equally harsh words of warning for any award or grant that might be thinking of attaching his name to its roster: "I've been arrested twice for showing my wiener," he says.

According to Legare, his life is not about writing.

"It's just something I do when I'm sitting on the toilet consti-
pated or when I can't sleep. Why do you think I've only written five
books in forty years? If I wrote one sentence a day you'd expect I'd
do better than that."

Ultimately, Legare hopes to be remembered for much loftier
and more enduring pursuits. Toward that end he has identified
a cause that is being neglected but which he promises is both an
important issue and a field in which he can make his own unique
footprint.

"I believe international piracy is the number one problem facing this country right now," he said, thumping his finger on the
table for emphasis. "I really believe that. I really do. Nobody can
deny that fact."

Legare looks out at the water and shakes his head.

"Just because certain entertainers glorify pirates doesn't make
it right," he says. "Pirates inflict real suffering. Pirates destroy real
families. If you're out on the water and some pirates get ahold of
you, that's a really big deal."

Legare shakes his head and looks down at the gun on the table.

"A pirate looks at forty? Not long as I'm around he don't."

Legare says he soon will be investing in a 70-foot sailing vessel
which will be outfitted with "all the latest killing technology," and
that he will use it to hunt pirates in international waters, where he
believes they can be killed without a trial and by a man traveling
absent the color of the law. He says he has recruited a band of mer-
cenaries to sail with him as enforcers.

"The hippies can scream about war crimes all they want. But
first, there ain't no war. And second, there ain't no crime. How can
you have a crime when you can't have a law? And besides, who's going to try me for it?" he says defiantly. "America? South Carolina?
I don't think so. Politicians don't want any part of that. Who wants
to lose an election because they stood up for the pirates? No, if
some pirates happen to end up dead in the water, nobody will ask

any questions. Nobody will even know about it if the ocean does its job properly," he says.

Although he is noncommittal, he indicates the sea craft will be named to honor former television star John Ritter.

"I can't say why," he says over and over again. "Now you're getting into an area where I'm really uncomfortable."

But will he turn his pirate hunting and killing adventures into literature for readers to enjoy in future years?

"No damn way," he says sternly. "There's a special bond there between the pirate and his killer. It's like doctor-patient or priest-penitent. It just goes way back and is older than man himself. Which is pretty old indeed."

When asked if he found it ironic that he would be going into the pirate business years after having suffered the loss of an eye rather than, as one would expect, before doing so, Legare becomes incredulous.

"No, there's nothing ironic about that," he says. "There's nothing ironic at all. All that's ironic is me living this long."

CHAPTER NINETEEN

Dreams now invaded the wiring in her brain and danced and sang to her in her sleep and played their imaginary harp songs. Twin midgets waved their little hands like a single child doubling and flapping its arms like a Hindu god in the reflection of a tall mirror.

There were cannons firing confetti and glasses of champagne and a replica statue in ice of Michelangelo's David urinating vodka from the penis and an old man in a black tuxedo collecting the vodka and making it into drinks and passing them around to the crowd. She was carried forth and hugged and taken from desk to desk and telephone to telephone where everyone in print and broadcast media wanted to talk to her.

Across the room a copy editor held up a telephone receiver and pointed to it, her face exploding in excitement. "Oprah's on the phone!"

Lee Ann put her hands up over her mouth.

"Oh my God!" she said.

Five days later she appeared on Matt Lauer's show. Lauer introduced her and she waved to all of America. On millions of televisions across the country was the face of Lee Ann Pickler above the name of Mary Dallas Page. It said so, right there, in one long blue banner with white lettering.

"So, tell us, how did you get Beau Legare to talk to you?" Lauer said.

Lee Ann gave a shrug. "I don't think it was anything that I did," she said. "I think he just decided it was time to set the record straight. Fortunately, he felt comfortable enough with me to sit down and answer my questions."

"The article makes him sound a little. . . eccentric I guess is the word," Lauer said.

Lee Ann laughed.

"He's his own man," she said. "He definitely marches to the beat of his own drum."

"Until now Legare has never commented, but does he read his own press? There's been hundreds, maybe thousands, of things written about him over the years."

"No," she said. "He just reads the sports section. That and the classics."

"What's his favorite book?"

She gave a coy and teasing smile. "I'm not saying," she said. "I can keep a secret."

She was sitting on the patio behind Beau Legare's mansion in a French patio chair and drinking a fluted glass of expensive champagne. She watched the light flash and wink at her off the curved glass. Beau brought the bottle over and topped off her drink. It was dry and sweet and alive with bubbles and it warmed her body as she drank it.

"So our little tale went over pretty well then?" he said.

"Hasn't anyone called you and asked you about it?"

Legare gave a shrug.

"I have no idea."

"How could you have no idea?"

"All communications go through my agent in New York and she has standing orders to tell anybody who calls that they can go straight to hell. Everybody except for three people, that is. And two of them are dead."

"They all want to know why you gave the interview to me."

"They can wish in one hand and shit in the other and see which one fills up first."

"I'm wondering too," she said.

Beau looked at her then looked out facing the water. He filled his glass again and lifted it to his face.

"Really," she said.

He began laughing.

"It was your turn."

"What?"

"Your brazenness, your guile, your deception. Your scheming, cold-blooded little ways. How determined you were to trick me. I was charmed, darlin. Charmed and surprised and amused. And I like to be amused. Your confidence won you your turn."

"My turn?"

"Life is a turning," he said. "It's like changing dance partners. Connecting and disconnecting. Seeing which ones fit and which ones don't."

"A dance?"

"Yes."

"And you thought we connected?"

"You were unlike anybody I had ever met. Nobody ever tried to trick me like that. Bribes, sure. Pressure, sure. But not outright bald-faced lying and then secretly taping me. I was quite shocked. Shocked and horrified and impressed."

"I'm sorry about that."

"No, I'm glad you did it. If I was you, I'd hope I had the courage to do the same damn thing. It was courage, my dear, and everyone loves courage."

"Does it bother you that your image will be different now?"

"I'm looking forward to it actually."

"Why?"

"Why you think I created this whole hermit routine?"

"I don't know."

"To get attention."

"Really?"

"Hell yes."

"Why would you do that?"

"Because I'm insecure, like everyone else."

"You're really strange, you know that."

"That's true but it's only part of it."

"Oh yeah?"

"Yeah," he said. "There's a logic to it."

"Tell me."

"People read your words closer if they don't get to ask you what they mean. The words mean whatever they mean. It gives you mystery and depth and bakes wisdom into any stupid little thing you happen to write down. James Joyce once spent five pages writing about a man taking a crap. But even that was beautiful because the words were true and Joyce didn't have to go on TV and talk about them. When people see you on TV, you don't look wise. You just look small."

"But that changes now, doesn't it?" she said. "For you?"

He nodded his head. "Everything changes. Even being a hermit novelist. Celebrities invent and reinvent themselves all the time. Why the hell can't I? The only way to restart my branding as a hermit is to briefly cease to be a hermit and then re-assume my hermit role. You sometimes have to stop being a hermit to remind people that you're a hermit.

"The god of this world has declared in stones and water that every living thing is movable, everything capable of transformation, of evolution. Isn't that right, Miss Mary Dallas Page?"

She nodded. "Yes it is, Mister Pirate Killing Whiskey Man."

She looked up and saw him looking down at her and for the first time in her life she saw herself looking into the eyes of a man who knew her and understood her and maybe even loved her. There was a softness there, the two of them. His hand brushed against hers. They came together and kissed. Legare pulled away from her.

"This might be a mistake for you," he said. "You might regret this."

"You're the first person I've felt comfortable around in forever."

"Maybe that ain't enough reason to keep going."

"I don't care," she said.

The feeling was a new feeling, but there was something familiar in the moment, as if her ancestral memory was reaching out beyond her own brief existence and devising to her some ancient bequest.

They held each other there. Her heart fluttered like hummingbird wings.

The room was spinning, her heart beating out of her chest.

She awoke sometime during the night. It was cold in the vaporous mansion and pitch black. She grabbed the covers and gathered herself in them. Next to her, she felt the rise and fall of a man's chest with a heavy breathing rhythm.

For a moment she became terrified at the thought of a stranger lying next to her. She felt alone, completely alone. There was no one in the darkness with her, only a stranger, a man she had just met. This man was no different than any other man. He too would leave her and she would be alone again. She knew it. She was all by herself in the world.

No, she told herself. That's not true. It's not, it's not. This man loves me. He loves me.

"Beau," she said, her eyes misting with tears. "Beau. . ."

She felt him stir and creak in his sleep.

"Yes, darlin."

"Beau, you wouldn't never leave me like that would you Beau?"

"No darlin," he said.

"Do you promise?"

"Leave you?"

"Yes."

There was a little pause and then he creaked again.

"I promise," he said.

CHAPTER TWENTY

After that, they operated as one. He was the invisible hand beating the drawers of ghosts in her head and guiding her through the mysteries of conjuring things from places where there had previously been none present. She was the reservoir and the faithful student.

He taught her how to write fiction. "If you're interesting, nobody will care if you're telling the truth," he said. "And if you're not, nobody will care period."

The two of them spent hours devising characters who might have populated the swamps surrounding the city of Charleston. They thought about outcasts and criminals and members of the occult. They made up story after story.

She took their collaborations to the eight o'clock editorial meeting, where she pitched the stories and then wrote them. She made several calls to Beau during the day and he would pretend to be her source.

The stories exploded off the page. They grew beyond themselves and entered the lore of the natives and became a part of the regional history. People talked about the stories in local coffee shops and bars. As if the land itself had ever been populated by those in the stories. The stories prevailed and prevailed and suddenly there was no stopping them.

There was the tale of Earl Duberry, a Vietnam veteran with a metal plate in his head and nineteen confirmed kills who now lived in a homeless shelter and collected cans and traded them for money at the recycling plant. He used the money to purchase old cars for fifty or seventy five dollars and then smashed them to pieces by wrecking them into trees. He then recycled them back into cans. He considered himself a performance artist meditating on the wheel of life. The story named him as a finalist for a MacArthur Fellowship but nobody from the Fellowship would comment on that.

And there was the woman named Sheila Sprangle who spent her time haunting the woods near Hanahan collecting squirrel bones which she believed levied special powers in the spirit world. She waited until the moon was full and then traipsed with a crippled gait to the cemetery where she recited curses over the graves of a long dead sheriff and his wife and children. The sheriff had allegedly killed her grandfather in a gunfight.

She was said to be suspected in a number of local murders but there wasn't sufficient evidence to arrest her for any of them. She became a local legend and if she was living or had ever lived at all she would have been startled by all the attention. The children made up rhymes about the witch and the evil she did in the woods at night.

Some of the stories were picked up in Charleston and beyond and one morning Beau Legare held up a copy of the New York World and smiled his crooked drunken smile and showed Lee Ann a story she had written. It said "By The Associated Press," but it was hers, word for word. They hugged each other and laughed at the absurdity of it all.

They were playing a joke on the whole wide world and getting away with it and it was so much fun that neither of them could stand it.

Some nights they lay there together and just looked into the eyes of the other without speaking a word but with both understanding the specialness of the moment. The world, rushing away, would leave them both on its plains but once they were here and once they left their mark by tricking all the others. Neither articulated it, but they both sensed the desperate fragility of their bond and their work and they both longed for it to continue.

Sheila Sprangle and Earl Duberry and all the rest emerged from decanter bottles, metastasizing in the brain folds in Legare's skull and moved from his lips to her lips, his fingers to her fingers and through her brain and into her eyes and the finger muscles moving her pen. Things only imagined by the two of them were distributed as calcified facts and upon arrival those facts became realities with which people in the larger world beyond now had to reckon.

The stories came on and on and all were beyond incredible. But they were entertaining and moving and sometimes they were even great. Beau guided Lee Ann through all sorts of characters real and imagined.

There was the blind man who used to be world chess champion and was now living in motels in rural South Carolina and the little homeless boy who was an expert pickpocket on King Street and the old grandmother who had poisoned two husbands and gotten away with it and couldn't be identified because of the need for anonymity.

She became a celebrity in the town. People came up to her everywhere, recognized her by the brightness and familiarity of her toothy country girl smile. They all smiled eagerly and stood next to her as their friends took pictures and all wanted to recount some story or another and to tell their own stories. She was everyone's favorite girl.

In the springtime, droplets of rain fell and the flowers opened and turned ripe in the sun and everything became a blur of colors. The keys of the Olivetti kept smashing blackened characters into the pulp of the broadsheet paper and Beau Legare, a glass of Tennessee sour mash melting in his hand, would throw back his head and rock backward and forward with laughter. She would hold him and the two of them together would compose little fabrications and watch as the following day people throughout the Lowcountry sat there transfixed at the stories.

CHAPTER TWENTY-ONE

He now found himself doing something he always said could not be done by any man. He was teaching another person to write.

No, he told himself. She was born knowing how. I'm just helping her find it inside herself. It's there. She just has to find it. And I can help her with that. She'll be a star at this.

He swore this as a validation and an affidavit of good faith to the part of him still doubtful of the whole enterprise.

He unloaded everything he knew about writing onto her and she grew with every story but always and from the beginning were present the natural lyricism and pitch. She just got better and better and she never made the same mistake twice.

One day he looked at her and shook his head.

"What is it?" she said.

"Reckon we're gonna have to teach you about other stuff too," he said. "If you're gonna be Miss Mary Dallas Page, you better start thinking and talking like her. One of these days you're going to run into a real debutante. What are you going to do then?"

"I don't know."

"See? There are some things you'll need to know."

"Like what?"

"Debutante type things. Cotillion things."

"Girly things?"

"Yes. Girly things. How to be a lady. A southern lady. I suppose so, anyway. Manners and such. You know, which fork to eat with. What sort of wine goes with what type of meat. All that."

He could see that she was skeptical.

"My dear, if you are to move among them undiscovered, you must know their little tricks and tropes," he said. "Otherwise it is no good. They will catch on."

"And you know those things?"

"Most of it. I reckon I can bluff my way through the rest."

"And you can teach me?"

"I'd be delighted to. It would be my long slumbering revenge visited at last upon them."

"Why do you hate them so much?"

"Never mind that," he said. "I have my reasons, but it's not what you think. It's nothing nefarious. It's just. . . . Training an imposter and sending her into their den to spill all their little secrets. Even the ones that aren't true but might as well be. Now, I can't teach you all the girl things cause I ain't no girl. You'll have to pick most of them things up yourself. But the rest, that I can teach you."

"How did you learn all of this?" she said.

"I was sired and reared by the landed Southern gentry and I am a rebel from their ranks. Rebel or outcast. I guess to me I'm a rebel. To them I'm probably an outcast. They probably think they ran me off and who knows, maybe they did. Who ran who off don't matter. I'm gone from them. But once I was one of them. Or at least they thought I was."

⊷⊶

"What turned you against them?"

"I don't know. Maybe it was just something to turn against."

"You don't believe that."

"No. I reckon I don't."

"What do you reckon, then?"

"It was their sense of entitlement, I think. The way they believed, and they did, deep down I mean, that the legacies being handed them were not tokens born of luck. Pure dumb luck."

"What's wrong with luck?"

"Not a thing in this world."

"I don't understand."

"I wasn't jealous of their luck. God bless them for that. I hated them because what I saw as luck they saw as a birthright. They honestly thought they were superior to other human beings. It sickened me toward them. I reckon that's it, anyway."

"But you've been lucky too," she said.

"Hell yes I have. But I saw it for what it was. And I was grateful for it and I was humble in the face of it. At least I like to think I was."

"What do you reckon they think of you now?"

"The landed gentry of South Carolina's enchanted marshlands?"

"Yeah, them."

He gave a broad, satisfied smile. "They don't think nothing of me," he said. "They don't know a person like me exists at all. I know that for a notarized fact because I know don't none of them read books."

As the days and weeks came on and then fell away, he watched a broken, frightened girl begin to straighten her gait and then walk upright. She became confident in who she was and what she was becoming. She was growing into her own lie and the lie was growing with her. She had subsumed the lie and it subsumed her and the two were now as unsplittable as water.

Her happiness infected those around her and her smile became warm and reassuring and the light in her eyes shone in empathy and everyone wanted to confide in her and be her friend.

"I can give you all of it. The look, the style, the moves, the confidence, all of it," Beau Legare told her. "If you trust me. Okay?"

"Okay."

"But I can't give you a life. What I can give you may resemble the trappings of a life. You might use these lies to obtain housing, food, shelter. That is a living but it is not a life. Only you can make it a life."

"What's the difference?"

"A life requires meaning and purpose. And nobody can give you that. That you must find inside yourself. It's all up to you. Don't look for help from me or nobody else. I mean it. Because you're the only one that's going to live it. Nobody else gets to, so nobody else has standing to tinker with the design. So think about it a lot. Just give yourself a good one. Okay?"

She smiled and put her arm around him, cradling him in a sweet and maternal embrace.

"Are you happy with the life you've had?" she said. "I mean, up until now."

Legare thought about that and finally said yes. "I was only good for one thing and nothing else," he said. "But I discovered what that thing was and I happened to be very good at it. That was enough for me. It's more than most folks get."

"I don't know what it'll be for me," she said.

"Let's hope it will be something."

"You say that like it might not be anything."

"It might not. That's true."

"That doesn't make me feel any better."

"I'm sorry."

"I'll take my chances I guess," she said.

"That's my girl."

"What do I got to lose?"

"Nothing," Legare said. "Not a thing in this world."

Hands joined, they walked among the marsh. The sky was cloudless and blue and the rotting smell of pluff mud flooded the bottomland. Orange waves of cord grass parted by dark and silvering spots of brackish water stretched out into the distant row of trees lined up against the sky.

As they walked, Beau pointed out the various natives of the marsh. In the distance was a snowy egret, elegant and white and feathered, its long crooked legs submerged in the black water. Overhead circled a red-shouldered hawk, its wings like black fingers against the sky.

They walked out onto the bridge of a rice trunk and she looked at the water and the grass and tried to untangle with her eyes the maze of canals and quarter drains hidden behind the green stalks of needle rush. He pointed to the water and there, not ten feet from them, lay an alligator, its horn back skin rising from the creek like chinks of armor. The giant lizard slept like a dragon guarding a Chinese temple.

He felt her pull away from him.

"Don't be scared, darlin. He won't hurt you."

"He's a crocodile," she said.

"No, darlin. We don't have any of them around here. He's an alligator."

"Whatever."

"His name's Jake. And he only eats people in the summertime."

"How do you know?"

"I read it someplace."

"But I'm scared of crocodiles," she said.

"Me too," Legare said. "But that there ain't no crocodile. That there is an alligator. And probably a big green chickenshit."

"Let's go," she said.

"Don't be afraid. Besides, bony little thing like you wouldn't tide him over for too long. Reckon he'd set his sights on me if he was hungry."

She smiled and looked back over the long range of marshland.

"It's so beautiful," she said.

"Yes it is."

"Is this all your land?"

Beau gave a thoughtful nod. "As much as land can belong to a man, yes."

"What's that supposed to mean?"

"It means there is a deed in some courthouse drawer saying I own this land and all the creatures upon it. Ferae naturae, as the Romans might say to one another. The grant goes all the way back to the king of England and now it has passed down to lucky ole little ole me. But to that reptile, I'm just another creature out here looking for food and sunlight. That deed don't mean a thing to him."

"It must be nice," she said, looking over the marsh plain.

"Land is land, I suppose. It was the cleave dividing royalty from the plebes in the olden days. But land is alienable. It can be given or sold or taken away. It can be destroyed and divided and laid waste."

"So can anything else."

"That's not true."

"Oh yeah. How you figure?"

"There are things that endure forever, believe it or not."

"I'm not sure I believe that."

"Well I guess I think you're wrong then."

"I mean it. What if I don't?"

"Then you don't. So what? We don't have to agree about it."

Lee Ann looked at Beau and then looked back out at the marsh.

"A smart man once told me nothing endures," she said. "I think he'd thought long and hard about it before he told me that. And I've thought about it a lot since then and I think he was probably right."

"Nope. He was wrong," Beau said.

"Oh yeah?"

"Yeah. I'm not saying he was dumb. I'm just saying he didn't think about it long enough."

"How do you know?"

"Because I happen to know that certain things endure."

"What things?"

"Things. The things we talk about but cannot touch. The things we can't see but we know are there. The big things. The invisible things."

"The invisible things?"

"That's right. It's like this. Can a thing not be invisible but real? A memory, for instance. Is there anything more real than a memory, or anything more invisible?

"If something cannot be touched, it cannot be harnessed. If it cannot be harnessed, it cannot be ended. Immortality is the world's inability to destroy everything that it creates. That is the magic. And a thing which is indestructible is a thing which lives forever.

"Memories of a thing, if not the thing itself, are immortal. They outlive even the human repositories holding them because they are themselves non-physical properties. Since they exist outside of the molecular universe as you and I understand it, they are in no way prisoners of the human mind.

"So not everything goes to the charnel house. Believe it or not. Things are identifiable and perishable according to the same principle. Think about it. Nature may only destroy that which it may touch in the physical sense and even nature is powerless to disturb something so elusive as a memory."

"You think so?"

"Yes ma'am. Once a thing is spoken or felt, it is moved into the ark carrying the record of time, the contents joined in covenant with their ancestors and descendants and passed from man to man and generation to generation. Ledgered and remaindered and preserved. The result is something invisible and yet permanently lasting.

"The Catholics believe that the substance of a thing and its shape are two distinct and divergent things, two severable things. It's like that. Think of a clock. You see its hands move but you never see time. Time is invisible, but its markings are everywhere. Things writ in words and in nature. The language and art of the world. Have you ever doubted its existence?"

"No."

"Of course not."

Legare squinted his eyes toward the sun. "The tangible world ages and burns and vanishes," he said. "It vanishes but it does not die. It is reborn into different shapes. Molecules and men. Death is not a destination but a middleman. It is an agency for the escheatment of the soul and the mechanism returning it to its very beginning. To the moment the lightning bolt first struck the primordial puddle.

"Moments are here and then they are gone. But then they are here again. Your birth, your death, this conversation, the creation and destruction of this world. All have been played and replayed endlessly since God first spoke. It's like a filmstrip winding and unwinding in the projector wheel. That's us darlin, you and me.

"This is our time through the viewfinder. Our bodies are antic clay and our goods are sentimental trash. All that is left is what we saw and what we did and what we felt. The time and the memory. There is nothing else."

She sat there looking at him and turning it over in her mind.

"What if you're wrong?" she said.

"It ain't a crime to be wrong. But I don't think I'm wrong. I'm pretty smart too and I've thought about it a lot and I know this much: The physical world dissolves and wastes away. It transforms itself, yes, and pieces of it die.

"But memory will outlive the sun. As a Roman poet used to say: Non omnis moriar. You see, darlin, I shall never completely die and neither shall you."

PART TWO

The Queen of King Street

CHAPTER TWENTY-TWO

At the end of springtime, she got the call that would change her life forever. She was invited to meet with Mary Ellen Snoffengrass, the editor-in-chief of Charleston's Lowcountry Gazette, to discuss matters unknown. The Gazette was Charleston's major daily newspaper. It appeared each morning on every doorstep in the city.

She had spent the previous nine months in Ravenel, less than thirty minutes from downtown Charleston on Highway 17. But she had never gone into the city, despite her deep and longtime fascination with it. The city was her magnet, but she was terrified to enter it. It was as though setting foot on its streets chanced cracking the glass of her fragile dream. Charleston was a place to dream about and not to visit, she told herself.

On the day she was to meet Mary Ellen Snoffengrass, Lee Ann got up before sunrise and vomited into a trash can. She got some coffee and waited for the bus that would take her to Market Street in downtown Charleston. As she crossed over the bridge, she was struck by the beauty of what she saw. A painted sand castle city hanging over a rolling sea. The houses blazed with colors.

She got off at the market and stood there for a few minutes watching the Gullah women weaving baskets from sweet grass and palmetto leaves. She crossed the street and found the rooftop bar overlooking the Battery. She looked around and saw a woman in a red sun dress and white long-brimmed hat with a blue band around it. The woman was seated in a pool of umbrella shade. She was smoking a long cigarette and staring through her dark sunglasses at Lee Ann Pickler. Lee Ann walked over to the woman's table.

"Are you Ms. Snoffengrass?" she said.

The woman allowed for a long pause.

"Miss Mary Dallas Page," the woman finally said. "Why, you look even younger than I had imagined. Please, have a seat. What would you like to drink?"

Lee Ann took a seat. "Do they have Chardonnay here?"

Mary Ellen Snoffengrass gestured to the waiter.

"A glass of Chardonnay, please," she said.

Mary Ellen Snoffengrass studied the child in front of her. "So," she said. "Do tell me about yourself."

As they talked, Lee Ann looked out over the rainbow colored mansions with their rounded porches turning clockwise toward the water. The ocean was a deep blue festooned with red and white sails riding up and down on the waves.

They talked for over an hour. Mary Ellen Snoffengrass asked her questions, and Lee Ann supplied her with fabricated and improvised answers. She had three glasses of Chardonnay and the wine relaxed her and gave her confidence. Mary Ellen looked at her through the enormous dark lenses. She smoked her cigarette and looked at Lee Ann for a long time, and then she spoke.

"I know you can write," said Mary Ellen Snoffengrass. "And I know you can find stories. If I wasn't sure you could do both of those things, you wouldn't be sitting here."

Lee Ann just nodded.

"What I want to know is whether you can do it here. Ravenel is one thing, but this is Charleston. I wanted to see you for myself and have a drink with you to see if we could deal with you or whether you would make us all want to kill ourselves."

"Oh," Lee Ann said.

Mary Ellen Snoffengrass took a drink of wine.

Lee Ann smiled. "Well what do you think so far?" she said.

Mary Ellen Snoffengrass looked out into the harbor and something in the distance seemed to remove the line of sight between her and her object of thought. Then she looked back at Lee Ann and took another drink.

"I'm impressed," she said.

On the bus ride home, Lee Ann sat in a window seat looking out at the world and thinking about the arc of her life. Everything was a beginning and an end. Don't get excited, she told herself. Don't do it or it might not happen. You might jinx yourself.

She cradled her head in the space between the headrest and the window and looked out the window and watched the blacktop and the palmetto fronds pass at a blur. She allowed herself for one brief moment to dream her dream and in that moment she was perfectly happy.

Ahead on the road was a young black girl, maybe thirteen. Her hair was frogged and braided with white beads and the beads went down her back and danced on the bicycle seat. The girl was peddling an old bicycle and balancing two bushels of green sweetgrass on the rack behind her. The blades fanned out around her like the feathers on a peacock's tail.

She tried in vain to hold onto the image and the beauty of the image as it paled into the vanishing landscape, the world and the brightness of its ornaments rushing on in a blur ever faster and then passing soundlessly away.

CHAPTER TWENTY-THREE

In July of that year she accepted an offer from Mary Ellen
Snoffengrass and went to work as a features columnist for the
Lowcountry Gazette. Her face was visible every Sunday morning
on the front page of the features section. Mary Dallas Page, it said,
under her smiling image. Columnist.

The words were corroborated in the masthead and on her business card. They gave her a three thousand dollar signing bonus
and an office overlooking the painted harbor. On the Sunday before she started work, she was so nervous she could barely breathe.

"This will be much more difficult, you know?" he said.

"I know."

"This isn't making up things for gullible rednecks who live in a
swamp. This is the King Street crowd. You understand? You may as
well be dealing with the Parisian gentry."

"Do you think I can do it?" she said.

"You'll have to be careful. Building a lie is like building a cave. There are physical laws and mechanisms. You have to bore straight into it but you cannot allow it to fall in on itself, because that's its natural inclination. So there's a balance you have to find."

"If I build it big enough, I can live inside it?"

"Yes," said Beau Legare. "You can in fact."

"I'm afraid, though," she said.

"What's there to be afraid of?"

"In the end all I have is me. And I won't even have that any more. I step onto those streets and Lee Ann Pickler disappears forever."

"There are always consequences. I'm not saying this is any different. You have chosen to assemble your life out of little cards of lies. You are a liar. Remember that. Never forget it. You have the ethics of a common marsh worm. But then don't be ashamed of it because the worm sure ain't. That's life, darlin. A great ruction full of riddles and externalities."

"What if they catch me?"

"It won't be good."

"Maybe I shouldn't risk it."

"The safest thing would be to go back to working as a motel maid."

"I'm not doing that."

"I don't blame you."

"I just want to be happy again," she said.

"Me too," he said. "I want that for you too."

⊶⊷

She spent the night with Beau at his mansion. She held onto him in the dark and fidgeted with anxiety.

In the morning, she lay on the enormous bed turning one of her business cards over again and again. The card was bone colored, with raised delicate ink and a thread-heavy linen stock. Her name and title sparkled in the light of the room.

He watched the girl there, watched her like you watch a butterfly foot onto a flower. She was finding her way and it was beautiful for him to watch.

He remembered one morning when the sunrise brightened the marsh and he opened the windows and made coffee and stood there in his bathrobe watching the changing sky. She opened her eyes and saw him standing there, the orange and blue curve of the world bending around him. She sat up and got dressed and poured a cup of coffee and sat up with him and looked out at the world rising with the sun.

"This world's one hell of a place," he said. "Whoever dreamed all this up has got some imagination.

CHAPTER TWENTY-FOUR

S he drove across the bridge and looked down at the harbor. She rode into the sunlit city with its colors bright in a rainbow of buildings with church spires rising and oak trees draped in Spanish moss. The city plunged into the maw of the harbor. Everything seemed so small from up there.

She could feel herself transforming as she crossed over the bridge. Entering the city was her turning point. A small town newspaper was one thing. You could get away with mischief there. But a major regional paper was another. There was no disclaiming her new identity now. It was a permanent identity.

The girl walking the dirt roads of Carthage and the girl turning the car onto King Street in downtown Charleston were two separate and discreet creatures and neither could ever again live in the presence of the other. It was a beginning and an end. It was the death of Lee Ann Pickler and the birth of Mary Dallas Page.

Mary Dallas Page was now a person with a job and a credit card and an apartment and a new Toyota Camry with a sunroof and leather seats. She was no longer the wonder girl from Ravenel. Greater things were now expected of her.

There were no surprises or congratulatory gestures for greatness. Greatness and perfection were things to be counted on. The entire city was there to hold her accountable now for any error or lie.

"This won't be the same," Beau Legare said.

"I know it won't."

"You can't go on making up stuff forever."

"I know."

"Eventually you'll have to learn to do it for real. It's the only way you'll last at it."

"You think I'll be able to?"

"It'll be a lot harder. People will be looking at you now."

"You'll be right there with me. Won't you?"

Beau Legare shrugged. "I'll always be there," he said. "In the shadows anyway. Always. But you will have to do it yourself from now on. Real people, real stories. Sometimes, at least. One false move and it all comes crashing down. A counterfeit bill is the genuine article until somebody starts looking at it too closely. Its value or illusion of value is only seeable from afar. So don't let them get too close. You hear me?"

She nodded.

"Just remember to have confidence. Never you doubt yourself, no matter what. Confidence, my dear. Confidence. Remember: some forgeries are better than the real thing."

Beau explained to her that she would have to infiltrate those from whom he had lived as an outcast and that to do so would be hard.

"Charleston is the most cliquish and provincial city in the world," he said. "There are two types of people in Charleston: Natives and Yankees."

"What do I do?" she said.

Beau thought about that for a minute. "I don't know," he said. "I really don't."

"You don't think I can just charm my way in?"

"I think that's all you can do. That's your only bet. Like anywhere, there is only one inner circle which is of any newsworthiness and all its members hang together like one festering puss blister."

Beau ran his fingers through his hair and looked up, hair wild like a mad scientist, a frosting of sleep coming over his eyes. "You going to tell them about Chapel Hill and the debutante thing and all that?"

"I plan to," she said. "Why shouldn't I?"

"Reckon you got to now. Just mention it in passing. Don't play it up or nothing."

"Okay."

<hr />

"Every city has a secret inner sect whose mystery is unfathomable to outsiders who look in on them in their silk dresses and polished loafers and hate them for their easy talk and their placing their hands around the shoulder or elbow of the other," he said.

"But how do they become them?"

"Nobody really knows," Beau said. "They kind of recognize each other and seek each other out. It's a mystery. Even to me."

"Oh come on," she said.

Beau smiled. "Okay," he said.

"What is it, then?"

"It's fitting in. And there is much going into that. There is breeding, pedigree, credibility, sameness, human connectivity. You're either one of them or you're not. And being born unto them gets you most of the way there. All you have to do is not be weird."

"Is that where you went wrong?"

"Yep."

"Will it be hard to talk my way in?"

"It'll be like trying to infiltrate Buckingham Palace."

"I'm nervous."

"Nervous about what?"

"What if I can't do it?"

"So what? Probably you can't anyway. If I was you I know I couldn't. Hell, if I was me I couldn't."

"So what then?"

Beau shrugged. "I don't know," he said. "So you fail at something? So what? Welcome to the human race. Failure is the grass of life. Success is the daisy. There is great freedom in failure because failure strips away all the pretentions and restarts the machine. Something else will find its way to you and you will probably fail at that too. All you have to do is be lucky at something eventually.

"But there is one great misconception which you may be laboring under. You might believe, for instance, that you are the architect of your own destiny. In fact, you have almost no control over it. Events intervene. Fate and luck. Good luck and bad luck. Being lucky, my dear, that is the most important thing of all."

"Really?"

"Yes. Napoleon and Caesar and Charlemagne would all tell you the same thing. Like old Kurt Vonnegut said, history is nothing but a series of surprises."

"So I don't have any control over it?"

"I didn't say that."

"That sounds a whole lot like whatever it was you said."

"I said luck matters and it matters big. Luck is your silent partner in life. And sometimes he isn't just silent, he's invisible. And he goes away for periods of time but when he comes back, he always brings something big with him. Sometimes it's a million dollars. Sometimes it's a dog turd."

"Okay. So I'm just a hostage?"

"No. Luck ain't everything. The rest of it is you. It's really something, how it all works together. Part of it is what you do, but part of it really is just your fate. So at least half of it is out of your hands. Maybe more."

"So what do I do then?"

"Don't worry about the luck. Just do what you can for yourself and hope the dice turn up for you. That's the best I can tell you."

"No," she said. "Please. You have to give me some guidance here."

"You could pray, I reckon."

"Pray for what?"

"Luck."

"No, come on. There has to be more to it than that."

"There's not. There's really not. Look, I have given you all the help I can give you. Now you must either go do it or give up on it. Confidence, my dear. Confidence. Remember. No one will doubt you unless you first doubt yourself."

"But I'm scared."

"I'd be scared too."

"No you wouldn't."

"You're right. I wouldn't."

"Why's that?"

"Because I know something you don't know."

"What?"

"I know that failure is nothing and success is nothing and that the struggle is the only thing that matters. I know that the world can be divided between those who join in the struggle and those who run from it. The former are the only ones I give a damn about. The rest of them are cowards who should be lined up against a wall and shot."

"You make it sound so harsh," she said.

Beau Legare gave a wide grin and pushed his hat back on his head so that the under brim showed over his shadowed and beard-dusted face.

"Life is not the destination," he said. "Life is the struggle."

"What do you mean?"

"The world's a beautiful place. It's got rocks and rivers and snow creased mountains and majestic wild creatures all living in some strange perfect balance. But it will kill you graveyard dead and keep on going without you.

"And it'll forget you ever existed. Making it remember you at all, that's the whole trick to it. That's the answer to the riddle everybody's busy figuring out. Because there isn't any other riddle. And in the end there ain't no riddle at all. You know what's waiting there for you when you're done picking flowers.

"It's always there. Walking beside you all the time. That conclusion raises the only one question worth pondering."

"What question is that?"

"Is there a God or not?"

"That's it?"

"Life promises the certainty of death. God promises victory over death. Could there be any other question? Is there anything else worth being interested in?"

"I don't know."

"That question is a doubly important question, because it deals with both present and future. How you answer that question determines what kind of person you will be."

"Why is that?"

"If there is a God, it is possible that he created us for a reason and that he might be interested in what we do. It is natural to think that such a God might place us where he wants us to be and at least give us a chance before sitting in judgment of us. If that is the true, you should be very afraid of angering God. You would order your steps very differently than if you believed he does not exist."

"What do you mean?"

"If God is nothing but a fairy tale, then this world is one big mean tragedy. He's the only thing holding it together. Over ninety percent of all people on earth believe in God. Can you imagine if they didn't?"

"Why do you think they believe in him?"

"Because they can't bear not to."

"What would happen if they didn't?"

"They'd all eat each other."

"You think so?"

"If God does not exist, you would be a fool to deny yourself any pleasure or ever place the needs of another person above your own. God is the difference. If there is no God, you're a fool for not murdering me in my sleep and taking all my money."

"I don't know if I believe in God," she said.

"I don't know either."

"He seems awful cold sometimes."

"Yes he does."

"He doesn't mind breaking your heart either."

"No, he doesn't. But the absence of God makes love impossible. Everything, even love, must come from somewhere and it cannot come from you if you come from nothing."

"Love is real," she said. "Love is something you know is real because you can feel it."

"Feeling it or not don't make it real," Legare said. "Feelings are just signals carried on the bullet heads of nerve endings. Whether a thing has any objective value depends on whether it can be judged by an impartial omniscient observer and characterized as a good or an evil. There must be some cosmic referee or else all is meaningless and random. You might pretend to love another person and they might pretend to love you, and you both might even believe what you're saying. But what does that mean? Such a love would answer to no authority and would be nothing more than the fantasies of dying sheets of carbon. The grass and the dirt might as well profess their devotion to one another. So what?"

"So that's the question I need to be asking myself?" she said.

"That is the only question. It is the question which answers all other questions."

"Okay."

"Don't worry," he said. "You don't have to answer it right now. Give it some time, live a little bit, see what you think."

"Well how come you know that and nobody else does?"

"I've had more time to think about it than they have."

"And that's it, you think?"

"There's nothing else to it."

"You're sure?"

"Pretty sure."

"So what do you believe?" she said.

"I don't pretend to know. I only pretend to know the question. The answer has been entrusted to another player in the game, I reckon."

"Well you must have thought about it."

"I've never thought about much else."

"And you still don't have an answer?"

"Nope."

"You didn't have to choose," she said. "You had a good life. You had fame and money. You had everything. You got to do whatever you wanted."

"Well lucky me then."

"Well lucky you."

— ❧ ❧ —

She walked down King Street in the cold admiring the orange flames dancing in the gas lamps, their iron holders affixed to the bricks by the hands of French artisans whose bone meal now fed the ground.

The torch lamps stood on either side of the doorframes. She stopped in front of a gray mansion. The mansion had green ribbons of ivy creeping up onto it and large oak trees in the tiny yard.

She looked at the wall surrounding it. Gray stucco, blasted away by time, the faded brickwork now showing. A cast iron gate with spikes atop its railing. Two balustrades, one on top of the other. A cantilevered platform with high arching porch doors and decorative columns curving in on themselves like gray hourglasses. The house stood there in the light like an enormous wedding cake.

She checked the number and then looked at the address in her notebook. This was it. Chimes rang out in the distance and somewhere deep within her breast she felt the beating of wings. Lee Ann Pickler looked through the spaces in the moss-threaded trees and saw the white columns and steeple of St. Michael's church. The weathervane on top turned in the wind and then stopped. The golden hands on the black church clock pointed to the Roman numerals IX and XII. Time.

She could see the tall thin cemetery stones stacked in crooked rows, the stained glass relief with a gaping blue hole indicating an empty perfect sky. The women at the tomb, the stone rolled away. Angel wings. He is not here, he is arisen. The story and how it all went.

She took a deep breath and crossed the street and again walked through the abstraction of self-made lies into the cold reality of a Tuesday morning in a strange and unknowable city.

CHAPTER TWENTY-FIVE

Mary Ellen Snoffengrass was impeccably dressed in knee-high deerskin boots and a long white party dress. Her wall of mascara hid her face from the world.

They sat in a large office decorated with bright flowers and blown-up magazine covers in frames on the interior walls. The outer walls were glass and looked out onto the harbor just downstream from the Cooper River Bridge. The bridge reached across the river as one long white rainbow splitting massive twin sails.

Mary Ellen Snoffengrass went over the expectations and the rules.

"I expect two columns a week," she said.

"Do you assign them to me or do I pick them?"

"You pick them. Write about whatever you want. If it's good I'll publish it and if it's not I'll fire you. But you know how that works. Or maybe you don't yet. Either way, that's how it works."

"I can do two a week."

"Good."

"Do I have to spend nine to five in here every day?"

Mary Ellen laughed.

"I didn't know."

"I don't give a damn if you're here at your desk or knocking back martinis at Thoroughbred's. I just want two columns a week. Be good and be on deadline. I don't want any excuses. I only want results. You can work out the other details yourself. I really don't care either way."

"Okay."

"What are some story ideas you have so far?"

"I got one or two. But I'm still pretty new to the area."

"What are the one or two you've got?"

"Well, I don't know. I just thought I could do like, you know, profiles of people around town. Colorful people and stuff."

"Colorful people are good. But not common colorful people. Maybe one or two a month. But I want you to home in on the big hitters. Charleston's old money set. Enough with the beggars and criminals already."

"I'll do the best I can."

"You got in with Legare. These people are just like that. Rich, pompous, self-pitying. Vain. Guarded. Just like that. Do you think you can get in with Legare again?"

"I don't know. He's a little unpredictable."

"Did you get the sense that his persona was a bit of a put on? I mean, I was wondering if you did because the interview made him sound so, oh what is the word I'm looking for, oh yes, so over the top?"

"I thought he was telling the truth."

"Really? Fascinating."

"He was nice to me though."

"Good. That's good."

"Are there any people that I should talk to in particular?"

Mary Ellen clicked open her purse and came up with a box of Winstons. She took out a long white cigarette and placed it between her lips and picked up a gold lighter and struck the ball of her thumb across the top of her forefinger and a blue flame appeared and showed Lee Ann Pickler her own distorted image reflecting in the metal. Mary Ellen bent her face down to the flame and drew in and the tobacco cinders hissed and smoldered.

"I was against hiring you you know?"

"I thought you said you liked me?"

"Not at first."

"I didn't know."

"As far as I was concerned you were a one-trick pony and everyone had already seen the trick. So prove me wrong, okay?"

"I'll do my best."

"Your best may not be good enough. It isn't always, you know?"

"I'll do my best."

Mary Ellen Snoffengrass laughed. "I know, darling," she said. "I know you will."

⊫⊣⊢⊐

She spent a hot Saturday afternoon looking at apartments from West Ashley to Daniel Island, finally settling into a one bedroom place in Mount Pleasant. The apartment bordered onto Shem Creek where she could watch the shrimp boats floating by with their tangled nets. The sun set in layers of colors behind them.

She found a riverfront bar where they made a good coconut rum and pineapple juice drink and she spent long afternoons on the outer deck working on fictional stories about imagined Charlestonians and wondering if they would be good enough for Mary Ellen Snoffengrass.

She fell in love with the sunset over the silvering marsh and the sulfur smell burning in the hot summer nights. The boats would go back and forth and she imagined what it would be like way out there on the ocean at night, away from any civilization and nothing but yourself and the stars and the moon and no part of the physical earth to hold onto. Beneath you, giant creatures slumbering in a deep, silent world.

She would call Beau and read the stories to him and he would do his little edits, a nip here and there, but it was becoming more natural to her and she could feel his steady invisible hand easing itself gently off the bicycle seat. She remembered his rules for writing. She repeated them to herself every day.

"First rule is you gotta be interesting," he said. "If you ain't interesting, you ain't worth a damn."

She remembered the stories he used to tell. There was the retarded boy who solved mysteries for old people and the compulsive thief who only stole metallic objects and the root doctor who sold criminals a spell to protect them from the cops but then snitched for money on the same people he had indemnified with his root dance.

She missed him but was grateful that he was letting her emerge into who and what she was becoming. At first she came into work every morning at eight and drank coffee and read the paper and tried to make friends. But the others were cliquish and insecure and offered what seemed to her a preemptive condescension. She was a girl living her dream and her dream was a lie and there were no friends to share it with. There was just Beau, and he was always there, somewhere, in the shadows watching her in the becoming.

"Why are they like that?" she said.

"Cause they're jealous of you, darlin."

"But why?"

"Cause there's plenty to be jealous of."

"They don't know anything about me."

"You might want to keep it that way. Besides, that's how it is sometimes," he said. "Everybody thinks they know everybody else. And you feel sorry for people beneath you and jealous for people you think are doing better than you. But nobody knows. Life is one of them things darlin. It's every man for himself. And don't nobody know the road you've had to travel. Or the road ahead. You don't know their road either."

"But they won't even give me a chance," she said.

She heard Beau laughing on the other end of the receiver. "When you fail, that's when they'll give you a chance. That's when you'll be the biggest star. That's when they'll all hug you and want to be your friend. Till then, you're the shark in the pool trying to eat them."

"But they would like me if they got to know me."

"Of course they would, darlin. You're irresistible. But people being people, they're either going to react to you with pity or re-sentment. Which would you rather it be?"

"Neither one."

"Take that up with the Creator, darlin. Cause he's the one made it that way."

"Well what about you?"

"What about me?"

"Don't you care how people look at you?"

"Not really."

"Why not?"

"I made peace with myself a long time ago. Why should I care?"

"Because you live in the world too," she said.

"I know exactly what I am, darlin," he said. "A person like me fits right into this little old world."

━◄╟ ╢►━

"I'm stuck," she said. "I don't know where to start."

"You need something good," Legare said.

"Do you have any ideas?"

"One or two."

"Really."

"Maybe so."

"Can I hear them?"

"You ever hear of the Great Brink's Robbery?"

"No."

"It was the biggest bank robbery of all time back then."

"Okay."

"There was a fella involved in that that has a Charleston connection. I toyed with writing a novel about him years ago."

"What's his name?"

"Trigger Burke. He was a hitman for the mob."

"A hitman?"

"That's right. He killed more people than Idi Amin."

"What's his connection to Charleston?"

"When he broke jail in Boston, he moved down here and rented himself a cottage out at Folly Beach. Out there with all the hippies and the goddern weirdos. Jesus' own people: the ones he loves but don't have no place for. The FBI got him there on Center Street waiting on a bus. He had a glass of whiskey in his hand and he was wet from swimming in the ocean."

"You think people would be interested in him?"

"Aren't you?"

"Yes."

"Well there you go then."

"What happened to him?"

"They took him back up north and fried him in the electric chair."

Lee Ann and Beau worked through the night. In the morning, they had a one thousand word feature story on a woman named Rosemary Addington. Rosemary Addington had been the teenage girlfriend of Trigger Burke and had helped shelter him while he lived on Folly Beach. Now in her seventies and dying of lung cancer, she finally had decided to reveal all of Trigger Burke's secrets.

She revealed that he secretly enjoyed dressing in women's clothing and dancing to Dixieland jazz tunes. That he was a big fan of German opera. That she once smashed a bottle of Pabst Blue Ribbon over his head when he was drunk.

Remembering the day he was arrested, she shook her head with sadness. "We had this plan to kidnap a rich man's daughter," she said. "We were going to hold her for a hundred thousand dollar ransom."

When they were done, Lee Ann looked at Beau. "It won't work," she said.

"Why not?"

"They'll want a picture. They'll want to see what she looks like. They're suspicious of me already."

"They ain't suspicious."

"They're suspicious. I'm telling you, they're suspicious."

"Just play your cards, girl," he said. "I can't tell you no more than that."

Legare left the room and went upstairs. After a while he came back down with a picture in his hand. It showed an old woman with white hair. Her skin was milk white and her face was covered in liver spots. She sat on a porch and smiled a crooked smile at the camera.

"Who is that?" Lee Ann said.

"That was my Aunt Mallie."

"Is she dead?"

"No, darlin, she lives on," Legare said. "She lives on as Ms. Rosemary Addington of Folly Beach, South Carolina."

The column was a hit upon delivery. In the Sweetwater Café on Market Street, the diners passed the article back and forth and remarked to one another with surprise that they never heard of Trigger Burke before. On Folly Beach, patrons asked the bartenders about Rosemary Addington. Does she ever come in here, they wanted to know.

Lee Ann followed up the Trigger Burke story by reporting on her discovery of the lost memoirs of Jasper Leon Sneed, a rakish Charleston socialite of the 1920's and the secret paramour of legendary composer George Gershwin. Sneed was a wealthy man about town who lived in an elegant pink townhouse on Tradd Street. Gershwin met him when researching Porgy and Bess and for several years made a number of visits that each lasted a month or more. The memoirs were acquired by a source whose identity could not be divulged for confidentiality purposes.

In his memoirs, Sneed reported that Gershwin had a habit of spitting on the floor and cursing every time the name Calvin Coolidge was mentioned in his presence and that he secretly loved to write dirty Irish limericks. Most of them were not suitable for publication in a family newspaper. One of them went like this:

> There once was a woman named Jill
> Who tried a dynamite stick for a thrill
> They found her vagina
> In North Carolina
> And bits of her tits in Brazil

They ran the story on a Friday, framed around a picture of Gershwin standing in front of a doughnut shop on Calhoun Street. He was smiling and wearing a straw boater hat.

At the King Street offices of the Lowcountry Gazette, Mary Ellen Snoffengrass smiled in satisfaction. She called Lee Ann into her office.

"Now this, my dear, is perfection. This is precisely what I wanted from you," she said.

Lee Ann nodded. "Good," she said. "I'm glad you like it."

"Come now, child," said Mary Ellen Snoffengrass. "Let us go over to the Francis Marion. I so want to show you off to my friends."

CHAPTER TWENTY-SIX

The man was a handsome young politician. His pretty wife was there beside him, her dress cinched at her delicate waist, a glass of white wine in her hand. Lee Ann Pickler leaned against the porch column. She looked at them. An image composed itself in her mind. Darkened heads in the plantation sun rising out in the cotton rows. A man's hat silhouetting in the sun and making his face a shadow. That's it, she said to herself. How perfect. How perfect.

He stood in the sun. He wore a dark blue suit with a red tie and when he smiled dimples formed at the sides of his mouth. He shook hands and grabbed hold of men's arms and looked them in the eye and smiled and pretended he had known them all his life.

"Good to see you old boy," he said. "Haven't seen you since the Woodbury game."

"We kicked up a ruckus that day."

"Rickety rack, rickety rack. Maroon and black, maroon and black. Eh, old boy?"

"I'll drink to that."

Lee Ann watched him working his way through the crowd, shaking every hand and touching every elbow.

The hostess leaned over and whispered to Lee Ann. "That's his honor, the mayor," she said.

Lee Ann nodded.

"That stunning creature to his left is his wife. They're quite the local celebrities. Some people think he could be president someday."

"Really?" Lee Ann said.

"Oh, yes. He's very popular."

<hr>

"There's this rumor I heard," Lee Ann said.

"Oh yes. Do tell me about it."

"It's probably nothing. You know how rumors are."

"Rumors are the highest form of information," said Mary Ellen Snoffengrass. "They are more accurate than statistics."

"But if it's not true, maybe I shouldn't say it."

"My dear, if it is a rumor it is probably true. My god, what business do you think you're in? Are we supposed to disprove these things? No, it is incumbent upon the rumor's subject to prove its falsity. They're not without responsibility here, you know."

"I heard two things," Lee Ann said.

"Well dish then. Do not hold back."

Mary Ellen Snoffengrass poured more cream into her coffee and stirred it with a tiny spoon. She crossed her legs and let one of her deerskin boots fall over the top of the other.

"I heard the mayor's wife was part black," Lee Ann said.

"Where did you hear that?"

"I promised the source I wouldn't say."

Mary Ellen Snoffengrass put her hand up. "Don't tell me then."

"You sure?"

"Yes. Someday a judge might order you to betray the source and then you can sort that out on your own. I'll support you if you decide to martyr yourself but don't expect me to join in any suffering. I don't do suffering. If I don't know who the source is, I can't be held in contempt. I won't have to sit in jail with you. Not that I would anyway."

"Okay."

"Is the source reliable?"

"I think she probably is."

"But his wife is white as milk. Has that occurred to you?"

"I heard she was octoroon."

"Really?"

"That's what I heard."

"How does that work?"

"I think it means she's an eighth black."

"Yes. But how is what I'm asking."

"I think you can be pretty white and still be octoroon."

"My dear, you are failing to understand me."

"Her grandmother descended from a slave on the Ashley Plantation, I think."

"Scandalous. That's his family home."

"I know. That's why my ears pricked up when I heard it."

"That's easily checkable, you know?"

"Yes, but I heard they covered it up. I heard they paid off her real grandma to go away. Her and her husband. I heard they moved to France and lived there till they died. I don't know where exactly."

"But wouldn't her mother be dark?"

"My source says she was supposedly light skinned. It was probably one of those deals where she came from a line tracing all the way back to the master of the plantation."

"That would mean the two of them are related."

"That's what I was thinking."

Mary Ellen Snoffengrass allowed the magnitude of the possibilities to distill within her. She held her head in her fingers as she spoke.

"The incestuous culmination of an ancient coupling between master and slave. Its hands on the gears of power in our fair city. My god. What a story."

"Yes. I know."

"We must run with this."

"Yes, absolutely."

"I'll talk to design. You have as many column inches as you need. We'll skip it inside, twice if we have to."

"Is it going in my regular spot?"

"No way. This is a front page story. Above the fold."

"I've got to check with my source first. To make sure everything is accurate."

"There's no time for all that," said Mary Ellen Snoffengrass. "I have a paper to get out and a story that will make it sell. We're just saying, 'Sources said,' that's all. What's wrong with that?"

Lee Ann broke the story and then used the hook to spin off a four-part series about how slavery's long shadow still fell over major cities in the modern South. Matt Lauer again flew down to Charleston and interviewed her about the stories. They filmed her on the deck of an elegant bar in the gas lamp district, the flood of harbor waves scraping behind her in the early morning breeze.

"So tell me about race in America today," Matt Lauer said.

"I can't much do that," she said. "But I can tell you about race in Charleston in particular and the South, generally speaking."

"Okay. Tell me about that."

"Well, Matt, it's a legacy from the past. It's a legacy that endures. It will always endure. It is an indelible part of the history of this city and its culture. The architecture, for instance. That's why some of the plantation homes have spiked fences. To protect against a slave rebellion. And those houses are still standing and people are living in them. And then you have the mayor and his wife. They're a symbol of the past, but they're also a symbol of reconciliation and hope. I know they're denying my story about their heritage, and I know they would rather keep the whole thing private. But they shouldn't be ashamed. I think they're living proof that we can overcome the legacy of our past."

She reached over and gently touched Lauer's knee. "Did you know," she said, "that William Faulkner once said that race itself is a myth. I think by that he meant that eventually the people on this continent will continue to commingle and procreate until you can't tell what race anybody is. Everyone will be equally exotic and equally plain, and equally accepted."

She was a natural. She was so beautiful and in such a simple way, and so young and smart. Commingle? My God. Where did that come from? She was such a warm, genuine creature and you couldn't help but to fall in love with her all at once. Lauer sat there enraptured, propping his chin up with his fist.

"You see, Matt, the race problem has always been here," she said. "It's been sleeping from time to time, but it hasn't gone anywhere. This story just goes to show that there are things in our past that still control us. Decisions we made back then influence the decisions we make today. Our destiny is linked to our past and vice versa. But as this story shows, we all share one common DNA and one common destiny."

Beau Legare watched quietly as she mouthed the platitudes and the host mindlessly nodded his head. He sipped from a frozen jar of homemade brandy as he watched the girl on the TV. There was frost around the jar from it being in the freezer and the white liquor was jolting and cold but nevertheless had a smooth pear flavor and was very pleasing to him. He was drunk as hell. It was eight o'clock in the morning.

That's my girl, he said. That's my girl.

CHAPTER TWENTY-SEVEN

I t wasn't long before she found herself at war with the queen of Charleston high society. It began at an elegant dinner party at the Rainbow City Club. There was a large ballroom with ornate chandeliers, and the place looked like a baroque museum with dark colors and vermicular patterned carpets and high ceilings colored sepia from decades of cigarette smoke.

The walls were adorned with paintings of men seated in big mahogany chairs and looking down in contemplative repose. One was an old picture of a Civil War general with a sharp white mustache and chin beard. He was standing ramrod straight, staring intently at something just over the artist's right shoulder, his right hand buried in his shirt as though he were Napoleon himself.

"That there is General Pierre Gustave Toutant Beauregard. He defended Charleston from the Yankees," said the grand dame.

Lee Ann nodded and took a sip of her iced tea. She followed the grand dame down the hallway and into a dining room where several elegant tables were decorated in various dishes, with glasses and bright silverware and a maroon napkin folded in each coffee cup. There were plates of crab cakes, little rolls with pulled pork barbecue, and poppy seed biscuits with cured and sugared ham.

The hostess introduced her around and there were many smiles and handshakes and cheek kisses and other exchanges of pleasantries. Finally the ladies stopped talking long enough to sit down and begin passing around the food. A waiter came and filled up their teacups.

"So where are you from, my dear?" one of the women asked.

"Greensboro, North Carolina, originally," Lee Ann said.

"Were you in the Daughters of the Confederacy up there?"

"No, ma'am."

"Well here in Charleston darling, you can get back in touch with your roots. We have a way of life down here. I think you'll find it right to your liking."

"It's very beautiful," Lee Ann said. "I think about how lucky I am every day. My office is right over the bridge. I'm inspired every time I look at it."

"I read your article on Beau Legare," another woman said. "I always wondered what happened to him."

"He's doing good."

"He sounds like he's crazy."

"A little bit, he is."

"How did you get him to let you interview him."

"I don't know. I guess I just asked him at the right time."

"Oh come on, dear. I'm sure you're being way too modest," said a woman.

"No, really," Lee Ann said.

The woman leaned in across the table. "Do female reporters ever sleep with men to get them to talk or does that just happen in the movies?" she said.

Lee Ann blushed and looked away. "I don't know anything about that," she said.

"I'd sleep with Bill Clinton," the woman said. "I would. Those adorable little hot dog fingers on my thighs. . . . Don't tell anybody though."

Lee Ann looked up and saw three tall figures in bright colors and with sharp collarbones. The middle one stood over the room and sighted them down the point of her chin like you might sight a duck down the rim of a shotgun barrel and then she looked away. She removed a fashionable red hat and turned her head back and forth and loosed the strings of blonde hair down her back. The woman across from Lee Ann sat up straight.

"That's Nicole Eisenhart," the woman said.

"Oh," Lee Ann said.

"She used to be a big time fashion model. Till she married Bud Greasson and had two little boys. Bud is the richest man in Charleston."

"She looks beautiful," Lee Ann said.

"She is utterly devastating. Such a pity that she is so unhappy."

"Why's she unhappy?" Lee Ann said.

The woman leaned across the table and whispered, delighting in the act of secret sharing.

"Bud is also the ugliest and crudest man in Charleston," the woman said.

"Really?"

"He's hideous. She tries not to bring him out in public."

"Really?"

"He would scare a cat off a fish wagon."

"Why'd she marry him then?"

The woman laughed and swatted her manicured hand at Lee Ann. "Oh you are too much!" the woman said.

Lee Ann saw Nicole Eisenhart and her friends coming her way. Nicole's eyes had homed in on Lee Ann and they walked her down. Nicole stood over her.

"Who's your friend?" Nicole said to the woman.

"Oh, Nicole. I'd like you to meet Miss Mary Dallas Page. From Greensboro, North Carolina."

Nicole started to giggle, and turned back to her friends and whispered something to each of them and then all three of them giggled.

"You have the hands of an angel," Nicole said.

"Oh, thank you," Lee Ann said.

She looked down at her hand and saw the white spots on her fingernails where the pink had chipped off.

"Those shoes are darling too."

The other ones giggled again.

Lee Ann stared up at Nicole and swallowed hard. She wanted to reach back and grab the air and smash Nicole Eisenhart's perfect little face into shards of glass, but then she remembered who she was and where she was and who she was supposed to be and all that she had endured to get here and what it might feel like to lose it. She thought about all that and then forced her lips to curl into a smile.

"Thank you," she said.

She saw Nicole Eisenhart again two weeks later, this time at a charity event at the aquarium. She saw Nicole point in her direction and then lean over to whisper to one of her friends and then both of them started laughing. Lee Ann turned away and looked at her program. She looked back up and saw Nicole putting her arm around the mayor and kissing him on each cheek. She could tell by the way they held their eyes that the two had been lovers.

Lee Ann Pickler now had an enemy who animated her imagination and stirred her long dormant impulses toward rage. She remembered the perverts in the bus station, the coldness of the woods, the feeling of having her face crushed in by Dusty McLeod's fist and sitting there in the cold dew, her eyes watering and nothing she could do about it. Not again, she told herself. Not again. Not ever again.

She set out on a plan of revenge to wreck the life of Nicole Eisenhart. She turned to her only weapons, imagination and prose and she summoned from deep within herself the dark spirit of vengeance. She sat before the keyboard and felt the hammer fall again and again and again. She worked late into the night.

She plotted out the tale in a paragraph or two, then set out on the long journey of marrying narrative to style. It was important to get it all out before the anger deserted her leaving only feelings of remorse and forgiveness. She pushed those things away and allowed the fire the burn. She wasn't letting anybody punch her in the face again. She wasn't smiling and walking home this time.

Nicole Eisenhart came alive before her on her eyelid screens burning in the ether and Lee Ann could see her there dangling and burning in the dream haze. A sad and snarling creature drunk on bitterness and martinis crying herself to sleep. The woman rumored to be the mayor's longtime paramour. The woman for whom the mayor was unwilling to leave his wife.

A woman in decline. Jealous of all the younger women at her feet and consumed with hatred toward the elephant man she had married. Weeping at the sight of her hideous children, the devil spawn of some redneck car salesman. All her beauty ruined.

She took everything that Nicole Eisenhart had ever been or loved or dreamed and burned it on a literary pyre and laughed at the pieces of her bones carbonizing in the redness of the glowing coals.

She delighted in picturing the soft chattering of the baroque museum set when Nicole Eisenhart's misery was brought out and displayed for everyone to see, rich and ornate and perfectly pre-served. Like a Joseph Turner painting under the footlights. All burning to ashes.

Nicole Eisenhart's life, her pathetic little life and all her insecu-rities and regrets, all were about to be laid bare on the front page of the Sunday Style section. Lee Ann Pickler saw not only to her enemy's ruination but to its enshrinement forever in the pages of the public record.

━┅┥┝┅━

When Mary Ellen Snoffengrass read the piece she threw her head back and uttered a deep cackle of laughter. She started choking and snot came out of her nose.

"What is it?" Lee Ann said.

"She'll kill herself!" said Mary Ellen Snoffengrass.

"Oh my God. We should do something."

"Calm down." Mary Ellen couldn't stop laughing. "She's prob-ably too vain for that anyway," she said. "My dear, where do you find such gems?"

"Do you like it?"

"Do I like it? This, my dear, is the reason I plucked you from that little country rag and brought you here to this enchanted city."

"Do you think it's too mean?"

Mary Ellen laughed again.

"Too mean?" she said. "My dear, what do you think we do here, charity? No, we are in business for the purpose of shining a bright light onto the pain of the Nicole Eisenharts of the world."

"I didn't know if it was a bit too much."

"It is perfect. And it will be a smash."

The piece hit on a Sunday morning and that was the last any-one in Charleston ever saw of Nicole Eisenhart. Later, it was ru-mored that she had changed her name and moved to the Middle

East, where she converted to Islam and married a Saudi prince who had a thing for American women.

After that, no one in Charleston ever picked on Lee Ann Pickler again.

CHAPTER TWENTY-EIGHT

When Beau visited, the two of them would walk in the afternoon sun down to the path fronting the Battery and overlooking the waves chopping and breaking against the harbor wall.

Down by the water there was a little sidewalk rising in a series of steps against the seawall. The pathway looked out over the islands and sailboats.

There were moss-draped trees. Armies of waves. Little lines of walkways and swaying palmetto branches. Panicles of flowers hanging down from them with tiny drupes on their leaves. The chittering of birds and the sound of the ocean breeze blowing through the live oaks.

Colorful mansions with tall Doric columns standing against the sun. Faded and veined with vegetation. The buildings crossed through with iron rods from the age of the great earthquake, when the city rattled and broke and the fires raged and charred everything in sight. Iron faces of lions forged onto the front of the buildings and onto the gates.

A park with a long white path leading to a gazebo. Men in tuxedos and a young woman in a long white bridal dress holding an armful of flowers. Cannons pointing outward toward the long-silent guns on the other side, cannonballs welded together in a small pyramid.

They walked along the water and watched the waves roll and curl in the churning spume of the sea. The seagulls roamed overhead, their mouths framing the architecture for the music of their yawning cries.

As they walked, Beau spoke on the subject of imagination.

"It's unusual and it's a dying art, you know?"

"What is?"

"What we do, you and me."

"What do we do?"

"We make stories. That's what we do. Some people make pies, we make stories. That's all there is to it."

She winked at him. "It's fun though, ain't it?" she said.

"It has its purpose."

"And what's that?"

"To try and make some sense out of this vast unknowable world. You tell your own little stories. If you're entertaining, you might even make some money at it. But it's mostly something else. You do it because it allows you to create something that has a chance to become immortal. You can see how intoxicating it must be to be God."

"You think?"

"Yes."

"Well you were awful lucky, then."

"What else was I going to do with my life? I was lazy and I preferred to make sense out of the world by telling stories about it over and over again. They say good fiction is truer than the truth. That's the idea, anyway."

"Do you believe that?"

"Yes I do."

"Really?"

"My whole life would be a lie if I didn't."

"I still feel weird about it," she said. "I feel like I'm doing something wrong. And I'm always afraid they're about to catch me."

"That's because you have a conscience, my dear."

"You mean you don't?"

"Not when it comes to writing, my dear, no."

Lee Ann looked out at the chopping water and then looked up toward the rise of the walk at the palmetto groves and the darkening sky. Beau gave a laugh.

"I reckon I just wanted to be good at the thing I cared about most. I don't care that I ain't good at nothing else. Screw all that, I guess. Besides, I was afraid people would forget about me."

"They'll remember you forever," she said.

"Forever's a long time, darlin."

Beau started walking again slowly and Lee Ann followed him. Then he stopped again.

"My favorite moment was after I published Whiskey Creek. It was my first book. I drove to Charleston and went to the bookstore right there on Market Street across from the church. I walked in half drunk. I found the book there and took it down off the shelf and threw it down on the ground. Hard as I could. There was a loud noise and all the people jumped at first and then moved away from me. Like I was some madman who had just snapped and gone crazy. Maybe it was the satisfaction in my face. The clerk called the cops on me. And I just stood there and smiled. Because that book, that binding of cloth and paper, that garish dust jacket, that was something real. It was a piece of real physical matter, and when it landed something landed which had not previously existed in this world. It was a tangible thing that grew out of my own imagination and I somehow felt that its life validated my own. In that moment, I felt like a real person and not a ghost. In that moment, I felt immortal."

"Do you have any idea how unusual you are?" she said.

"Unusual or same. We're all just interruptions in the undertow. But for a time we did exist and we moved against it."

"If that's supposed to be profound, it's not," she said. "It's stupid."

"Yeah," Beau said. "I know it."

They kept walking and Beau stopped and turned to look down at her and smiled.

"That's what I love about you, darlin," he said. "You keep me straight."

"You keep me crooked," she said.

At this time her role with Beau was deepening and hardening and though she wrapped herself in its comfort, she was afraid of the inner realities of the moment. Beau was her refuge, her last harbor in the world. She didn't know what she was to him but she sensed it was something very dear and important. She decided to embrace the rightness of the moment and allow herself to defer to another time all questions beyond the moment and its rightness of feeling.

Their love was like a play, each scene a piece of something larger with an arc and a shape. She sensed that there was a purpose and design to it, as though it was fed to them one scene at a time, and the words they said to each other were pieces of a dialogue passing through them as brief vessels existing only for that purpose.

CHAPTER TWENTY-NINE

The Monkey And The Pigeon

(Beau Legare and Lee Ann Pickler lie in bed in each
other's arms.)

BEAU

An old man and a young girl. It ain't right, you know?

LEE ANN

I'm not a child. I'm almost twenty years old.

BEAU

You're way too young to be with a broke down old man like me.

LEE ANN

You think so?

BEAU

Nope. But everybody else will. So it may as well be true. There are
a million subjective realities and you can deconstruct them all
away and none of them mean a goddamn thing. But objectively,
that would probably be the consensus if you asked enough folks.

LEE ANN

I don't care what they say.

BEAU

I never gave two shits about them either. But facts are facts. If you are linked to me in the romantic sense, people will look at you differently. That's a fact.

LEE ANN

They don't look at me any way or another now.

BEAU

You're wrong about that. They're looking at you more and more. And if you don't believe me, just let them catch you kissing on a crazy old man. They will see you different. They might not respect you. You and me both. It don't make a damn what they think about me. I'm way too old for all that. But I do care very much what they think about you. You still have a whole life to live. It's your choice either way. I'm just warning you.

LEE ANN

(Looking up at him and touching his weathered face.)
You're the only man who's ever spoken to my heart.

BEAU

(He smiles and leans back and eases Lee Ann back with
him. He puts both of his arms around her stomach and
holds her hands in his and rests the side of his head
against the softness of her hair.)
God speaks to man in two books you know.

LEE ANN

No, I didn't know.

BEAU

Yes, ma'am.

LEE ANN

What do you mean?

BEAU

He speaks in words and in physical matter. Earth and water. He created the earth and her sciences. He made all her laws to encourage the species and help them along and preserve them and then, when man was ready, he handed down the Commandments. Each law is divisible in the other and the totality of human existence is summarized in that sacred and crystalized moment. Laws in flesh, laws in stone.

LEE ANN

I never thought of it like that.

BEAU

It's largely perfection, it really is. But there are still spaces in it all. Between God and earth and man. Between the individual and the everything. Even the firmament is not uninterrupted by holes. That's all that stars are, you know? Holes in the night sky. It's all a giant miracle but like any miracle it leaves shattered pieces of detritus behind. When he creates, he is also careful to destroy so as to keep the balance of things. That's why there are broken ones out there. Folks like you and like me. And there's other ones too. Don't think there ain't. And he just leaves them out there. Hanging out there. He don't put them back together. That's one of my few objections to his otherwise sublime work.

LEE ANN

(She rests her head against Beau and listens to his words ringing softly in her ear.)

I don't give a damn about any of that.

BEAU

But there is a thing which transcends God's laws, transcends physical matter, transcends space and time and the passage of time. This thing is the destroyer of kingdoms and the conqueror of death. It lays waste to all of God's laws and is God himself.

LEE ANN

(Sitting up and looking at Beau.)

What are you talking about?

BEAU

You know what I'm talking about. Don't make me say it. It's embarrassing.

LEE ANN

No I don't. Really I don't.

BEAU

Yes you do.

LEE ANN

No. I promise.

BEAU

Let me tell you a story.

LEE ANN

Tell me.

BEAU

There was a macaque monkey in China who became an orphan and was raised in this zoo with a white pigeon who had also been orphaned. Two broken animals from different species. One made to master the sky, the other to walk upright like a man. Both broken and consigned to the creator's workshop of failures. Both unable to perform their given task. Both weak and limping. Both sickly and abnormal. Freaks and rejects from their own kind. Each alone by himself. Just the animal and the world and nothing else. But there they are, the bird soothing its white feathers over the monkey's wrinkled and frightened face. The monkey's long arms and protective fingers holding onto the crippled bird with tenderness and compassion. Two desperate, lonely creatures joined in loneliness and longing and the capacity for love and each carrying with it the heart of the other and promising the other to stand there till the end. There is nothing in the laws of nature more perfect or more mysterious than that. Science has no answer for such a thing. But this unlikely coupling sustains both creatures and replenishes them and gives them wings. Their love seems as natural to them as it seems mystifying to the world. Some desire anteceding time binds them to one another, joining them and giving them symmetry. Two lovers sheltering against the despair of the world. That, my dear, is love.

158

LEE ANN

Love?

BEAU

Yes, love.

LEE ANN

So it's true what they say about love?

BEAU

What do they say about it?

LEE ANN

All the sappy, romantic stuff. You know what I'm talking about.

BEAU

All I know is that it the stirrer of my every noble gesture and the nucleus of my every redeeming act. It is the only part of me that shall outlive death.

LEE ANN

I love you Beau.

BEAU

I love you too darlin.

CHAPTER THIRTY

S he was walking in the market on Sunday morning among the fudge makers and cart vendors selling food and hot chocolate when she found a real feature story.

It was cold in the square and the absence of trees left the people there naked against the wind. They pulled their coats over their faces like robbers. Children ran across the patchy sprawl of grass reaching out from King Street and dying in the sea plain.

The triangular soar of cathedrals blocked out the sky at both ends of the park. The parapets on the pink castle walls of the old Citadel stood out like tombstones against the sky.

She walked among the vendors and the smells of their food. She stopped at a booth selling hot shrimp and grits and waited for the lady in front of her to pay and walk away.

"How much?" she said.

"Five bucks," the vendor said. "Fifty cents more if you want cheese."

Lee Ann bought a bowl of shrimp and grits and then found a clear space out on the grass overlooking the square and sat down and enjoyed the mash of the cornmeal and shrimp meat. She thought about how she might spend the rest of the day. Most days she felt like a tourist, just playing in a foreign city, nowhere to go in particular. She had a date with a computer screen at some point, but until then, there was nowhere she had to be.

She began thinking of the artists and vendors at the market and wondered what their lives might be like. She finally got back up, threw away her trash, and began walking through the booths, looking at the wares and trying to gauge the craftsmen and merchants.

At the edge of the midway she found a black eldress kneeling in the grass with her hands upon a wheel that was wet with clay and spinning endlessly. The woman worked her wet fingers into the puddled clay and soon Lee Ann began to see the thing take shape.

The woman looked straight ahead as she worked. Her eyes were white as larvae and there was no pupil in either of them. Lee Ann watched her staring blindly into some dark universe unseen by others and watched the mastication of clay in her hands.

The clay began to take on a familiar form. It curved out on both sides in symmetry like the lines on a bell. The old woman would run her finger up and down the cylinder and a ripple would appear and then vanish into the smoothness of the clay. Behind the woman on a wooden rack sat dozens of kiln-fired pots, glazed in turquoise and some with primitive faces adorning them.

"Hello, ma'am," Lee Ann said to the woman.

"Hello there yourself," the woman said back in a thick Gullah accent.

"What's that you're making there?"

"Making a pot."

"A pot?"

"Yeah. Something wrong with that?"

"No ma'am."

"Well then."

"How long have you been doing that?"

"About twenty minutes, I reckon."

"No, I mean how long."

"Oh. Maybe sixty five years, seventy years. I don't know."

"How old are you?"

"Eighty seven this July."

"What do you use the pots for?"

"Look, missy. I ain't out here to chitchat. Ain't got no time for chitchattin. I'm out here to sell pots. You wants to buy a pot or don't you?"

"No, ma'am. I'm with the Lowcountry Gazette. I'm interested in doing a story on you."

"A story? What kind of story?"

"A story about you making pots. I think people would be interested. It might even bring you business."

"If you're with the paper you could afford to buy a pot."

"I might could," Lee Ann said. "But we have ethics rules. If I buy from your business, I might not be able to write about you. I couldn't be objective that way."

"Suit yourself," the woman said. "But I think you're just a cheapskate."

"I just have a few questions."

"Good," the old woman said. "I ain't got more than a few answers."

"What drives you to come out here every Sunday and make clay pots?"

"I like to stay busy. The idle mind is the devil's workshop. That's what the Bible says. Plus I need the money. I sew during the week too, you know."

"Really? How much do you make?"

"I could buy and sell you two or three times."

"I mean, what do you need all the money for? Don't you have family?"

"I got family," the woman said. "My granddaughter going to have a baby come July. I'm saving up money to buy some college books for my great grandbaby."

"July, huh?"

"That's what the doctor say."

"You can celebrate your birthday and your great grandbaby's birthday at the same time. Maybe even on the same day," Lee Ann said. "Who knows?"

"Probably not," the old woman said.

"Why's that?"

"I don't figure on being around that long. Doctor say I got three months, maybe four. Got the cancer in my bones. Say I better get right with Jesus. But I been right with Jesus for a long time. So I just try to pass the time."

"My God," Lee Ann said.

"Don't take the Lord's name in vain, sweetie."

"But. . ."

"But nothin. The Lord don't forgive no blasphemy. That's the one sin the Lord don't forgive."

"I'm sorry."

"Don't be sorry to me. Be sorry to God. He's the one going to judge you."

"You're right. I'll ask him to forgive me."

The blind woman smiled. "Dying ain't nothing special," she said. "Not if you know where you going."

⟞⟝ ⟞⟝

Lee Ann wrote the story and it triggered a mountain of letters to the editor. People sent cash donations to help the old woman's cancer treatment. They sent money for the great-grandchild's college fund. The mayor himself wrote a letter to the editor praising the article. But Mary Ellen Snoffengrass was not pleased.

"Won't this exposure make readership go up?" Lee Ann said.

"Probably not," said Mary Ellen Snoffengrass.

"Why not?"

"Nobody wants to read articles like this."

"But even the mayor said he liked it."

"That's the worst endorsement possible. If the mayor is happy with you, you are certainly not doing your job."

"But I thought my job was to find good and interesting stories."

"No. Your job is to find interesting people and then find out interesting things about them. And by interesting, I mean scandalous, embarrassing. Am I making myself clear?"

"I'm sorry," Lee Ann said. "I thought I was doing something right."

"Don't let it happen again."

"I won't."

CHAPTER THIRTY-ONE

Columns of sunlight fell through the long windows lighting the dusty hardwoods. She lay in bed, eyes wide open, thinking about the woman in the market.

"What is it, darlin?" he said.

She wiggled against him and turned to look away.

"Come on," he said. "Spit it out."

"It's nothing," she said.

"It's something. If it involves me I'd at least like to know. I might even think it's funny."

"No," she said. "It's just something I was thinking about."

"Well tell me. Maybe I can help you not think about it."

"Do you ever wonder why we do anything at all?"

He gave a snorting laugh. "I rarely think about anything else," he said.

"I mean, what's the point. We're all going to be dead anyway."

Legare laughed out loud.

"How cute," he said. "Portrait of the existentialist as a young girl. How utterly goddamn adorable. Now that's prettier than nine silky ponies. Soon you will put on a beret and start reciting poetry at some coffee bar. I cannot wait. This is going to be so much fun."

"Stop making fun of me."

"I wasn't making fun of you."

"Yes you were."

"Okay. Yes I was."

"Nevermind."

"I'll stop. I promise."

"No. Nevermind."

He sat up and ran his fingers through his hair. "Have you ever seen a cathedral?" he said.

"I'm not talking to you."

"No, really. Have you seen one?"

"Duh."

"I don't mean one of these eighteenth century British firetraps besotting our fair city. No. I mean a cathedral proper. An honest to God one. Something in Europe, something perhaps exceedingly old and beautiful."

"No," she said. "Never saw one."

"The Cathedral at Rouen is this little gothic masterpiece in France. It took them seven hundred years to build it. You know that? And this was in the Middle Ages, when the life expectancy wasn't more than twenty five or thirty years. Imagine that. You think you're young now, think again. That's twenty eight of your lifetimes stretched out in a chain, each link grasping the preceding and following ones and holding onto them both at the same time.

"An unbroken chain with seven hundred links reaching all the way to God. And what a sight it is. Walls of saints set off in white stone, frosted like a wedding cake. Every little piece of it the life's work of a man. Each carving memorializing a single life. One tiny piece. A funny little gnome in the rock perhaps.

"Every single day spent chipping and polishing that solitary little figure. The man would be born, rise through childhood and adolescence and adulthood. All of this happened very fast, you understand.

"And somewhere in there he would fall in love and sire children and they would grow up at his knee and then comfort him in age and ease his journey into death and they would bury him in a church graveyard perhaps and memorialize his life in a dignified manner and then grass would grow over the spot where lay his bones.

"But he memorialized himself in the rock. His life is its agent -- the figure. Through the figure he will live forever. People will come for hundreds of years and place their fingers against the stone and look at the figure carved there and, without even knowing it, they will bear witness to the validation of the carver's life.

"His children would die just like him and their children and on and on, but the figure was immortal and he was its creator and today he lives because it endures. To this day, his breath. It yet passes. All the way now to you, as your being charged with the mere knowledge of the gnome validates the carver's purpose and his life. Can you imagine the love he must have felt for it?"

"That's stupid if you ask me."

"I think it's maybe profound."

"Why?"

"I don't know. There's something to it, I think."

"But why would they do that? Give up your whole life just to help build something you'll never see finished?"

"I don't know."

"But I bet you have an opinion on the matter."

"Could be."

"What is it?"

"Faith maybe."

"Faith? That's all you've got to say about that? Faith? Jesus. I'm disappointed."

"It could be something else, I guess. But faith is probably what it is."

"Faith in what?"

"Something bigger. Maybe in being part of that."

"What good is that?"

"Nothing, by itself. But a small faith becomes an agency for the larger thing it's a part of. Faith in that larger thing becoming something greater than its pieces. The possibility of the communal soul chaining itself to that place and staking a claim in fee simple for all time. About being a part of all that, maybe."

"Maybe they just didn't know any better," she said.

"Maybe so."

"But you don't believe that, do you?"

"No," he said. "Reckon I don't."

CHAPTER THIRTY-TWO

I t was Christmastime in Marion Square. There was an enormous lighted tree among the cathedrals and castle walls. The palmetto trees lining the streets were spaced out along the sidewalks wrapped in white lights.

They walked hand in hand. It was a warm night and they walked slowly. Beau pointed to things with his cane and told stories, some of them serious and some of them in jest. Occasionally, he took a flask from his coat and put it to his lips.

"General Longstreet is reported to have once taken a dump under that tree yonder," he said.

Lee Ann smiled and held onto him. They bought some coffee from a street vendor and took a seat on a park bench.

"I got you a present," she said. "Here, I hope you like it."

She took a small box out of her coat pocket and handed it to him.

"This is a token of my love for you and my gratitude," she said.

He took the box and slowly turned it over, admiring the gold wrapping paper. He carefully unwrapped the paper and opened the box and saw a beautiful blue fountain pen engraved simply: Beau Legare, Writer.

He looked at her and then looked at the ground. She put her arm around him.

"It's very beautiful," he said.

"It's more of a symbolic gift than anything. I can't give you anything you don't already have."

"It's the nicest gift anyone's ever given me."

She kissed him on the cheek. "I'm glad you like it," she said.

"I'll put it on my desk and use it exclusively from now on."

"I was hoping you might get back to writing fiction with it."

"We'll see about that. You never know."

She squeezed his hand.

"Why don't you write anymore?" she said.

"What's the point, really? I've said all I've got to say."

"No you haven't. I think there's more."

"No, trust me, there's not," he said.

"When's the last time you sat down and wrote something?"

"I don't remember."

"That's so sad. You should be writing."

"It tends to interfere with my other activities, such as it were."

"Like what, exactly?"

"Whatever it is my days are made of now."

"Oh." She looked away and then looked back at him.

"That's not true, is it?" she said.

He nodded and said, "Stories. They don't come to you, you know. You can't just make them up. You find them. The act lies in discovery, not creation. Nobody understands that, but it's true."

"Really?"

"Writing is archaeology. Not art."

"Like looking for dinosaur bones?"

"That's right."

"You just haven't had a site to excavate."

"Not in a while, no."

"It's okay," she said.

"I know it is."

"Maybe you should get out more."

"No, it's not that. It's something else. It's something that was there when I was younger but isn't there no more. Something in my heart maybe."

"You think it went somewhere?"

"Yep."

"Where you think it went?"

"I don't know."

"Have you thought about going looking for it?"

"Not really. It's something that's been gone a long time now. I wouldn't know where to start."

"It had to go somewhere."

"I guess so."

"So where'd it go?"

"In a bottle," he said. "That's where it went to."

CHAPTER THIRTY-THREE

The letter came from New York City. It was addressed to Ms. Mary Dallas Page. She opened it and saw the iconic stationary. A globe with a news ticker circling it.

The New York World. It was the greatest newspaper in the world, with bureaus from Dublin to Jalalabad. Her heart stopped beating and her life shrank into the moment. She was afraid to open the rest of the letter or even to look at it.

The letter said to contact a woman named Amy Diamond, editor in chief of the paper. Lee Ann called the next morning. She could feel her heart beating in her chest. An assistant answered and when Lee Ann said Amy Diamond please, the woman said, "Hold on."

A woman then came to the phone with a soft Brooklyn honk in her voice.

"Amy Diamond?"

"Yes. Who is this?"

"This is Mary Dallas Page."

"Oh yes. Thank you so much for calling."

Amy Diamond explained that she had read Mary Dallas Page's column for the last year and saw steady growth and dynamic storytelling. "I'd like for you to come to New York and meet with us."

Lee Ann didn't know what to say. There was a long pause. Finally, she said, "I'd love to."

"Good," Amy Diamond said. "How's Friday morning?"

"This Friday?"

"Yes."

"It'd be expensive getting a flight out this late."

"I'll have them get you a ticket. There will be one waiting for you there. I'll make arrangements for you to stay at the Helmsley Carlton House."

"Okay."

"Okay then. I'll look forward to seeing you here on Friday."

Lee Ann became stuck again. "Oh," she finally said. "How do I get to your offices?"

"Don't worry about that," Amy Diamond said. "I'll send a driver."

She found herself sitting in the lobby of the offices of The New York World. She tapped her feet together in a nervous tick. The offices were in a giant glass and bronze building at State Street Plaza on the southernmost tip of lower Manhattan. Lee Ann took the elevator to the forty fourth floor. All of the walls were made of glass and it made her feel like she was floating high above the Financial District.

Beyond was the blue harbor and Liberty's lighted torch. The Verrazano Bridge. Bayonne and the little green trestle-wheel bridge way off in the distance. She was choked with the beauty of it all.

After awhile an assistant wearing a headset came walking out to greet her. She stuck out her hand.

"I'm Claudia Goodchance, executive assistant to Ms. Diamond. Thanks for waiting."

"No problem," Lee Ann said.

"This way, please."

Lee Ann got up and followed her. They turned a corner and descended a spiral staircase and emerged into the newsroom. It was a maze of cubicles partitioned with short carpeted walls. There was the constant chatter of human voices.

Along one wall was an octagon shaped desk with eight copy editors reading text as if fixing parts on an assembly line. To their right was the large screens of the graphic design department. Reporters and copy editors and layout girls all jostled and joked, people sitting on each other's desks and wearing jeans and tennis shoes.

At the other end was the advertising department. As Lee Ann well knew, they were the underclass. They were like used car salesmen but worse. It was beneath the dignity of any reporter to even speak to one of them.

She remembered Chris Ellers telling her: "Stay away from the ad people. They're trash. They're worse than the guys who deliver the paper. They're all just drunks and pill poppers and criminals who can't or won't get jobs anyplace else. So stay away from them. Only associate with fellow editorial staffers and you'll be alright."

The World had exiled the ad people to a dark corner of the floor and she could tell who they were as soon as she saw their condition. They were gathered behind a glass partition like quarantined lepers.

She thought of Chris Ellers and saw his face there. Smiling, bald on top and with the sides shaved. Graying mustache and thin face and crooked teeth and that bashful, intelligent, playful smile. A face and a smile full of adventure. The flickering ping of light in his eyes when he looked right at you. What would he think of this sight? What would he think of her now? She thought of him as she toured the newsroom. What would say to all this? He'd laugh his ass off, that's what he'd do.

She remembered where she was when she heard about him dying in the wreck. She remembered the picture in the paper, the car upside down in the ditch. She remembered the memorial service, his desk festooned in pictures and kitschy knickknacks, a clown head on a spring bouncing back and forth that he used to play with all the time. She remembered the sight of his empty chair and of watching the light come in through the newsroom window, illuminating particles in a space that should have been occupied by him.

The assistant led Lee Ann into a bullpen in the middle of the newsroom. Inside was an attractive young woman seated at a desk. Two older men in dark slacks and dress shirts were seated around her. Lee Ann saw them all watching her.

"Right in there," said the assistant, and then the assistant vanished. Lee Ann walked into the office. A large but attractive woman with chestnut curls and a black pantsuit swiveled in her chair, turning away from her computer to face her visitor. She crossed her legs and nodded. A gray-haired man sat at the table just to her right.

"Close that door behind you," the woman said.

<hr />

"I'm Amy Diamond," the woman said. "And this is Gavin Murphy. Gavin is our managing editor."

"Nice to meet you," Lee Ann said.

She shook his hand and he offered her a seat and she sat down in it.

"You probably know why we've asked you to come here," Amy Diamond said.

Lee Ann shook her head. "No," she said. "Really, I don't. I'm honored to be here all the same, you understand?"

"We want you to write for The World," she said.

Lee Ann Pickler was knocked back in her chair. It was like she'd been hit by a meteor.

"Me? Write for the World?" she said. "Are you serious?"

"One column a week. You'll carry one paper every week. We're thinking of giving you Friday. Friday is perfect for a cheeky and mercurial talent such as Mary Dallas Page."

"But I. . . ."

"You what?"

"Nothing."

"No. Go on. What is it?"

"It's nothing. It's just that I don't know if my column will translate to all those readers. I know Charleston pretty good but I don't know anything about New York or most anywhere else," Lee Ann said.

There was laughter from the other three. Amy Diamond looked at her and smiled.

"We're offering you a shot," she said. "But of course if you don't work out we will find somebody else to carry Friday. This is the NFL, you understand? That's just business. We're the New York World and we'll do whatever we have to do. But the shot we're offering you is every writer's dream. Friday columnist for the World. You get the last say every week before the weekend. And since it's Friday, you can be sassy and even mean and really rip your claws into people. That's why we're offering you the job. Do you want it or not?"

"That sounds wonderful," Lee Ann said.

"It's unbelievable pressure. Now understand that. You've never seen anything like it. But you will be a star. Immediately too. Success here is big, and so is failure. So swing for the fences, alright?"

"I just. . . . I just never imagined anything like this."

"This opportunity will never come along again. This is your shot. You either take it now or you never take it."

"Okay."

"Okay what? Okay you understand or okay you'll do it?"

"I'll do it."

Amy Diamond smiled. She got up and walked over to Lee Ann Pickler and hugged her. She bent down and kissed her on the cheek.

"My dear," she said. "I simply can't wait to unleash Mary Dallas Page on the Manhattan clubrooms and salons."

CHAPTER THIRTY-FOUR

"Your column will have to have a name," said Amy Diamond. "What kind of name?"

"Like our other columnists have."

Lee Ann shook her head. "I don't know," she said. "I'll have to think about it."

"I have an idea," said Gavin Murphy.

They turned to look at him. His placed his hands on the table and gestured with them as he talked. "Column's running on Friday, right? It's going to be sassy, irreverent, maybe even a little bit mean. Great. Okay? How about simply, 'Your Girl Friday?' How's that sound?"

Lee Ann looked at Amy Diamond and Amy Diamond shrugged.

"Okay," Lee Ann said. "That sounds good to me."

＊＊＊

She knew she had to tell Beau that she was leaving but she couldn't summon the words. Finally she wrote down the words and sealed them and put them in the mail. When she boarded the plane to LaGuardia, she cried as she thought of him. She hated the idea that he was alone now, no one there to care for him and listen to all his fascinating little stories. She trembled at the thought of his loneliness and its potential depth.

She prayed for his health. She knew his drinking would get worse but that it would get worse anyway. With or without her. She could feel his stinging grief in her own chest, his heart breaking next to hers. It was over now. The two of them parted silently like one heart dividing in two.

PART THREE

Ghosts in a Dream

CHAPTER THIRTY-FIVE

When she landed at LaGuardia and retrieved her luggage, she got in the line at the cab stand and waited for a car to take her to the Marriott. She checked into her room on the 16th floor. She unpacked her things and then walked down to the street and stood there at the crossroads under the lights and looked up at the soaring billboards and lighted advertisements for musicals. The street was choked in the smells of burning garlic and grime riding the hot breeze.

She descended into the burrowing hole of the subway where she bought a fare card and set out to see her new home. She rode the C train to Fulton Street and got off the train and walked up the stairs and out onto the street.

Broadway crashed through Canal Street. Twists of blacktop bottomed out under a gray sky full of hammered clouds. There was a metallic bull, its hoof raised and head lowered and ribs sagging through the hide. People crossed the street in a long gassy blur.

She knelt there, where the road divided, and stared into the narrow terminus of water. The enormous square of the Custom's

House blocked out the sky with its white columns and gray marble and wrought iron gates. She took a picture. The orange ferry gave a loud honk and she got up and walked to the church across the street. Before entering the church, she squinted to see the end of the long rows of buildings forming a gray fjord above the sidewalks.

She opened the gate to the church and went inside. She walked into the darkened alter room where candlelight rose dimly on things over a certain height. She knelt and closed her eyes and said a prayer to Jesus and asked him to look after her mother and father. Not being a Catholic, she was intimidated by the ritual of candles and incense and she broke from the scene as soon as she rose.

She walked out into the graveyard where empty stones were smoothed and names of the dead erased. They stood askance in the gothic meadow.

She thought about the magnitude of the thing. She was now a writer for the New York World. No, not a writer. She was a featured columnist. The greatest newspaper in the world now carried the Mary Dallas Page column. The entire literary world now hung on every word she wrote.

The next morning, a truck would pass by that very cemetery with a picture of Mary Dallas Page on the side of it. It would be Lee Ann Pickler. Runaway girl from Carthage, South Carolina. Lee Ann Pickler. A picture of her with her arm propping up her chin and her smiling out at the world.

The job and its looming nature and all the many dangers all were terrifying to her. She was responsible for writing one column a week. Five hundred, eight hundred words maybe. But all of them had to be perfect. Everyone would be watching.

She knew she could write, but the material was strange and un-familiar. And if she got caught telling stories, it all came crashing down. All of it.

Beau was not here to help her. There was no safety net this time. She would succeed or fail on her own now. She lay awake at night looking at the darkness of the ceiling and watching the fan blades turning and listening to the Brooklyn street sounds and thinking about the future and worrying about it all.

꒰꒱

Sometimes, when she closed her eyes, she saw herself with a man. He was young, but older than her, and he had dark waves of hair and an angular build. He would hold her in his arms and stare lovingly into her eyes across a table at a Midtown restaurant. They would meet for lunch and he would regale her with funny stories and gaze captivatingly at her with love glowing in the pearls of his eyes.

She remembered her mother's warning to her. Someday girl. Someday some boy's gonna come along. And he's gonna break your little heart. And I'm just gonna hate him for it.

She wondered at what would be the form of her love. Would he be tall? Yes, tall was important. Short was a deal-breaker. Strong jaw, short playful hair. Funny. He had to be funny. She remembered the boys in her high school. They were so stringy and sallow faced, like frightened skeletons hiding from the world. They were all so ordinary. Her love would be different, she told herself. Her love would be special.

꒰꒱

She remembered a church service in Charleston. She walked into the church with the humble reverence of a sinner and pilgrim. The sanctuary was built like a Greek temple, the steeple a massive colonial tower. An enormous white clock, the black hands standing out in the whiteness of the clock face and announcing the time as fugitives from some ancient god-cursed order.

Standing there she watched the brass organ pipes and the sunlight as it passed over them. The light shimmered on the brass curves and mirrored outward.

She looked at the altar and the deep blues and reds sparkling in mottled colors in the stained glass windows. The immaculate ceremony of robes and candles and incantations to the Almighty. Bejeweled peasants walking through incense and begging for alms, kneeling, their hands raised to God.

When the priest began to pray, she closed her eyes and called up the face of her mother and then said her own prayer. She moved her lips silently, earnestly, praying for God to deliver her from the loneliness she carried in her heart and to somehow reunite her with the spirits of those she loved and missed.

When she finished, she stood among the worshipers. She noticed that she was in a hall full of strangers.

Weary faces and gnarled hands pushing themselves up onto the dark pine ledges and filing into the aisles.

The music began and then all pushed their way into a line and began walking, as if to nowhere in particular. They moved down the aisles and disappeared from sight like ghosts in a dream.

CHAPTER THIRTY-SIX

Alone in a new city, a thoroughly scrutinizing and unforgiving city, she set about the task of finding new and interesting stories. She was alone in a city of strangers where there were millions of stories waiting to be discovered or invented. One day the method occurred to her.

Standing in the shadow of Grand Central Station, below the cast iron eagles and the Beaux-Arts facade with Mercury gesturing the swells onward above the reposed figures of Hermes and Minerva, she observed a crowd of elegantly dressed gentlemen going into a large townhouse on the corner. Lee Ann walked over to a hot dog vendor and said, "What's that over there?" The vendor gestured with her head and said, "That's the John Brown Society."

"What do they do in there?" Lee Ann said.

"I don't know," the dog vendor said. "I never been in there. Don't know anybody that has."

She sat on the curb and watched the movement through the dark windows and imagined all that might be happening inside. She took out her notebook and wrote down some lines. She saw men, all attired in tailored suits, sitting around a large oval table. A tuxedoed servant brought them glasses of scotch and cigars and he cut the tips of the cigars and lit them with a gold cigarette lighter. The men smoked their cigars and discussed what she imagined were secrets.

She invented a new source, and according to this source, the men inside had set into motion a number of conspiracies that affected the lives of all New Yorkers. There was a plan to manipulate global currency markets and make a play on the Japanese yen. Another plan called for the gradual dissolution of the New York City Council and its replacement by the triumvirate rule of the New York City mayor and the governors of New York and New Jersey, who could be bought or bullied into doing their bidding.

No, she said. That's too big. They'll see the bullshit in that one right away.

CHAPTER THIRTY-SEVEN

S he moved into a boxcar apartment in Greenpoint, Brooklyn. It had long painted hardwood floors that winked in the sunlight and an exposed-brick wall and windows opening onto the raindrop-painted lights of Manhattan mirroring in the East River below.

Way off to the left was the Williamsburg Bridge. To the right was the 59th Street Bridge and Turtle Bay and the Empire State Building. The lights danced on the water like ragtime piano notes giving symmetry to the skyline.

Lee Ann delighted in searching out the neighborhoods. She visited the Greeks in Astoria, the Italians and Germans in Williamsburg, the Koreans in Flushing, the Dominicans in Washington Heights, the Russians in Coney Island. It was a parade of nations with no borders between them. It was as if she could go to any country on earth for the price of a subway token.

She fell in love with the thorough strangeness of her own adopted home in Greenpoint. The old worldness of it. The newspapers and magazines in Polish and the pink glow of the Europa nightclub and the bakeries and kielbasa shops with their sausages hung upside down stuffed in sacks and the constancy of a language she did not understand. Sunday morning and the smell of the bread baking on the bricks. Church bells ringing from the big gray cathedral on Driggs Avenue.

On the first night in her new apartment, she drank a bottle of Australian wine and went up onto the rooftop and felt the easy fall wind blowing through her hair and brushing gently against her neck. She remembered the swing set, the priest, the rolling of her digits in fingerprint ink and their dull applications in paper smears.

There were airplanes lifting off and landing at the two airports and several helicopters swooping down unevenly around the bridges and the skyscrapers on the other side. It was all so much. It was the capital of everything that mattered and now she was a part of it all too. All her dreams had come true.

She took another drink of wine and then she heard Beau's ragged Southern voice.

"Life is one big stomping parade, darlin. You either stomp or you watch it stomp past you."

She could see his face and follow his lips synched to the sounds articulating the words in her head.

"Why be like everybody else? Why be ordinary? You don't have to. Who says?"

Why indeed?

She smiled and thought of him. What would he think if he saw me now? She thought about picking up the phone and calling him but decided to go one more night without reaching back. Still the old memories flew in like bats. She remembered the secret gardens and the faded tombstones and Spanish moss hanging down like elegant brown mosquito netting. She remembered the moon hanging over the waves.

Charleston was lovely, incandescing in the coals of its own gothic charm and shining against the harbor. But New York City was that and everything else.

It was skyscrapers and water and bridges and it carried in its ancient liver the history of the species along with its every author. It swallowed Charleston and Calcutta in one gulp as a blue whale swallows schools of krill.

⊨⊣ ⊢⊨

The subways were something out of a labyrinthine dream. There were veins of darkness carrying strangers through the bowels of the earth. She took the G train to Hoyt and Schemerhorn, then took the A or the C to Fulton Street, then changed over to the 4 or the 5 and rode the Lexington Avenue line uptown. The 6 if she needed to make local stops through the East Village or Midtown or the Upper East Side.

She held onto the pole tightly as the car began to rattle and the windows grew dark. She became immune to the noise of metal friction.

One day she boarded the train's lead car. She stood against the glass and steadied herself by placing her hands on both sides. The train began moving faster and faster and she felt herself flying away from the platform and crashing through the tunnel darkness.

The car leaned with the turn of the machine, throwing fun-house flashes of light. She saw the paint-scarred cement curves visible in the flashes of light. The exiled waste of the great city came at her in white bursts of graffiti. She saw up ahead a broken moon of light moving closer and closer and then she emerged into the glare of the terminal on the other side of the river, where people dressed in black coats with casual looks of defeat on their faces stood on the platform.

There was a hissing as the doors opened and the people embarked and disembarked and the train's gears began to move again.

⊨⊣ ⊢⊨

One day a fiddler appeared on the platform at 14th Street. And then a magician in a tuxedo with orange balls and a cup and then a mime painted silver with a change cup in front of him. Buskers working up and down the platform.

A Chinese man sawing at some ancient wooden bow organ, pulling a string and making the device dance like a spinning dreidel, its notes mixing sweetly with the burning incense and the smell of rain on the sidewalk.

CHAPTER THIRTY-EIGHT

The newspapers. There were so many of them. And the magazines and TV stations and online media. It was switchboards and headsets and gossipy whispers into ears, the trading and guarding of secrets. She had a front row seat in the nerve center of the greatest city ever devised by man.

Work was terrifying and overwhelming. Everyone was a genius. She knew she could not compete with any of them. They could all write. They could all develop sources. They could all dig out stories and organize them and turn them over quickly.

Lee Ann introduced herself around the newsroom and tried to memorize everyone's name and what they did. The newsroom was sprawled over three floors and she was on the third floor with the editorial board and the other opinion columnists. The newsroom had mazelike partitions and glass on all sides and the harbor flooding underneath it and the Statue of Liberty standing beyond the gray floor in a solemn gesture against the black water rolling and chopping in the harbor.

There were small bullpens with the desks all assembled like a giant puzzle and computers and keyboards were everywhere. The capacious room rippled with energy and the constant noise of conversation.

Lee Ann met a young woman only a few years older than herself at the coffee machine and introduced herself. "Daphne Sabiston," the woman said.

"Wow, that's a pretty name," Lee Ann said.

"Thank you."

"So what do you do here at the paper?"

"I review TV shows."

"Oh. That's got to be fun."

The woman shrugged. "Where you from?" she said.

"The south."

"Duh. I know you're from the south. But where in the south?"

"Charleston, South Carolina."

"Oh. I went there for a TV conference several years ago. It's a quaint little city."

"Yes. It's very beautiful."

"So you're doing what here?"

"I'm the new columnist," Lee Ann said.

The woman's eyes shot open wide. "You're kidding me," she said.

"No," Lee Ann said. "I start next week."

"You? A columnist? No disrespect, but you can't be more than 25. What the hell do you know about anything?"

"I don't know," Lee Ann said. "I wrote a column down in Charleston and people liked it."

The woman shook her head and started to walk away but then stopped and looked back.

"Well welcome to Manhattan," she said. "You will soon be nostalgic for the quaintness of your former life."

——⟨+ +⟩——

Her first day at work featured the usual HR formalities. She found out about vacation and sick days and the group insurance plan. She filled out an application for a charge card for her expense account.

"I want to see a lot of activity on that thing," her editor said.

"What do you mean?"

"I don't know how you did it down south, but here we get in with our sources the old fashioned way: by using the expense account. You take them out to dinner. You get them drunk. You take them to a Knicks game. Whatever it takes. Buy them a porterhouse steak at The Palm and a good bottle of French Merlot. Ours is a schmoozacracy here."

"Okay," Lee Ann said.

"Can you do that?"

"I can do that."

——⟨+ +⟩——

Mary Dallas Page turned on the southern charm and began introducing herself to the Manhattan social set. She quickly realized that the sophisticated elite snobs were nothing but a bunch of suckers. She would invite them to lunch at Poleska or Nobu and chat them up and ply them with wine and learn all their secrets.

Her first big story hit on the morning of January 9. The headline marched across the page and curled under itself in sly repose. "Deputy Mayor In Tryst With Anchorman." The story recounted a sizzling gay love affair between a City Hall bigwig and a prominent local anchorman with blow dried and frosted locks. Heated denials and threats to sue immediately followed. Everyone in the newsroom laughed. They took Lee Ann Pickler across the street to the Carriage House and bought her a drink.

Other fables appeared next. They included stories about the chairman of a major state agency taking kickbacks and using the money to fund a sex trip to Thailand and a pitcher for the Yankees who used cocaine and beat up his girlfriend, a famous actress and a regular on the club scene.

She was having the time of her life. She became good friends with Amy Diamond and Claudia Goodchance, and one night the three of them went out for martinis and ended up at the male revue. They giggled as naked men shook their G-strings at them and flexed their muscles.

The next day Lee Ann sat at her desk with a hangover. She drank a cup of strong coffee and held her throbbing head in her hands as she read the papers. There, in the first item of the Page Six column, above an article about Madonna, was a story detailing her exploits from the night before. The article referred to the three of them as "nocturnal news nymphs." There was a drawing of a martini glass with a smile hovering over it. Naughty Newsgirls, it said at the top.

CHAPTER THIRTY-NINE

"Alright, you ready for this?"

"Go," said Amy Diamond.

"I heard from a cop source that Senator Fingerman is being investigated by the feds for bribery."

"Shut up!"

"I'm serious. Apparently some developer who wanted to build condos in Bay Ridge sold him out. Fingerman demanded a payoff and the man went to the feds and they put a wire on him. Apparently they have the whole thing on tape."

"A cash payoff?"

"Two hundred grand plus a brownstone somewhere in south Brooklyn."

"How good is your source?" said Amy Diamond.

"Pretty good. He's a NYPD detective who has a good friend in the U.S. Attorney's office. He says it's real hush-hush over there."

"Why is he telling you?"

"I pretended to be interested in him. I went to dinner with him and he told me all kinds of stories to impress me about all the people he knew. Movie stars, politicians."

"Will you burn him as a source if we go with this?"

"Not necessarily. He knows what I do for a living. We just have to make sure it doesn't come back on him. Maybe we can just say, 'Government sources said.'"

"I like it," said Amy Diamond. "I like it a whole lot."

⚊╫ ╫⚊

"Mary Dallas, pop into my office for a minute."

"You got it, chief."

She walked into the office and closed the door behind her. She took a seat in one of the chairs facing Amy Diamond's desk.

"Senator Fingerman called. Then his lawyer called. They're denying your story and threatening to sue us. I just need to know. Are we on solid ground here?"

"Did you call the U.S. Attorney's Office?"

"They're denying it too."

"I'm not surprised," Lee Ann said. "Of course they deny it. Because of the wire taps."

"How sure are you that we're right on this?"

"My source says we're a hundred percent."

"So you still hang with your source on this?"

"Absolutely."

"Have you talked to your source recently?"

"Not in a day or two."

"Follow up with him."

"I will."

"Okay. No big deal. But we better be right or this gets ugly."

"He knows what he's talking about."

"You might have to name him, you know? If the court or Congress subpoenas you. They might hold you in contempt if you don't name him. They'll put you in jail if you refuse. It happened to Loretta Perkins two years ago. She spent six weeks in jail before she cracked and told them. She came out mad as a hatter. I think she lives on a yak farm in Wyoming now."

⊨⊣⊢⊨

Amy Diamond was already on her second glass of wine when Lee Ann Pickler entered the wine bar. She was seated behind a bar table smoking a cigarette, an elegant silk white handkerchief tied around her neck. When she saw Lee Ann, she smiled an immense smile.

"Did you hear about Fingerman?" Amy Diamond said.

"No."

"Feds took him away this morning. He's cooked apparently."

Lee Ann Pickler was so astonished that she couldn't speak. The words tumbled over themselves. Finally, she managed to say, "I told you."

"You weren't one hundred percent, you know? The indictment doesn't say anything about bribery. It just says he embezzled campaign funds to pay off a hooker and then lied about it to the FBI."

Lee Ann stared back at her.

"Oh well, it doesn't matter. A felony is a felony. No. No, that's not true. His felony is worse than the one you predicted he would be charged with. So he can't complain. Or go ahead. He can complain all he wants. A respected United States Senator is one thing. But a disgraced one like him? Ha! Bring it on. Fingerman's whole biography has changed overnight. He has no friends anymore. He's nothing but a sex pervert now."

Amy Diamond took a long drag on the cigarette and then crushed it into an ashtray. "Oh well," she said. "Fingerman is yesterday's news now. Now the story becomes who the governor is going to tap to replace him. Do you have any good sources in the governor's office?"

"I sure do," said Lee Ann.

CHAPTER FORTY

One night she went to sleep and found herself alone in some far distant land. Or perhaps it was the same land but in a parallel dimension. She couldn't be sure. It was familiar but unsettling and everything there was distorted. There was a tunneling effect to the world, with concentric rings of darkness drawing back and forth and dimming away at the edges of the frame.

She was sitting on the porch of her childhood home. She was listening to the crickets and watching the leaves in the night fields moving in the wind. On a long familiar white road extending into the dead horizon, she saw a figure wearing a long white shawl emerging out of the darkness and taking shape and ascending the low roll of the dusty plain.

The figure walked a familiar walk down the middle of the pebbled street and when the figure got close enough, she saw under the shawl the contours of her mother's face. The image flashed at her for one brief moment in the moonlight and then was dark again.

Lee Ann called out to her, but she kept walking, never looking back at the girl. It was as though she was a stranger on the road to some appointment. The figure pulled the shawl over her head and the features of her face disappeared into the darkness.

Lee Ann got down off the porch and ran after her, her bare feet raising up the white dust from the road and powdering her legs and the trail behind her. She caught up to the figure and touched it from behind.

Mama, she said. Mama, it's me, it's me.

But when the figure turned around, the face was the face of a stranger. She recoiled from it. The stranger looked at her cold and unknowing and then turned away and started down the road again walking away from her. The stranger became smaller and smaller in the distance.

She stood there and watched the figure go and then after awhile she started walking behind the figure and saw her depart from the road and cross over a field and go into the woods. She followed from a distance and watched the figure. There in the darkness was the glow of a large bonfire. There was the crackling of burning wood and the acrid smell of wood smoke.

In the fire's light she saw what appeared to be some sort of ghastly Medieval carnival. Drunken skeletons shorn of skin and tissue were dancing hideously around the fire, moving their feet to the music, bright ribbons of silk flowing all around their white staccato bodies. Empty skulls with black holes where eyes had once been.

One skeleton stood up on a tree stump and lifted a flute to his bare jawbone and sent a haunting moan sawing up into the night woods. Another player stood beside him and turned a wooden peg on a pear-shaped lute which he began to pick and strum and a ragtime chorus began.

Swaying and clapping and singing. Gray bones animated in jerking rhythms and visible in cinders which rose from the fire and drifted upward and disappeared. A young female skeleton wearing a bridal veil and a wreath of ivy and carrying a bouquet of dead roses reached out her hand and it was taken by another and the two skeletons danced to the music and the others moved back, making a circle for them to dance in.

Lee Ann looked into the distance and could see that there were many more of them coming to the dance. A crowd of skulls ranging the darkness and coming up the hill toward them.

The stranger made her way into the firelight and there she took down the shawl and she was no longer a face but a skeleton herself. Around the fire, the dancing skeletons made one turn, two turns, and bowed and sashayed and the young skeleton girl spun and was caught in her lover's arms.

They danced as though they had always been dancing in that place and that time neither moved nor stopped there and that each in his reverie knew he was without origin or destination.

One of the skeletons looked at her. He motioned for her to come to the dance, his bony finger gesturing her onward toward the firelight. Come to the dance, he was saying. Come here. Come to me. Come to the dance.

She came awake soaking. She got up and went into the bathroom and turned on the light and looked at herself there in the mirror. A child no longer stared back at her. It struck her that she was older now. Her face was the face of a grown woman. She moved her fingers over the creases around her eyes.

She went to the refrigerator and took out a bottle of water and unscrewed the cap and threw it into the trash and took a long drink. She walked over to the window and looked out onto the dark landscape and over the sleeping rowhouses and lines of shops and bodegas.

In the distance lay Manhattan, tolling away in the dead hours of the world.

CHAPTER FORTY-ONE

It was the summer of her twenty third year and Mary Dallas Page was now a staple of American journalism. She was the snarky voice of the not-so-common man and the bringer of social justice to the Manhattan champagne set. She mixed her stories with original reporting and sarcastic humor. Her easy smile and curl of brown hair, pixilated in black on gray paper, was now iconic.

In the springtime the council of wise men met at Columbia University and made their annual trip to the podium to announce the Pulitzer Prizes. In the category of Best Commentary, the editors articulated three words. Mary. Dallas. Page.

⊫ ⊨

She got drunk that night off expensive champagne and walked up to the rooftop. She wore the silver medal around her neck like an Olympic champion swimmer. She climbed up on the fire escape railing, arms outstretched as if to hug the Brooklyn street. She drank down a mouthful of the sweet champagne and allowed

203

herself to swim in the lights of the Chrysler Building, bright like teardrops raining down across the river.

She would stake herself to this moment. This moment would stand. She had taken the talent devised to her by the Almighty, carried it in her own cradled hands down the dusty Carolina back-stops. She had nurtured it and cared for it with food and water and love, fertilized it with the mind and genius of Beau Legare, and now here it grew, at last, straight and tall and bulbed with bright colors.

In her hands was the Pulitzer Prize. Whatever else she was, she was now a person in this world. And not just a person, but a successful person, a famous person even. A Pulitzer Prize winner.

She now had a place to stand and a voice with which to speak and an audience who would listen to her. She had a marker in the world, even if it was not under her real name. She would live on. She would not vanish from the earth. She would not die, she would not ever die.

Her mother was right after all. And Beau was right. The words had come true. She said the words over and over until tears crowded her eyes. This was it. All her dreams and more, the sparkling world bedight with the rapture of her arrival. Love flowing over her like a waterfall. This is it, she whispered to herself. I did it. This is it.

CHAPTER FORTY-TWO

The Manhattan Press Club met in an office overlooking the South Street Seaport and the cliffs of Brooklyn Heights on the other side. The officers and board members met around a large black walnut table covered by a thick sheet of glass. Agents of all the major papers and magazines were there. Amy Diamond introduced Lee Ann Pickler around the table.

She had met with Lee Ann earlier that week in her office.

"I'm the president this year," she said. "I can probably get you in as vice president. What do you say?"

"What do I have to do?" Lee Ann said.

"There's nothing to it, really," said Amy Diamond. "You administer the accounts, you organize the annual press club awards. Basically, you throw a big party. There's prestige attached to it to, of course."

Lee Ann looked at the men and women around the table. They all looked at her with boredom in their eyes. They gave half-waves and several said, Nice to meet you, and then they went back to staring at the papers in front of them. Someone made a motion.

Someone else seconded it. All in favor. Aye. Lee Ann Pickler was vice president of the Manhattan Press Club. She smiled and thanked everyone around the table and wondered whether any of them even remembered her name.

CHAPTER FORTY-THREE

Lee Ann Pickler and Amy Diamond spent all day shopping on the Upper East Side and then settled into a cozy trattoria near the river. Amy Diamond ordered garlic bread in gorgonzola sauce and they sat under the throbbing red lights and ate the gorgonzola bread and drank their glasses of wine.

"So, you meeting any men or what?" Amy Diamond said.

Lee Ann shook her head. "Not really," she said. "I kind of stay in my apartment most of the time."

"We need to get you out some. I know, I'll take you to the yacht club. My friend's getting married there next weekend. There will be men galore. Handsome men. Rich men."

"I don't know," Lee Ann said. "I won't know anybody there."

"It'll be fine. They'll all be excited to meet you. You're a celebrity now, you know?"

"You think so, really?"

"Your face is printed weekly in the pages of the World. You are a star."

"It's not a big deal."

"Yes it is. It happens to be a very, very big deal."

"I just like telling stories," Lee Ann said.

"Well good. Come and tell some of them at the wedding."

When the bill came, Lee Ann reached into her purse for some cash but Amy Diamond told her to put her money away. "This one's on the press club," she said.

⊷⊶

"Oh, I didn't tell you," Lee Ann said. "Bernadette Summers is interviewing me."

"Oh my God!" said Amy Diamond.

"I can't wait."

"That's great news. She's the biggest suckup in the biz. You'll get slow pitch softball all day."

"I'm kinda nervous though."

"What could you possibly be nervous about?"

"I don't know. I just am."

"Well relax. What's the worst thing they can say about you?"

CHAPTER FORTY-FOUR

THE BELLE OF THE BALL
By Bernadette Summers
Staff Writer

Mary Dallas Page is beaming. Her black evening dress cleaves tight to her narrow sides and tapers and plays gently at her ankles. She stands on the observation deck of the Empire State Building pointing the view finder out somewhere over the ocean.

"You know, if you look far enough, you could probably see the coast of Ireland," she says playfully.

Mary Dallas knows all about looking far enough. She launched her career by looking out over the ocean and dreaming. A child of manner and culture sired and reared by North Carolina nobility, she knows well that her status is not accidental. But it was not automatic either, and what most impresses is how willing she has been to pay her dues without complaining.

"God never made an easy road," she says, this time over a sundae at an Upper East Side sundae shop. We are upstairs by the spiral staircase and the checkerboard floor distracts her.

"Anyway, my family was very supportive of me. That's what makes all the difference."

Her modesty befits a Southern belle who looks at least five years younger than her twenty nine years and has already won a Pulitzer Prize for her groundbreaking weekly column in The New York World. However, American journalism does not deal in soft platitudes, and even in a celebrity culture where instant news is available at the click of a mouse, something just doesn't seem right about the girl.

She is, to put it mildly, a throwback.

"I don't think I'm different than anybody else," she says. "I was in the right place at the right time and it happened for me, that's all."

That something was the interview of a lifetime. An interview with the legendary novelist and professional recluse Beau Legare.

"He was ready to talk about his life, and I happened to be there when the lightning hit," she says, smiling and then finishing her sundae off with her spoon.

She coyly refuses to answer the inevitable questions about her possible romantic relationship with Legare. Rumors of an affair between the two began to spread almost immediately following the exclusive interview with Legare.

"Beau Legare trusts me not to violate his privacy," she says. "That's why he agreed to talk to me. He knows I can keep a secret. At first, he was a subject for a story. But then he called me out of the blue a week later and we started talking pretty regularly. Obviously he's an interesting person to talk to. Eventually I came to see him as a friend. I'm particularly protective of him because I know how much he values his privacy."

When editor Amy Diamond hired Page as a columnist for the World, she knew she was taking a big risk. Page had succeeded in writing sizzling features and regularly breaking scandalous news for the Lowcountry Gazette in Charleston, South Carolina, but Diamond knew that success in New York wouldn't come easy.

"Charleston, which is a lovely city, is very regional in terms of its news coverage," Diamond said. "The World obviously has a much more diverse readership and a much wider reach, with readers all over the world. I expected the transition to be hard, but I had confidence that she could pull it off. And she has, spectacularly. I never once doubted her talent or ability."

Diamond originally foresaw Page writing a Friday opinion column that mixed insight with sardonic wit. However, Page's column has taken on a larger role than originally envisioned. She regularly breaks news, as she did in Charleston, and while she is never shy about offering up a snarky remark, she is also capable of serious and thoughtful reflection."

"I don't like being pigeonholed into this or that," Page said. "I don't consider myself an opinion columnist or a reporter per se. I see myself as an observer and a storyteller. I try to bring my readers the best stories I can find and offer them serious and humorous observations about those stories."

Page's efforts have so far garnered praise from her colleagues and readers alike. The World, which does extensive research into its readers' interests, has noticed significant spikes in sales and clicks when a Mary Dallas Page story appears. Media specialists, like Columbia University journalism professor Irv Morton, say that Page is breaking new ground in journalism. "She's quickly becoming the face of the paper, as well as its most important voice," he said.

But Mary Dallas Page shrugs off the accolades and says that she's just lucky to have a job that she loves and wonderful colleagues to work with. She has achieved enormous success at an early age in life and there is no indication that she won't be a major force in the media world for years to come.

CHAPTER FORTY-FIVE

The Hudson River Yacht Club was open on all sides with tall sheets of glass looking out over the water to the lights of Jersey City on the other side. Lee Ann stood next to Claudia Goodchance, the two of them drinking from their champagne glasses.

"This is really a nice place," Lee Ann said.

"It's okay," said Claudia.

"You seem bored. Is everything okay?"

Claudia shrugged.

"I've never been to a wedding this nice," Lee Ann said.

Claudia gave a disgusted laugh and walked away. She went back to the bar and ordered another drink.

Lee Ann stood there drinking her champagne and noticed a tall, handsome man in a black suit and pink tie watching her. He had high cheekbones and a muscular jaw and brown wavy hair slung like a mop over his head. He gave Lee Ann a confident smile and then began walking over toward her.

"Name's Drake Newport," the man said, pushing out his hand.

Lee Ann smiled and took it.

"Charmed," she said.

"May I buy you a drink?"

"I already have a drink."

"Well, may I stand here and bore you with conversation for awhile?"

She threw her head back and laughed.

"Oh why not?" she said.

"So to whom do I owe such a divine pleasure?"

"Mary Dallas Page, that's who."

"Mary Dallas Page? I do say that is an extraordinary name. That accent. You're not from around here are you?"

"I'm from Charleston."

"Charleston? Lovely town, Charleston."

"You've been there?"

"Once or twice. I've sailed into there before. I seem to recall listening to a jazz band at a bar called Henry's. That's in the Market, right?"

"Wow. I feel like we're friends already."

"Did you grow up there?"

"Not there exactly. I grew up in North Carolina. Made my debut there."

"A southern debutante. Why you might be called on to teach the ladies of this yacht club some manners."

She smiled and took a drink of her champagne.

"So where are you from?"

"The Upper East Side. My father ships things back and forth across the ocean. Mom was a fashion model. She's a dilettante now. She sits on the board of the Met and goes back and forth to Europe, buying up clothes and paintings. It's very tedious, you know."

"Sounds glamorous to me."

"Not really."

"No?"

"No."

"Did you grow up here?"

"Mostly. I spent a year in Paris at the Sorbonne after I finished my bachelor's degree at Princeton. Then I went on to the London School of Economics."

Drake waved his hand.

"It's really very boring you know. I'm in commercial real estate now."

"Wow, you really get around."

"There's nothing to it really."

"Well I'm impressed," Lee Ann said.

"Don't be," Drake said. "Did you finish school in North Carolina?"

"Yes."

"Duke?"

"Chapel Hill."

"So you are a Tar Heel, then?"

"That's right."

"What is a Tar Heel, anyway?"

"I don't know."

"You went to school there and you don't know?"

She smiled. "I don't know if anybody knows for sure."

"What did you study there?"

"I studied journalism."

"You're a journalist?"

"I sure am. I write a column for the New York World."

"The World? Fine paper, the World. I read the financial pages every morning. The news. It all comes so fast it's impossible for me to keep up. Plus, it's so damn depressing usually."

"It's huge, all the information we process," she said. "I still can't believe how big it is."

"So you are on the opinion page?"

"Yes. My column is part feature column, part news, part opinion column. It's sort of its own little thing."

"Now that you mention it, you do look familiar. You're that Friday girl, aren't you?"

She smiled and nodded and took a sip of her drink. "That's me," she said.

"My father is a major shareholder in the paper. He's a big fan of the editorial page too."

"Your dad must be mighty rich."

"He does alright."

"So what kind of shipping does he do?"

"All sorts of things really. Oh, let's not talk about shipping. It's really so tedious. It's just moving things back and forth from place to place. There's nothing to it really."

"Okay."

"Do you belong to the club?" Drake said.

"This club?"

Drake nodded.

"No."

"I see."

"This is my first time coming here. It sure is pretty though."

"I've been coming here since I was a child. I had drinks with Bill Clinton here once."

"That must've been cool."

"Oh it was."

Lee Ann sipped her champagne again.

"So what's it cost to be a member of this club, anyway?"

Drake gave a dismissive wave. "Money," he said. "It's boring."

Lee Ann giggled.

"How would you like to go out on my yacht sometime?"

"I would love it."

"I usually go back and forth during the summer. From here to Montauk. We have a summer home out there."

"Montauk, huh?"

"Yes. It's very lovely. And the yacht allows us to avoid all those gawking tourists. They're really a nuisance you know."

"I wouldn't know."

"Have you ever been to Montauk?"

"No."

Drake shook his head sadly.

"Well," he said. "You must come out there one weekend. It really is the place to be. Everyone goes there in the summer. Presidents, movie stars. They're all very lovely people."

"I'd love to go there."

"How about next weekend?"

"Next weekend?"

"Yes. Do you have plans?"

"No."

"So you can go then?"

"Maybe. We'll see."

�️⟨+ +⟩

Lee Ann visited with Drake at his townhouse overlooking Central Park. There were marble tiles running the length of the floors and white columns and everything opened onto a terrace spilled with greenery and the grayness of skyscrapers floating above it.

She marveled at the pictures displayed all around.

"That one is me in Park City with Hunter. Please do not make me talk about her," Drake said.

Lee Ann giggled.

"She was the girlfriend you acquire and then hold onto for far too long," he said.

"Was she crazy?"

"Oh no. She was just. . . what's the word I'm looking for? Average, I think. There was just no sparkle to her. I felt sorry for her mostly, because she did seem to love me very much."

"She's really pretty," Lee Ann said.

216

"We met at Andover. She was from new money. Software money, I think. Really. You know how crass those people are."

"I guess," Lee Ann said.

"Her parents were Penn State grads. Imagine that! I mean really, Penn State! And – get this – they actually traveled down to the football games every weekend in a Winnebago. I mean, how embarrassing is that?"

"I think it's sweet."

"Oh, my dear," Drake said, admiring Lee Ann. "My dear, you are something. Did your redneck Carolina friends observe those same rituals?"

Lee Ann felt her eyelashes rise and fall twice in rapid succession.

"Yes," she said.

Drake stepped into her space and put his arms around her and she did not turn away.

"Enough about her," Drake said, taking her hand. "Tell me all about Mary Dallas Page."

⟞⟨⟩⟝

She told him lie after spectacular lie. About how she grew up on the golf course in Greensboro, went to private school, vacationed in Sun Valley and Mexico, made her debut at sixteen, studied journalism at Chapel Hill, dated the football coach's son, did an internship at Paramount Pictures, settled on writing and chose to start small and work her way up.

She filled the room with images of success, of the blazing village lights of nighttime Charleston, the gas lamps burning and illuminating the green sculptures in the shaded gardens. She told him about interviewing Beau Legare and what an interesting man he was.

Drake listened to the stories and his fascination grew. She told him about her ambitions, she told him about her dreams. She told him everything about herself except for that which was true.

CHAPTER FORTY-SIX

"Drake, do you ever think about things?" she said.

The two were lying together in the silk blankets of the Newport home in Montauk. The bedroom wall was a sheet of dark glass and the morning sun was coppering the sand. The black ocean lay beyond under the last few stars hanging over the rim of the world.

"What kinds of things?"

"You know. Things like death. Like why we're here at all."

"Oh goodness," he said. "I sure try not to."

"Do you ever think of the ones you know who've already died?" Lee Ann said.

Drake looked surprised.

"Have you ever lost anybody close to you?"

Drake put his hands behind his head, making butterfly wings out of his elbows and lying with his head on the pillow. "My grandfather," he said. "I was eight years old when he died."

"Do you remember much about him?"

"Not really?"

"Nobody else?"

"Thank goodness, no."

"Do you miss him?"

"I wonder what it would be like to sit and have a drink with him now. Me at my age and him at his."

"Do you ever lie in bed at night and wonder whether you'll see people again when you die?"

Drake laughed. "What?" he said.

"Do you?" she said.

"No, dear. I try to keep my mind on more serious pursuits."

"You're not curious about it?"

"I'm not interested in superstition. I'm more curious about things that are real."

"Like what?"

"Less morbid things."

"I'm being serious."

"Okay, like my sailboat then. I think about sailing all the time. Or my Ferraris. Things like that."

"Don't you get bored with material things sometimes?"

"No. Do you?"

"Yes."

"I can't imagine why. Who doesn't like nice things? You're a liar if you say you don't."

"It just gets boring, that's all."

"What would you rather talk about?"

"I don't know. Ideas. Art. Things like that."

"Art is a tonic for the hoi polloi and the vocation of bored dilettantes. My mother is a prime example. It should be of no interest to people like us."

"I love art. Art is what makes life worth living."

Drake gave a condescending look.

"Such abstractions should only occupy your time if you do not know or cannot afford more. . . sophisticated pursuits."

"Your Ferraris are just going to rust."

"No, they won't. I keep them all in a heated garage."

"That's not what I meant."

"They will be in mint condition for years to come."

Lee Ann rolled over and looked at the wall.

"You don't understand," she said.

"My dear, you must remember that you are no longer in the company of that old gasbag Beau Legare. You're in the civilized world now."

"Don't say that about him."

"Don't be so sensitive."

"I mean it."

Drake laughed.

"I tried to read that book he wrote. The one about the negroes. Just to see what you might have seen in him. I can't imagine what it was. It was overwritten gibberish."

"Stop it. I mean it, Drake."

"Oh please, my dear. Beau Legare should be in some cornpone museum somewhere. Not on the arm of a debutante."

"You don't know what you're talking about."

"You aren't still infatuated with him, are you?"

"I don't want to talk about it anymore."

"I have tried to be patient with you, my dear. But Beau Legare? Really."

"He's a wonderful man. And a genius."

"He's an old drunk. What kind of man wastes his time making up stupid little stories? I mean really, spending your time imagining people who aren't even real and having them talk to one another. Has anything ever been sillier?"

Lee Ann began to cry softly. Drake reached out to touch her.

"My dear, you and I can go anywhere together. We can sail to the coast of Spain. Or fly to my mother's home on the Riviera. We have the finest homes and cars at our disposal and we know all the most interesting people. You can drink martinis with Paris and Lindsay not two miles from this bedroom or you can sit in a swamp and listen to that old gasbag drone on and on about the poor suffering negroes. I mean, really."

"You don't know anything about him."

"I just thought you'd be over all that by now. I mean really, how tedious."

"People will read his books a hundred years from now."

"Why would I care about what people read a hundred years from now?"

CHAPTER FORTY-SEVEN

To celebrate having been a couple for one year now, Lee Ann and Drake decided to sail to the Amalfi Coast with Drake's parents. Drake's father had rented a villa on a hillside in a little Mediterranean town. Lee Ann had never seen the other side of the ocean and she could not wait.

When they shoved off from Long Island, she stood on the starboard bow and felt the wind in her face. The yacht sliced the endless plain of water and cradled itself in the arms of the waves. Soon the land disappeared and after a while she began to feel sick from the rocking of the boat.

She spent the first two days afflicted with severe motion sickness. She heaved and purged her stomach over the sides of the boat until she choked. Mrs. Newport held back her hair and soothed her with gentle words and touches. "You poor dear, you poor dear," she kept saying.

The third day her vestibular center righted itself and she sat up in the captain's chair and looked out over the ocean and felt that she was no longer being churned in its waves but was now riding atop it. She felt like a passenger and a human being again.

That night Drake brought Lee Ann dinner in their private cabin. He uncorked a bottle of French Merlot and poured them each a glass.

"Alone in the middle of the sea," he said. "What could be more romantic than that?"

She pressed against him and held him tightly and made a faint mumbling noise.

"You've been to Italy before, I take it," Drake said.

"No," she said.

Drake sat up surprised. He took a drink of his wine.

"Really?" he said.

"No. Never."

"Well," he said. "It's really quite beautiful."

"I can't wait to see it."

"But I thought you won a scholarship to Europe in college?"

Lee Ann looked away. "I did," she said.

"Where was that again?"

"Scotland."

"Did you go anywhere besides Scotland?"

"Not really."

Drake shook his head. "Pity," he said.

"I always wanted to go to Italy though," she said.

When they arrived at the port of Positano, it was pouring rain. Lee Ann walked out onto the deck and felt the warm droplets of rain shattering against her. There was water everywhere. The sky and ground were water and sheets of water seemed to hang in the air.

She looked across the short run of ocean to the rock-cropped coastline rising in the spray like a Mayan pyramid. Blurry lights flashed at her through the rainstorm up and down the hillside. She wiped the shattering wet globules from her eyes and felt the blue and white surges of lightning flooding the hillside and the sky. The rain beat against the world and flooded the world and everything swirled together.

The beauty of the moment and its unifying effect on the natural world took hold of her, as if she could step out of the boat and walk upon the waves, and it occurred to her that maybe there was a binding together of things on the earth and that this unity was a blessing and not a curse and that maybe that was what Beau was talking about. Unity and transformation and rebirth. To eternity and beyond and back again. She stared at something there in the ocean plain and she had seen its face before and she would see it again and now she knew its name.

After awhile Drake came to the deck and tugged at her hand.

"Please, my dear, have you lost your mind?"

She pulled away from him and stood there for another long moment looking at the hillside and then finally broke her gaze and looked back at him. She looked up and immediately felt the warm bursts of rain hitting her face. She looked back down and put her hands up to wipe her eyes. Then she opened her eyes again and looked upward and smiled.

Positano was a hill town in Campania retreating from the water and ascending a series of green Mediterranean hills. The ocean surrounded the mountain and there was a steep rise of rocks heading straight into the mouth of the waves.

They stayed in a little yellow villa high on the mountain and overlooking the ocean. Lee Ann spent the mornings and evenings on the porch holding onto the white columns and looking out over the sea. She made strong Turkish coffee and warmed up some milk on the stove and made café au lait and drank it on the porch and marveled at the colors on the hills and the steepness of the rocks. She thought about why people living at the verge of different oceans might come to such independently different conclusions about how to live by the sea.

She thought of the Atlantic Ocean rolling its black oily waves onto the wet sand at Folly Beach. She pictured the ghostly lighthouse, stained and abandoned and tilting on the sea plain, submerged just off the shore of Morris Island. A relic from a world that had passed and perished and been forgotten, a world that would never return.

She closed her eyes and called up the smell of the Charleston swamp marsh. She heard the language of the sea birds. Then she opened her eyes and felt her stomach plunge with the sensation that she was falling into the bottomless expanse of the caldera dying below in the rim of the sea.

"Only problem with a counterfeit life is that there's always a thread loose. That thread gets pulled on hard enough and the whole fabric comes apart. A person can be untrue just as a bill can be untrue. A fake masquerading as an original and nobody knowing of its false status. Hiding among the originals and being not one of them. There is considerable danger in that."

Beau Legare looked at her through the distance of dreams.

"What do I have to lose?" she said.

"Nothing."

"What do I have to gain?"

"Everything."

"What do I do?"

"Life ain't chess, darlin. It's poker. You do what you do in poker. You look them in the eye and you bluff them and you try to win."

Down the mountain there was a short canvas of beach. There was a long run of smooth pebbly rocks with the ocean washing over them. Lee Ann and Drake walked along the beach. Little fires on the shaly sand sent up orange bursts like torches in the horizon, the waning gibbous moon high overhead. She walked barefoot, feeling the cold seawater washing over her feet. She held Drake's hand in her own and breathed in deeply the night air. When they reached a little cove, Drake stopped and got down on one knee and took a diamond ring out of his pocket.

"Will you marry me?" he said.

＊＊＊

The wedding was set for the following summer, in Corsica. They would announce their vows before a small assembly standing at the mouth of the sea and then carry the honeymoon to a hideaway cradled in a meadowed alpine village in Switzerland.

There would be champagne in a tub and a single flower on the windowsill and through the narrow window a view onto the sky and the valley below and the long run of the land sparsely populated by goats grazing the bajada's green sweep, their horns curving inward like beasts on the African veldt.

CHAPTER FORTY-EIGHT

S he sat at her computer looking at her byline on the screen. Mary Dallas Page. She still had trouble answering to that name sometimes. Mary Dallas Page was a person she did not entirely know or understand. She was an intimidating, condescending presence, especially to Lee Ann Pickler.

She thought of the names. They were hard to tell apart sometimes for a girl split in two by them. She was Lee Ann Pickler, she would always be Lee Ann Pickler. But not to them. Not to anyone.

Lee Ann Pickler was a secret person she carried around inside her, hidden from the world by the pasteboard mask of Mary Dallas Page. Columnist and debutante. To them she was Mary Dallas Page and would always be Mary Dallas Page. Always and forever. When she died, they would bury her under a tombstone with the name Mary Dallas Page.

And the name of the other girl would be forgotten, with no record or memory recorded of her. Her timeline would simply end, making it impossible even to classify her among those who had lived and died. It would be as though she had never existed at all.

She would be just another runaway from a South Carolina dirt town. A girl who vanished into the dust and the smoke and circulatory ramps of blacktop. Just bones in some dusty ravine probably left there like trash by some nameless killer.

When she died, her true self would be removed from existence and there would be neither thing nor ghost left of her. Only a girl on paper filed away in a government drawer somewhere, a girl existing not but for contributing an atom of thickness to the bureaucratic wall.

A stamp and a file sticker and maybe a grave marker. But even the bones and the names would forever be unmatched. She had severed the chain between herself and the ones who had gone before her. She would be alone now. There, in the graveyard, under the moonlight, forever.

Alone was no longer a place or concept or condition. It was now a state of being disclaiming the promise of heaven and rising to become eternity itself.

CHAPTER FORTY-NINE

She was at her desk talking on the phone to the hostess at Basta. The two were laughing and talking about a party from the week before. Lee Ann had a copy of the New York Post on her desk and she flipped through it as she talked and giggled.

When she turned to Page Six, her heart stopped. There was his picture. He was smiling his drunken smile, and there were the words: "Not dead. . . yet."

"Reclusive author Beau Legare was found unconscious in his South Carolina mansion yesterday by his cleaning lady. Sources say the secretive scribbler lost consciousness and crashed after taking a dangerous mix of prescription drugs and alcohol. Legare is listed in serious condition in Charleston's Medical University of South Carolina Hospital."

⊷⊱ ⊰⊶

She saw the Cooper River Bridge from the air and was able to see her old apartment building there in its shadow. The lighted span and cables looked like a giant blue dolphin leaping from the water and returning to it. The city sank lower and lower into the glaze of the Ashley River, smooth as poured metal, as the plane crossed the ancient church spires and rowhouses and rattled home on the tarmac.

When they reached the terminal, she got her luggage and took a taxi to the hospital. She tipped the driver and walked into the lobby and found the information desk.

"Where's Beau Legare's room?" she said.

"Are you family?" said the information lady.

"I used to be."

"What's that mean?"

"Nevermind. Which room is it please?"

"I can't tell you. We've had reporters trying to get in there ever since Mr. Legare was admitted."

"I'm his daughter," she said.

"Oh," said the information lady.

She looked Lee Ann up and down.

"You look familiar," the woman said. "Have I seen you before?"

"Please, ma'am. I've just flown in from New York to see my daddy. I haven't seen him in five years. We've had a really difficult time these last few years and I wouldn't be able to stand it if he died without me seeing him."

"I didn't know he had a daughter."

"Neither did he. At least that's what I told him last time I saw him. Please, I have to see him. Please."

"Oh. Well dear, he's in room 316."

Lee Ann nodded and walked to the elevators and rode to the third floor. She got off and followed the green arrow and began counting off odd-numbered rooms. 322, 320, 318. . . .

She came to the door and reached out to touch it but then pulled her hand back. She didn't know what he might say. Finally she opened the door slowly and entered the room quietly.

It was dark inside. The light from the hall illuminated a dark green curtain and everything was visible only in grayscale and black. She could hear the hissing of machines. She closed the door slowly behind her.

There, in the bed, was Beau. He was smaller than she remembered him and his skin was creased and wrinkled like gray elephant skin in the darkness. His arms were crossed over his chest. She could hear him taking labored breaths. She took a seat in the chair across from him and started crying.

"Don't be like that, darlin. There's nothing to cry about, really."

Lee Ann looked up. She saw the ragged, beaten smile. The light in his eyes had dimmed and he looked very tired.

"Did you come all the way here from the big city just to see little ole me?" he said.

She nodded.

"How sweet."

"I was so worried about you."

"Nothin to worry about, darlin."

"You could have died."

"Oh, I suspect that's not too far off. I reckon anyway."

"Don't say that. Please don't say that."

"Oh, there's nothin to it really."

"Please don't," she said. "I'd miss you so much. This world wouldn't be the same without you."

"This old world won't miss one beat."

"Yes it will. I promise you it will."

"Death is nothing, darlin. It's like they say. At first you're afraid of it. Then you want to run from it. Then you beg and bargain with it. You try to make deals. But then you learn to stand there and shake hands with it. It becomes your friend. That's what I'm finding out. And the peace is real. It's enough. I didn't think it would be, but it is. I think about it like this: I'm going to win either way."

"How can you say that?"

"It's very simple really."

"Tell me then."

⇥+ +⇤

"You know how when you go to a party and you don't want to leave because everyone is having so much fun? You know how that is?"

"Yes."

"It's like that. But eventually you have one drink too many. It feels like everything changes. You feel like it happens in one instant but you know it's been changing all along. Your legs go wobbly or you spill something and then your head begins to spin. You're drunk off your ass. You might deny it at first, but then you finally accept it and then you decide to find some dignity in it. You find the dignity to lay down and go to sleep and leave the partying to everybody else. So you don't overstay your welcome and ruin everything."

Beau blinked his eyes and looked away. Then he looked back at her. "The world collects bones and makes them into other things and life goes on. The world is transformation, baby, and everything cycles from infancy to death and back again. But once you were here and you lived and loved and other people loved you," he said.

"That sounds almost beautiful."

"It's like this. You lay down on the bed. Something changes inside of you and that's okay with you and you pass that point between when it's fun to stay awake and go on making noise and when it feels better to lay down and go on and go to sleep. Eventually sleep becomes what you'd rather do."

"But it's not sleeping," she said.

Beau smiled. "I'd be depressed too if I believed that. But I don't. I believe it's a sleep you do wake up from. You wake up refreshed. A new body, a new home. This is all a mere prelude to the journey to come."

"So you believe in God then?"

"On a good day. Yes, darlin."

"How about on a bad day?"

"On a bad day I still believe in God, but I wonder whether he's much interested in what happens to people."

"Really?"

"Really. I told you that before."

"Did you? I guess I didn't believe you."

"Oh well."

"I don't want to lose you," she said.

"You won't."

"Promise me."

"I promise," he said. "You will always be with me. My heart will always belong to you."

"Stop it."

"No, no. I mean it. That part of me is yours and yours alone. That may mean nothing to you now because you are still very young. It might sound trite and easy to say. Wait till you get old. It means a lot. It means everything. It's all a person has to give."

"I've missed you so much. I don't think I can stand to let go of you again."

She got up and stood over him and looked into his weak eyes. He reached up and touched her. He held her delicate face in his hands and kissed her on the lips.

"You don't need me no more," he said.

"Yes I do. I'm nothing without you."

"You're wrong," he said. "You are Lee Ann Pickler. "You're the girl who went from a creature in the forest to star columnist for The New York World. You went there with nothing more than a smile on your face and the guts to try. You traded a locker at the bus station for a Pulitzer Prize. You are a person of superhuman talent and will and you have the bravery of Joan of Arc. You can endure anything. You have already endured everything. You will endure happiness as well."

"No, I'm not. I'm nothing. I'm not even a person. I'm just one big lie. That's all I am. Even my name is a lie."

"You are who you've always been. The girl who wouldn't shut up and get in line. Who wouldn't be ordinary."

Beau looked at her with tenderness and love. He spoke to her softly.

"They laid out the life you were supposed to live. It was a nothing life. It was just one long parade of minimum wage jobs and boring sex with some man you didn't love. You were gonna clean ashtrays in motel rooms and mop the floor in fast foods joints and then you were going to marry a construction worker and settle down and learn how to make a nice casserole and live in a single-wide trailer. And you were going to hate it. You were going to be constantly tormented by the uncontrollable aches and longings that come when you know that you are special.

"But you were better than that and you knew it. And so you refused to live that life and instead appointed yourself a new life, a different and meaningful and interesting life. Good for you. And so far it has been a great life. The life you actually live is your life and not some other life they wanted you to live.

"That life is dead. It never happened and was willed out of existence by you as fast as it was conjured by them. Life is you and your own two hands, darlin. That's what matters, not the names. When you're my age, you'll understand. When you die, who cares what name they file you under in the warehouse of names?"

CHAPTER FIFTY

She stayed with him for five days. When her editor called asking where the hell she'd disappeared to, Beau got a smirk on his face.

"Tell her the truth darlin," he said.

She put the phone to her shoulder.

"Tell her what?"

"Tell her you're in Charleston with me and that you are doing a newspaper story on me and my condition. We'll write it together. It'll be like old times. Tell her to be patient and you will deliver to her the last interview with the great Beau Legare."

Lee Ann couldn't contain her smile. She put the phone back to her ear and said the words and then put the phone down. She leaned over and kissed Beau on the lips and reached for her notebook. When she turned away from him she felt a tear roll down her cheek.

CHAPTER FIFTY-ONE

A MARSH LION GAZES DEATH
By Mary Dallas Page

CHARLESTON, S.C.— When the machine beeps and the hospital staff comes running in, they see a naked man dancing on the tile floors. He has ripped the tubes out of his arms and penis and freed himself from the monitors stacked around his bed.

"I've never seen anything like it," said Dr. Donald L. Donkeyfisch, a surgeon at Charleston's Medical University of South Carolina Hospital. "It's one hell of a sight. I probably shouldn't say this, but I can't wait to get that old man out of here."

The old man is famed writer Beau Legare, a youthful-looking man of 60 with a mane of thick white hair and a boyish face dusted with white beard stubble. Legare dances to the radio. In sickness or in health. His favorites are Huey Lewis and the News, Night Ranger, and anything by Scott Joplin.

"Not Janice Joplin, though," he says adamantly. "She's a dead skank and her voice sounded like a dinosaur eating trees. What would I want with her?"

Legare is anxious to be discharged and return to his life. Although he shot to literary immortality with seminal works such as "The Negroes of Whiskey Creek" and "The Colossus of Marshbanks," Legare has not published a novel in more than 10 years.

"I'm through with writing," he says. "The next thing I write is gonna be a damn suicide note. I want everybody to know exactly what they did wrong. So it'll probably be pretty long."

Legare, long known as one of the most reclusive artists in the world, has only granted one previous interview over the course of his career. That interview was given to this writer when she was a reporter for the Ravenel Reader, a local newspaper located near Legare's South Carolina rice plantation.

Legare recently made international headlines when he was found unconscious in a puddle of his own drool by his housekeeper, an illegal immigrant who came to America in search of a better life. The housekeeper has since been deported to Guatemala.

"I learned a lot about myself," Legare says of the incident. "For instance, I learned that ten or twelve Xanax and a fifth of Grey Goose will mess your world up, jack. It was educational like that. So it was good in a way. Next time I won't take more than six or seven."

Legare refuses to be confined to a bed, and instead often takes trips down the hall. He has on occasion left the hospital to get a shrimp burger at The Blind Tiger, where he has been observed doing shots of tequila and was last week issued a written warning for urinating on the bar. He is also known to have snuck out of the hospital on at least one occasion to sing karaoke there.

"I was back before the nurses came by in the morning, so I don't know what they were so upset about," he says. "So what if I was still drunk and singing real loud. Sister Christian is a great song and will withstand the test of time. You just wait and see. Besides. It's a song with a melody and you don't really need instrumental backing. You can pretty much just wing it solo and that's what I was doing. If you weren't there and you didn't hear the performance, it's really not fair for you to cast judgment. Some people thought it was quite good. They told me so afterward."

Legare says he is gaining strength every day and should be released soon. He hints that when the day comes, he may not return to his previous activities.

"I tried to kill pirates for awhile," he says. "But it was frustrating. I never got any confirmed pirates, only suspected or alleged or possible pirates. You could never really tell. It was hard because people kept changing course on us. We never could see them. Lucky we had GPS-guided water missiles. It's a shame to have to shoot down some strange boat in the water, but it's better to be safe than sorry, I guess.

"After that, I did some mercenary work on behalf of the government. I'm not at liberty to say which one, but it's a pretty local one. I recruited a band of Seminole Indians and we set up this commando training camp on Sugarloaf Key. That's down in Florida. They were Indians, so they were already pretty good at sneaking up on people. Eventually we crossed the ocean in a raft and landed on Hispaniola's shores. We attacked the beaches in the early part of dawn and tried to liberate the island. One of my men shot this guy but it turned out he was a lifeguard who saw us in the water and figured we was drowning and came out to help. We tried to revive him but we couldn't. So that was unfortunate. We were all really sad about that. But we pressed on because the mission is the mission.

"We told the people we were there to free them. But none of them listened or even spoke the language. Nobody. Not a goddamn one of them little brown bastards. So eventually I mated with a prostitute and got a urinary tract infection which set me on a course of pills. Then I had to come back home. It got to my brain and I self-medicated and then they found me naked and curled up on the floor. And so here we are."

Always the optimist, Legare is positive he will make a full recovery and says he already has projects in mind for when he leaves the hospital. He wants to open the first drive-through liquor store on the Galapagos Islands to serve the thousands of tourists who visit there each year and he wants to learn more about the African diamond trade and perhaps profit somehow from its spread.

"I'm also thinking about buying a chinchilla ranch in Challis, Idaho," he says.

CHAPTER FIFTY-TWO

On the third day she was there, she told him what she had previously been unable to tell him.

"I'm getting married," she said.

His eyes blinked twice and then he spoke.

"Well congratulations are in order, darlin."

"I'm sorry."

"Nothing to be sorry about. Getting married is something to celebrate, not be sorry for."

"I just don't want you to be hurt, that's all."

"Oh, think nothing of it darlin. It's really nothing. I promise you."

"Tell me about him," Beau said.

"He's handsome, rich. He has his own yacht."

"Sounds like a winner."

"You would hate his guts."

"You think?"

"Yes. No question. He's inherited money. He can come off as obnoxious. He'd be a caricature in one of your novels."

"I'm not as close-minded as you think. Everybody has their little place in the world. Even people like that."

"He's very nice. His dad's a big time international business guy. They have houses all over the place."

Beau smiled. "When you were growin up in Carthage, you didn't have no idea you would live like that someday, did you? Sailing around the world, living it up in New York City."

She shook her head no.

"But tell me darlin. Is he good to you?"

She looked at the floor, then looked up at Beau.

"He can be sweet," she said.

Beau sensed something in her hesitation.

"He's been very good to me."

"Good," Beau said. "You deserve someone who'll be good to you. New money. Old money. Hell, it beats no money."

"I miss you."

"Don't think about me darlin. A pretty young thing like you, you need somebody your own age. Somebody who'll take good care of you. You deserve to be happy. Don't ever apologize for that."

She nodded.

"Do you love him?"

"Do I what?"

"Do you love him?"

"I don't know," she said.

"Well you either do or you don't. It's okay either way."

"I think I do."

"Oh well," he said. "Marry him anyway. If you decide later that you don't, you can just end it. Fate will sort all of that out. It always does. It accounts for every human externality and it will not be denied. But you carry its burden with you into any human coupling. So marry him. I mean it. At least then if it don't work out you'll leave with some of his money."

⊷╫ ╫⊷

Her mind kept going back to the funeral week.

When the elders and eldresses had retired from the kitchen, Aunt Detra came out and greeted the little girl. She put her arms around her and held her tightly and allowed the child to rock back and forth against her bosom.

"Just remember how much your mama loved you," she said.

The little girl just nodded and cried. "It's not fair," she said.

"No," the woman said. "It's not. It's not."

The woman soothed her hands through the child's hair and looked into the mirrorglass of her wet eyes. "You can come live with me now. I love you too, you know."

Lee Ann nodded and hugged her back.

⊷⊶

She pulled up to the curb and sat there watching the house. She watched her Aunt Detra walk out and put her hand up above her eyes as if in military salute. She squinted into the burning sun. She watched the girl in the car wondering who she was and what she might be doing there. The girl's eyes were hidden behind two dark round lenses. The woman went back inside and returned with a broom and began sweeping the porch.

It was all so eerily familiar to her, but everything seemed smaller. The houses, the landscape, everything. She remembered Aunt Detra and her mother talking and cooking in the kitchen on Sunday afternoons after church had let out. The sounds of children playing would ring through the halls of the farmhouse. Lee Ann watched the woman on the porch. Her body was lankier and more bent. She leaned over at an odd angle and scraped at the porch dirt with her broom.

Lee Ann opened the car door and got out and leaned against the car. The woman stopped and looked at her. She leaned the broom against the house and began walking down the steps of the porch and into the front yard. Lee Ann walked to meet her there. They met each other at the white picket gate at the front of the yard and looked at each other for a long moment. Then, without either saying a word, they came together and hugged each other tightly and began crying uncontrollably.

CHAPTER FIFTY-THREE

She stood in the kitchen for the first time in six years. She looked at the things which had not changed. The Grandma Moses painting and the long oak dinner table unclothed.

"I was worried real sick about you. So was Tommy."

"Is he working today?"

The woman looked out the kitchen window and then looked back at her. "Tommy died two Christmases ago."

"I'm so sorry," she said. "I don't know what to say. I should have written you."

"Well you're here now. That's all that matters."

"How have you been?"

"I've been doing good. I've been doing real good."

"I've certainly thought of you a bunch. Almost every day sometimes."

"I've thought about trying to reach out to you too. But I figured you left for a reason and if you wanted to call, you would call."

"How were you going to find me?"

The woman laughed. "I was going to call the New York World and tell them I had a hot tip for Miss Mary Dallas Page."

The old woman reached over and touched her arm gently.

"You see, baby. We might still be small town South Carolina, but we do have televisions and some of us watch Matt Lauer every morning. Some of us old ladies even have a crush on him."

Lee Ann smiled and chewed on her lip. "How many people know?" she said.

"Nobody but me, as far as I know. Nobody's mentioned it. We listed you as a missing person and then later we found out you had been in jail twice. You were gone by the time we got there. We were real worried. When I saw you on TV, I almost had a heart attack. I thought to myself, I said, 'That there is Marla Pickler's little girl.' And I thought about how your mama would be so proud if she could have been here to see it."

Lee Ann wiped away tears. "I thought about that too," she said.

"If there's anything I did to make you want to leave, I want you to know how sorry I am."

"You had nothing to do with me leaving."

"I've missed you very much."

"I've missed you too."

"It's never too late to come back to your family, you know?"

"I don't know about that."

"It's not. I mean it. We all love you."

"I love you all too."

The next morning she knelt by Beau's bedside and tried to summon the will to tell him goodbye, this time probably forever.

He pressed her hand in between his two hands.

"Don't get too smart," he said.

"Don't worry about me," she said. "I know what I'm doing. I had a pretty good teacher."

"You had an arrogant jackass for a teacher. I just hope you have more self-control than me."

"What do you mean?"

"You've had success. Success brings about the expectation of more success. A certain arrogance settles in. The Greeks called that hubris. And they believed that hubris summoned the god Nemesis. So watch out for him, cause Nemesis is one bad son of a bitch."

She left Charleston with tears in her eyes. She watched the lights spilling across the dark water over the wing of the plane as it lifted higher and higher and tilted in the sky. She felt the jarring bump of the wheels on LaGuardia's tarmac.

She waited for her bag at baggage claim and then got in the long line at the cab stand. Eventually she got a cab to her apartment in Brooklyn and there she saw the wedding invitations spread out before her on her kitchen table. They were black with silver lettering. Looking at their beauty and thinking strangely about the formality with which the ceremony would proceed and knowing of its false nature, she felt a low sickness spread through her stomach.

She turned and closed the door behind her and then walked up the stairs and onto the roof deck and stood marveling at the towers of light as the wind moved through her hair like cold fingers.

"Oh Beau," she said.

She closed her eyes and saw the chapel and the whiteness of the bridesmaids and the grooms fitted like penguins. All of them smiling and not one of them knowing her name. She saw Drake standing there in a black tuxedo, his mop of brown hair flopping to the side and the crooked seesawing of his grin. She walked on and on toward a man she did not love.

She wiped a tear from her face and opened her eyes. The naked city lay in rows before her. She thought about disappearing into the madness. She would get a job in some rough and tumble Alphabet City bar serving beer and chicken wings to drunk cops and firemen and she would become a real person again. She would be Lee Ann Pickler. Country girl from Carthage, South Carolina.

She would put a palmetto and crescent moon sticker on her window and on the bar for all to see and she would work late at night and sleep until mid-afternoon and she would dance on the bar and drink Captain Morgan's straight from the bottle. She would have real friends, people who knew her and called her Lee Ann Pickler.

She shook her head sadly. A life once assembled cannot be dissembled without destroying itself, she said. Such a knot cannot be untangled and can only be cut in two dividing what had been one whole life into two broken ones. Beau told her that.

She went back inside and poured a glass of wine and drank it. She took out the bag of wedding invitations and began filling them out.

CHAPTER FIFTY-FOUR

Nemesis was born in Brooklyn as the sun set on the year's darkest day. At the moment of his delivery, the boy cried out and then fell silent for a period so long that his physicians and caretakers thought there was something wrong with him.

He was surnamed Goldberg and forenamed Stanley, the appellation a tribute to a long-dead uncle. The nurses put a Santa hat on the boy and pranced him around the hospital ward and called him Mr. Big Shot. His mother brought him home the day after Christmas.

The child was a sickly and slow child and he clung to his mother when she tried to set him down. He did not speak until the age of four and his parents initially thought he might be retarded. His first word was a word of profanity he repeated from his father.

He grew up isolated, playing with his toys all by himself. He sat alone at the edge of the room and watched the other boys and girls playing their games and they would sometimes look back at him and sense a smoldering in his eyes. The other kids and their parents saw nothing but strangeness in him.

When Stanley was a boy, his grandfather Abel gave him a small transistor radio so the boy could listen to the Yankees games. But the boy never listened to the games.

He turned the radio sideways and put it on his wooden night stand and propped his head up on a pillow and looked out over the tin rooftops of Cobble Hill. He liked music no one else liked. He would find the one radio station playing ancient country music and he would lie there on his mattress and watch the lights from the skyscrapers dancing to fiddle strings in the bilge of the river.

He looked out into the world and dreamed enormous dreams, keeping them all to himself. He sang along with the music but only in his head.

One day a neighbor kid left a Kurt Vonnegut book on the subway and Stanley picked it up and read it cover to cover. He went home and took out a pad of paper and a pencil and wrote a story about a detective in outer space. Then he wrote another one. Eventually he shared them with his English teacher and she encouraged him to keep writing, so he did.

He graduated fifth in his high school class, missing valedictorian only by a pair of lousy math grades and a B-minus in biology, but he skipped the graduation ceremony and spent the afternoon sitting under a tree in the arboretum alone drinking a bottle of British navy rum. He went away to liberal arts school in Connecticut and spent the next six and a half years drunk and stoned.

At night, he lay awake in drink singing songs to himself and then he missed class the following morning. He struggled to wait for the approach of greatness which God had told him would one day roll over him like sea foam.

He wrote for the campus paper, The Confessor, critiquing theater and film. He wore jeans and a black silk shirt and let his hair grow long and put it back in a ponytail. He carried a copy of The Last Temptation of Christ in the green netting of his book bag and often quoted from it and from Nietzsche.

He believed most of all in his own destiny and believed that destiny was both preordained and willed by the preternatural acts of man. There was a duality that determined the outcome of things. He knew that. Inevitability was certain to him because it stood astride the actual and the possible and tested whether God was God anymore or whether he was now something else. Whether he had moved on, as some of the philosophers had suggested.

Stanley left college without graduating. He took literature courses and read all the greats. There was Joyce and Hardy and the Russians and Garcia Marquez and Thomas Pynchon. Charles Dickens, the master of master storytellers.

He hoarded the books and collected them in boxes that grew to stink of mildew. Eventually he returned home to Brooklyn and moved back into the bedroom he had lived in as a child.

He worked for temp agencies and spent time in the movie houses and bars of Court Street submerged in the smoke and garishness of night lights. He submitted story after story to everyone with a post office box. Editors, agents, writers he admired. Newspapers, magazines, trade journals, alternative newsweeklies. Nothing.

He began drinking heavily. He carried a pint of Rebel Yell in his overcoat and would go to restaurants and order a Coke and then sneak two or three shots of the whiskey into the drink when the waiter wasn't looking.

One day Stanley came home and found his father dead from a heart attack. He held his mother and the two of them wept in each other's arms. Together they sat Shiva, greeting the calling mourners and inviting each of them inside. One of his father's oldest friends came over and patted Stanley on the back. Stanley shook the man's hand.

"These things are always so hard on everyone. Everyone except, well you know." The man gestured indicating Stanley's father.

"You don't think it's hard on him too?"

The man shook his head. "No," he said. "The dead do not even know they are dead."

The next month, Stanley came to the conclusion that there wasn't enough money for them to live on, so his mother went to live with her sister in Clearwater, Florida and Stanley moved into a windowless box in Fort Greene. Lien creditors seized the house and its goods and sold them at auction. Stanley got a job bartending at night and wrote during the day.

One day the mailman pushed a letter under Stanley's door. He picked it up and held it in his hand and noticed that it had professional looking stationary and he was hopeful that it might be something good. Inside was a letter from a startup newsletter called The Borough. There was an invitation from the editor to write on spec. Stanley took him up on it.

He first wrote a review of a jazz concert that he didn't like, and then a review of a wine bar that he did like. He then published an essay on the creeping gentrification and loss of ethnic identity in neighborhood Brooklyn. He added a poem about the Brooklyn Bridge. It went like this:

Desire
Like a lost star
Falling alone
Atone
To the river
Below

Stanley said the words over and over again. Standing on the deck of the bridge between the brickwork support columns and the web of cables and looking down at the floating cities of light crossing beneath. Giant barges spanceled to tug boats moving in a perfect line through the water.

He watched them pass under the bridge. He stood there drunk and thinking about things and there was a clarity to it all. There on the bridge.

He decided that a man could be great even if he died anonymous. Even if no one knew about his greatness. He could be. He really could be. Invisibly great. That would be the title of his memoirs. He stood on the bridge and watched the city, his long black frock coat blowing open in the wind.

Later, Stanley met a girl and they briefly had a love affair. She read his plays and didn't understand them but then he would explain them to her and she would nod and say now she understood. Eventually she told Stanley to marry her or she was leaving him. He was alone after that.

He stayed in his apartment and wrote for hours at a time. He consumed bottles of green label whiskey and cheap Australian Shiraz with a cartoon kangaroo on the bottle and he smoked cigarette after cigarette and the stale smoke odor attached itself to his body and clothes.

He finished a one-act comedy called The Town Idiot of Dumas, Texas, and then wrote another one entitled John Hinckley, You're Crazy As Shit. It was his hope that he might play the part of Hinckley himself.

After he wrote, he walked down the stairs and across the street to the bodega where he bought packs of Lucky Strike cigarettes from the Palestinian man there and then he walked down to the piers and watched as the darkness mounted the land and the sun's pink face died in the spaces between the towers. The black river water chopped and curled in the waves at his feet.

CHAPTER FIFTY-FIVE

S he stood on the starboard bow feeling the wind on her face. She sliced right through it and imagined that she was a mermaid on a seashell riding atop the white surf and smashing into the beach.

Drake was in the captain's chair wearing his white cap and pink shirt and boat shoes. He had a glass of Chivas Regal in his hand. The air was salty and warm and everything cooked on a low setting in the gentle elixirs of Long Island Sound. She thought about her mother and father.

She remembered her father out in the field, dark spots staining his overalls, his face slick and wet in the sun. She remembered him taking off the baseball cap with the green mesh backing and the gold tobacco leaf on its front and wiping his face with his arms and then looking up and smiling at her playfully from afar.

She remembered Mama bringing a tray with glasses filled with ice and a large pitcher of sweet tea and setting it down on the porch. She remembered rocking back and forth and looking out over the long green horizon and wondering what it would be like when it came to be her turn.

Drake stilled the blades of the motor and the bow eased back into the water. Ahead there was nothing but the unchangeable nothingness of ocean flattening into a blue cloud-blasted sky.

She put her straw hat back on and looked up at Drake and smiled. He gave a confident smile back and climbed down out of the captain's seat and walked out on the bow and put his arms around her.

"I'm really getting sick and tired of this old boat," he said over the chopping of the engine.

"I think it's great," she said.

"You're being too kind, my dear. Really, it's time we upgraded to something else. Imagine the embarrassment of sailing into Montauk next season in this thing."

"How old is it?"

"It's nearly ten years old now. Can you believe that? I told mother last night. What will people think if I take this old thing into the club again next season, or God forbid, the season after next. People will start laughing at us behind our back."

"What did your mom say?"

"She said we would talk about it when she returns from Ibiza next month. But really. We can't have people thinking we're poor white trash. We're not Massepequans, for God's sake."

She looked out over the water and thought about the Lowcountry's clustering patches of sawgrass. She looked back at him and then looked out over the water again.

She remembered an Easter sunrise service. She remembered her mother on her knees in the river, cupping her hands in the water and bringing them over her head, showering herself with river water. She remembered the preacher and how he pinched her nose and dipped her under the brown water and then brought her back to the surface. She was slick with wetness and her hair was painted against her body. She wiped the sting out of her eyes and smiled and then hugged the preacher. She looked at the little girl and winked.

Lee Ann thought about Drake's words. She answered, almost robotically.

"No," she said. "I suppose we can't."

CHAPTER FIFTY-SIX

Dr. Gerhong Korang looked his patient over and shook his head.

"That cop said I hit him?"

The doctor nodded.

"I don't remember hitting any cop," Stanley said. "I don't remember anything like that."

"You have no memory of it?" the doctor said.

"No."

"How can he say I hit him?"

"He will say it. He has the scratches and the bruises to prove it and he has witnesses."

Stanley put his hands over his eyes. They were swollen and bloodied.

"What about me?" he said.

The doctor shrugged. "You are a drunk. They are police. Whose word do you think the courts will believe? Besides, you are lucky you are not worse. Those police. They were not happy with you. It is dangerous when police are not happy with you."

"How long have you been an alcoholic?" said the doctor.

"What?" said Stanley Goldberg.

"How long?"

"What do you mean by alcoholic?"

"I mean how long has alcohol been a part of your daily life?"

"What makes you think it has been?"

"Because I live in this world too. I see people like you all the time. I can tell by your complexion. The way the skin is drawn and caved around your neck and jaw. You should probably have your liver examined."

"I drink at night. So what?"

"So how long have you been an alcoholic?"

"I don't know."

"If you had to guess."

"Seven years, eight years maybe. Eight years. Maybe more. I don't know."

"What do you drink?"

"Bourbon mostly. Or beer. Maybe some wine with dinner. What the hell difference does it make?"

The doctor nodded and wrote something down on the chart and then he set the chart aside and took a seat across from Stanley.

"You drink every day?"

"Yes."

"Do you feel sick when you wake up in the morning?"

"Yes. So what? What am I going to do? Lie to you? What the hell does it matter?"

The doctor nodded.

"They sent you to me to determine if you were legally insane," the doctor said.

"I'm not insane."

"You don't think so?"

"How am I insane?"

"I didn't say you were. You said you weren't."

"Am I?"

"No, you are not. You know right from wrong and you can appreciate the consequences of your actions. Your disease is one of self-incapacitation coupled with a previously-undiagnosed and possibly untreatable somnambular disorder that causes you to stumble around in an automatic and destructive state. You intentionally consume things you know will craze you but you do so regardless and then you feel sorry for yourself for causing the wreckage afterward. But no, you are not insane. Not according to the law. At least as I understand it. I'm not a lawyer."

"I've never been in trouble before," Stanley said.

"Well," he said. "I got busted with a joint in college. But the charges were dropped after I did some community service."

The doctor nodded. "It doesn't matter for my purposes," he said.

"I'm just telling you because you're trying to figure out if I'm dangerous or not and I'm telling you I'm not."

"People tell me things every day."

"And you don't believe them."

"Usually I don't. Usually they are unworthy of belief and they speak out only in self-interest. It is fairly easy to see through."

"You got me figured out then?"

"Yes," said the doctor. "I think I do."

"You don't know anything about me," said Stanley.

"Sure I do."

"How's that?"

"You are no different than anyone else. I don't mean that to insult you or to judge you in any way, but that's just being frank. I hope you will see that by being honest with you I am treating you with respect. Even if I'm not telling you what you want to hear."

"I appreciate that," Stanley said, nodding his head.

"I'm no different either," said the doctor. "People forget that we are but animals and that our behavior, within certain ranges and excluding certain obvious outliers, can be predicted as easily as the weather. More easily. Winds can change direction without warning. The human heart cannot."

Stanley looked at the tiles on the floor and noticed small bugs squirming in the cracks.

"My life wasn't supposed to be like this," he said. "I'm better than this. My work is better than this."

"You think so?"

"When I was a boy, God told me he had some special purpose for me and I always thought I knew what that was but none of it ever happened to me. That's hard to accept. I'm getting older and it's hard, that's all. That probably sounds crazy though."

"I'm not judging you," said the doctor.

"Yes you are."

"No. I'm just evaluating your psychological condition to comply with a court order. You have no moral accountability to me."

"So what do you think about me?"

"You want the long version or the short one?"

"Just tell me."

"Although you've been pleasant and agreeable to me personally, I find you to be an impulsive, potentially violent personality. I think you are probably fairly dangerous to other people around you given your narcissism and recklessness and this aggressive sense of self-pity."

"A violent person?"

Stanley Goldberg stood up and started to say something but then suddenly began weeping and sat back down. He held his hands up over his face.

"I told you I was drunk," he said. "You ever been drunk?"

"Alcohol is an inanimate object, Mr. Goldberg," said the doctor. "You still had a mind and an opportunity, and more importantly you had the ability to act or refrain from acting. You were still in a conscious state of choosing. You made a choice. That you made a bad one does not mean that you are insane, only that you were wrong in your choosing. Do you understand?"

"Yes, I understand."

"Good. Any psychiatrist worth his salt will tell you that there are things that go beyond medicine and things which we are powerless to treat because they exceed mere biology. You did not do what you did because you were sick but because there is something broken in you. Something beyond my ability to diagnose and beyond medical explanation. That is my opinion, at least. Alcohol did nothing to cause the act, it only loosened your inhibitions. It allowed you to do in an altered state what you volitionally would have done in a sober one but for your fear of certain penalties, like the ones you are facing now. I hope I am wrong about you, but I wouldn't be surprised if someday another person died at your hands. Negligence, you understand, I'm saying. It will be an accident, I'm sure. And you will feel very sorry about it. It will haunt you. But still. The result is the same. The person will be dead and it won't matter to the person's family that you were in a diminished state or that you are very remorseful or that you have had many frustrations and disappointments in your life."

"So you're going to say I'm a monster?" Stanley said.

"I didn't say that."

"Well what exactly, then?"

"You are a very complicated person, I think."

"How so?"

The doctor cleared his throat.

"I think that you are dangerous, mostly in a way that I would characterize as reckless but containing voluntary actions, albeit ones decided by a maimed frontal cortex caused by years of substance abuse. I think you are not an evil man, if that's what you're after. I don't think you are a sociopath. You seem to have empathy for people and remorse for your actions, or at least the capacity for those things. And you are not, so far as I can tell, a pathological liar."

"Well that's something."

"Yes it is. Believe me it is."

"What the hell does that matter?"

"Most of the people who see me are liars. It prevents their recovery. A diagnosis is meaningless until the instrument of repair is readied. Do you understand?"

"Yes."

"That's good."

"What else?"

"Nothing else really. I feel sorry for you because I think you are a very troubled young man probably facing further escalating troubles because I think that although you wish you were strong enough to stop what is coming your way you are in the end powerless against it. Your weaker parts are stronger than your stronger parts are. Do you understand?"

"I understand."

"And so I suspect your nature will ultimately win out. And I feel most sorry for those around you because they will suffer from your disease more acutely than you will. They will be the victims, not you. For you, it will be mostly painless. It will be like going to sleep. I'm only trying to be candid with you."

"I understand that."

"Good. I'm glad you understand," said Dr. Korang. "In any event, it was nice meeting you.'

CHAPTER FIFTY-SEVEN

Stanley went on the appointed day to the courthouse on Centre Street carrying with him the crumpled pink citation and found a seat in the gallery and waited for the district attorney to call out his name.

When they called him up, he stood before the judge and entered a plea of guilty, his Yankees cap crumpled into a fist at his waist. He took responsibility for punching the police officer and apologized. He said he remembered nothing of the incident but didn't doubt but that every word of the police report was true and that he was drunk on bourbon and cold medicine and that he was just so sorry. That's not an excuse but it's the truth of the matter, he told the judge.

I'm sorry about the whole thing and I've never done anything like that before, he said. If you let me go I'll never do anything like that ever again. I'll quit drinking from now on, starting today. Swear to God I will.

Then the officer spoke and told the court about what had happened. He was wearing his uniform, walking his beat near Astor

Place in the East Village when he came across a short, disheveled man urinating onto the brick wall in an alley next to a bar.

He waited for the man to finish and then told him to turn around. He informed him that his actions were criminal and that he now would be answering to the law.

The officer said that the man became irate and drew his hands into fists. Let's go, then, he said to the officer. If you think you're such a big goddamn deal. The officer drew his stun gun and shot the man full of metal hooks attached to cables. He shocked the man to his knees, then placed him in handcuffs and called central booking for transport to the Tombs. He mashed the man's head against the sidewalk with his boot and told the man many times to shut up. This could have easily been a shooting, he told the judge.

"Did this man ever apologize to you?" the judge said.

"No, sir. Not till just now."

The police officer turned and faced the judge. He told the judge about his wife in Milford, Connecticut and their two little girls, and about how he commuted to the city every day wearing a bulletproof vest to walk the dark streets never knowing which goodbye hugs from his daughters might be his last.

He told the judge about how punks like this punk here make it so dangerous for honest cops just trying to keep this city safe. About how good people will someday stop choosing to live in the city if bums are allowed to piss on the street and assault cops. Booze and dope, said the officer? Everybody's got some excuse. Every single one of them.

The judge nodded his head and sentenced Stanley to sixty days in jail and then the jailer took Stanley through the side door, cuffed him and searched him, put him on a bus back to the Tombs for processing, and then on to Rikers. Stanley was in Rikers by suppertime. He stood in a long line and held onto a tray and then sat alone and ate a corndog with no stick and a couple forkfuls of corn. The banging metal noises were jarring to him and ruined his appetite.

The first night was the hardest. It was something to be locked up with nothing save your mind. Only in isolation could a man rise above the level of animal and that was an ironic thought to Stanley indeed. He realized that a man's humanity was never more acute than when everything else was taken away from him.

He did his time there by retreating inside himself. He had long leaned on alcohol and other drugs and now the detox was the worst part. It was excruciating at first when coupled with the boredom. Every moment made itself be known. Time moved forward slowly, then backward, then forward again, all at a crawl. His hands shook and he watched them shake and he was powerless to stop them or look away. He held them before his face and they trembled even when his brain told them to stay still.

He did not know whether it was day or night and days of the week and hours and minutes all became confusing and arcane concepts.

Time was no longer a linear thing. It was a friend you used to know but couldn't fully remember now. The face kept changing on you. The pale light shone through the outer screen on the narrow window looking out onto the gray-walled circle of the yard.

He lay on the floor of the cell and composed a play in his head. It was called Miracle at Rikers and was about a futuristic society where men invented robots and infected them with human qualities, including the capacity to understand the complexities of life and distill them into artistic forms. The robots became able to do this more quickly and with greater accuracy than could the humans. The robots were made to look just like the humans except that there was a colder look in the glass of their eyes, the affectation slightly flatter and more even. That was how you could tell. There was something about being human that was visible in the eyes, and despite the amazing breakthroughs in science, that something was still incapable of being reproduced mechanically.

But unlike humans, the robots could be repaired and replaced, piece by piece, so they would never die. They prospered at first and were a great help to all mankind, and their art led to greater understandings of things and these understandings led to a new Enlightenment which eventually assigned error to the source of its very becoming. Mankind came to regret not only the creation of its machines but the concept of creation itself. If man could create immortals where God could not, God was obsolete and his miracles ephemeral.

There was no God. There was only fraud and superstition. Art, it was decided, was a thing to be destroyed because it gave hope where hope was not warranted and mankind set out to destroy the machines in order to destroy the art. The robot artists became fugitives with prices on their heads.

They hid like rabbits in the woods and when they were discovered they were chased and shot like rabid dogs and their metal corpses were left on the floor of the rain-blown hills of the forest to rust there in an eternal junkyard.

Man, in his long evolution and aided greatly by his robot philosophers, came to discover, as man once discovered the roundness of the earth, that the human animal was what it was, a biological being which lives briefly and then becomes extinct, and in this knowledge he recognized the impossibility of an afterlife and so had soured on the notion of a living god. First they mocked the gods, then they outlawed them, then they came to persecute their believers.

It was now a common truism that faith itself was a cruel institution that enslaved people in unattainable yearning and that art preserved hope that in turn inspired faith and was thus the greatest evil of all man's devices, far more destructive than murder itself because where murder promised only death and was thus consistent with the laws of nature, religion and art promised hope and eternal life and thus subverted the natural form and propagated lies and falsehoods. The gods were the makers of the misery and the removal of the misery meant the removal of the gods.

Only the robot artists objected. A young robot playwright named Nikos was the protagonist. Brave and an undiscovered genius, he was the work of one of the last of the old believers, an eccentric tinker who forged robots out of the spare parts of obsolete cars salvaged from a thieves' junkyard, a man who had perished in the fires on Calvary Rock where one by one god worship was extinguished in the executioner's sunset. Men lowering their heads and facing the invisibility of their maker for his own obscure sake and in his own faceless name. Their heads rolling down, one by one.

Nikos was a robot like many, sensationalized with the capacity for longing and pain, but uncommonly he set out to conquer them and deny them any consideration in his mortal life. Unlike any remaining humans or the past humans in the history books, he knew well who his creator was and he had no hope of any afterlife. This strengthened and restored him. He reckoned that he was ignorant of all events before his birth and so had already experienced death and that actual death would be no different than history before his creation and this rendered the intervening years all some brief fortunate happenstance and that bold or meek he would lie cold in the same mechanical grave.

Incarcerated and starved of energy by the human regime, he creates a story in the machine of his head and tells it to the other robots through the pulses in their transistors and they tell it and retell it among themselves and the story restores them and gives them hope. When some of them escape from the regime of man, the story gets out to the masses of people and causes them to question the measures taken to persecute the robot believers. Something in the human form reawakens in some and a great disturbance occurs. By some this is seen as a strange and possibly miraculous occurrence and by others a talisman of the final days described in biblical narration.

Mankind divides in insurrection between the believers and non-believers and civil war tears the land between the warring halves. The play ends at the beginning of the war. The audience is left unknowing of its success or failure and clueless as to the story's contents beyond the meager details provided.

He closed his eyes. He could see the backs of darkened heads watching the actors speak the lines. He could see them all rise from their seats and begin to cheer.

"I didn't think it would be like this for me," Stanley Goldberg said.

"Nobody here say no different."

"But I've sensed it since I was so young. I always knew it. It was what kept me going even when there was no reason to have any hope. I just didn't think it would take this long, that's all. It can still happen. I'm just getting older and it hasn't happened yet and I thought it would have happened by now. I thought I would do my part and God would put me where he wanted me to be."

"God going to do what God going to do."

"But I did what I was supposed to do. I wrote the plays. They're there, all of them. They exist. They are a part of this world even if nobody else knows they are. Okay?"

"You write plays?"

"Yes."

"No shit?"

"Yes I write plays. I can write anything. Really."

"Can you write my appeal?"

"I'm not a lawyer."

"Me neither."

"I'd just mess it up."

"Lawyer probably mess it up too."

"Probably so," Stanley said.

"That's how I got in this mess to start with."

"Really?"

"Lawyer done me wrong, man. Pled me guilty without even getting my motion of discovery."

"Sorry to hear that."

"Come on then," the man said. "What do you say?"

"No," Stanley said. "I can't do it. I'm not talented in that way."

"Nevermind then. Suit your own self."

"It's just so frustrating."

"Yeah."

"I know what my destiny is. I've seen it so many times. It's in art, I can tell you that much."

"Well mine's to get out of here."

"You will."

"That's not what the judge say."

"Well maybe he's right."

"I hope not."

"You know how it is. Overcrowding and all. You'll probably be out before you know it."

The man shook his head. He spat in the toilet. "I wouldn't worry about God if I was you," he said.

"Why not?" Stanley said.

"Cause ain't no God in here," he said.

"Maybe there was never a God to begin with," Stanley said.

The man shook his head. "Naw," he said. "Probably they wasn't."

CHAPTER FIFTY-EIGHT

He rolled over in the filthy blanket and woke up to another day in the shelter. He put on his flipflops and took a shower, then grabbed a coffee and set out for the day walking down Bedford Avenue and crossing McCarren Park. He got on the L train and rode it to Union Station, then caught the Lexington Avenue line going uptown. The train smelled of grease and urine and all the travelers held their heads down like condemned prisoners.

He stopped at the A.P. building in Rockefeller Center and rode the elevator up. The receptionist gave him an application and he explained to her that he was looking to freelance for cash and would go anywhere in the world to do it. Bosnia, Iraq, I don't give a shit, he said. Please fill out the form, the woman said.

Then he went downtown and found the Gotham City News. He was stopped by the security guard and told to go home.

"I'm just looking to do some freelance," he told the guard. The guard radioed upstairs and got one of the editors.

"There's a guy here says he's looking to do freelance. Says he'll work cheap and write about anything. He don't give a damn. Says he has experience. Says he writes plays."

"Send him on up," one of the editors said.

⊨⊣ ⊢⊨

"What kind of writing have you done before?" the editor said.

"All types. Movie reviews, hard news, opinion, obituaries. Whatever comes down."

"You have clips?"

"Got them right here."

Stanley opened the photo album and turned it so that the editor could flip its pages. The editor nodded his head.

"Do you know anything about crime?"

"Yes."

"You been arrested?"

"I went to jail for hitting a cop. I was drunk then."

"You don't drink anymore?"

"Not like I did then."

"We pay twenty bucks a story. I can give you a couple stories a week. If you make an impression, I'll give you more."

"I can handle whatever you got."

"We'll see. Stringers are a dime a dozen in this town, you know?"

"I know."

The editor nodded. "Well, kiddo," he said. "Let's see what you got."

⊨⊣ ⊢⊨

Stanley Goldberg began writing general assignment beat stories about the City Council and mob hits and problems with the subway system. He was aggressive and bullying and his headlines blazed across the top of the Gotham City News. Within six months reader-ship had increased by eleven percent but he had been suspended twice for writing libelous inaccuracies and warned three times for showing up to work drunk.

"Why don't you just fire me if I'm such a pain in the ass?"

"Because you can teach an asshole manners," said the editor. "But you can't teach a nice guy how to write."

Stanley immediately appreciated the kind words and vowed to never again disappoint the editor. The idea of having a mentor who cared about him and believed in him and looked after him was of tremendous import. He polished the stories, sharpening them line by line until they practically mugged the reader of his attention.

Stanley worked late into the night on his plays. He drank brandy and wrote drafts of the plays by hand. None had ever been performed or published but his passion to write them burned on. He had been hard at work on one for three months now and he couldn't seem to break through the opacity and find the play he was supposed to be writing. Everyone told him the story idea was great.

Storytelling was not the problem. Staging was. It was a retell-ing of The Memoirs of Ulysses S. Grant, but set in Grand Island, Nebraska in 1952. He stayed up into the dead hours to compose his thoughts, he wrote until his wrist cramped and sprained and his hand became a claw. Thy River Divideth. That was what he was calling it.

He chewed his fingernails until he freed the blood in the swol-len quick. Someday, he told himself. Someday. Someday.

CHAPTER FIFTY-NINE

He was following an expedition of MTA cops and engineers through the cavernous recesses below the East River. He followed the light and saw it stabbing against the tracks.

Then there was the screaming of train shoes on rail irons and a long yellow light and then the blue circle with the letter A inside. The machine roared toward them and by them. It made a crashing sound like a wave at the beach.

They shone the lights and swished them against the wall and there was a small passageway that led to a larger opening in the tunnel. Inside were mutants lying in their own filth and hiding their eyes from the light.

Stanley went in and crowded the man holding the light.

"Jesus God Almighty," somebody said.

Stanley started asking the mutants questions.

"What's your name?"

"How long you been living down here?"

"How often you go up on the street?"

"How you get down here with all the trains running back and forth?"

"Has any of you or anyone you know ever been hit by the trains?"

The mutants retreated from the light and held their hands over their faces and made primitive groaning noises.

"Goddammit," Stanley said.

There was a joke and then police laughter all around and then they were handcuffing the mutants and taking them back onto the track and now the light followed them and pointed into the station terminal. They emerged into the light like captives in a Roman parade. The light was blinding to them.

Stanley Goldberg followed them up into the terminal and then stood on the platform and crouched down and looked back into the hole. Damn, he said to himself. You'd never know it but there was a whole civilization of mutants hidden down in there.

What is a mutant, anyway? He asked himself.

A mutant is someone who does something unusual for too long and mutates into that thing. A person is no more than the sum of his base desires. When you take everything else away from a person, the base desires are all that is left, and this condition makes a person vulnerable to any abhorrent condition. It could turn you into a person who hides from the social order in a man-made cave and survives on insects and vermin.

That's what a mutant is, he decided.

He put his notebook into his coat pocket and then walked down Broadway and found an Irish pub and ordered a hamburger and a Guinness draft. When he returned to the newsroom, his editor called him into the office.

"You know how shit rolls downhill?" the editor said.

Stanley nodded.

"Well here it comes. We have to appoint someone to do volunteer work for the Manhattan freakin Press Club. This year it's your turn."

"Okay," Stanley said.

"Good," said the editor.

"What do I have to do?"

"I don't know. You go to meetings and shit."

"Okay."

"You think you can handle that?"

"Sure," Stanley said. "Why not?"

CHAPTER SIXTY

The Manhattan Press Club had its annual awards banquet in April at La Verna among the coneflowers blossoming in the park like yellow tree ornaments. Horse drawn carriages ticked past the black limousines.

The members and their guests arrived tuxedoed and gowned like princes and princesses getting out of black Lincoln Town Cars and holding hands as they walked down the carpeted runway through the frenetic splash of camera fire. It was an overflowing scene. Expensive champagne, open bars in every corner, sharp tuxedoes on crisp white linen shirts, bright dresses hanging on the painted women, their fingers and necks adorned with diamonds and gold, a raised platform decorated in orange bunting and a podium in the middle with the lights shining down on it.

Lee Ann Pickler took a seat at one of the tables in the front and looked at the program. There was a listing and biography for every nominee for every award. Amy Diamond slid in beside her. She was drinking a martini and wearing a red strapless dress and matching heels. She tossed back her hair, throwing it over her left shoulder, and stirred the drink with her olive.

"Isn't this just lovely?" she said.

"It's really something," Lee Ann said.

"After tonight, this will all be your baby."

"What?"

"You will be president after tonight."

"I doubt that."

Amy Diamond laughed. "It is done," she said. "You will be elected president at our wrap-up meeting on Tuesday and after that I'll be stepping away and you will be in charge."

"Are you sure?"

"The vote will be unanimous."

"I've never been in charge of anything like this before. I don't know if I can do it."

"You've done all the work this year," said Amy Diamond. "What you will do is find a loyal and hardworking VP, a lackey really, and then you will coast and go to parties and be introduced as president of the press club. You will love it."

"I don't know who I would pick."

"You might want to start putting some names together."

The program began and the music rose and the performers came out and did their little routines and told their little jokes and then one by one the presenters came out from behind the curtain holding a single golden envelope sealed in red wax and stamped with the press club seal. They made their way to the podium and said a few words and then got down to business.

"In the category of best investigative reporting, the award goes to. . . ."

"For best political reporting, the award goes to. . . ."

Lee Ann Pickler clapped and smiled as the winners made their way to the stage and stood in front of the balloons and thanked their editors and copy editors.

She noticed the man seated to her left and saw him repeatedly click-clacking the top of a silver Zippo lighter.

He was wearing a black suit with a yellow tie and he was drinking whiskey and not clapping at any of the awards. He just turned and read the program and drank his drink. Lee Ann was intrigued with the sad, self-deprecating way he had about him. But when she spoke to him, she found him to be jovial and charming in a sarcastic, thoroughly New York kind of way.

"Are you a writer?" she said.

"Allegedly," he said.

"Who do you write for?"

"The Gotham City News. I cover the Brooklyn courts. I write plays too."

"Off Broadway?"

"Off Off."

"Interesting."

She could tell the man hadn't shaved in several days and his hair, although combed, had not recently been washed.

"What are your plays about?" she said.

He laughed. "About things that aren't very lucrative, apparently. About poor people doing crazy things," he said.

She smiled back at him.

"I've tried all sorts of things," he said. "Basically it's like Ibsen, if Ibsen lived today, you know? Ibsen's probably my biggest influence. Hedda Gabler, especially. And Ghosts. It's like Ibsen meets John Cassavetes. Maybe a little Sam Peckinpah in there too."

She laughed.

"I know that sounds like a joke but I mean it."

"I wasn't laughing at you. It just strikes me as a wild combination, that's all."

"It's a passion and I do love it. I think theater can take from cinema and literature and music and everything else. It allows you to comment on the human condition. You know? But I do enjoy writing about the courts too. You get a lot of good stories there," he said.

"I'll bet."

A waitress came by and brought the man another whiskey. He held up the glass and looked at it lovingly.

"This is quite an event," he said. "This is the first time I've been to it but I'm glad I came."

She touched the man's arm. "I'm probably going to be president next year," she said.

The man held up his drink as if to toast. "Well congratulations," he said. "Let me know if I can be of any help. God knows I love a party. Make me minister and appropriator of whiskey and I'll work my ass off for you."

"I'm Mary Dallas Page, by the way," she said. "I write a column for the New York World."

"I know who you are," the man said. "Everybody knows who you are."

The man smiled a crooked smile at her and stuck out his hand. His fingers were short and thick and his fingernails were bitten to the nub.

"I'm Stanley Goldberg," the man said.

She was elected president of the Press Club by unanimous consent. She thanked them all and promised to work hard on their behalf. She took over the budget, the planning, the administration of the awards selection and awards banquet. She named Claudia Goodchance her top assistant. Most of the other positions went to colleagues from the paper, people she knew would be loyal to her. For the position of treasurer, she reached out and chose Stanley Goldberg, who she knew was a drunk and would be easy to control.

CHAPTER SIXTY-ONE

After a year of planning and traveling and spending money on the press club credit card, Lee Ann Pickler found herself standing around the chess tables in Washington Square Park. Greenery leafing out all around her. She took a seat there on the park bench looking at the pigeons stabbing and juking their way over the long circle of pavement. It was all set. Things were all in place. She waited for nightfall and her coronation.

When the night came, she found herself reclined on a pile of silken pillows. She enjoyed a restful satisfaction in her work. She lay in the Victorian suite of the hotel drinking champagne and eating grapes. Her peers sat like courtesans at her feet.

They drank pink champagne and ate prime rib and brie on water crackers and talked about all their adventures over the last year. Lee Ann Pickler threw back her head and laughed and sucked on grape stems and told a story about sailing with Drake to the Amalfi Coast.

"I suggested we rename his yacht the Arawak, like those doomed Indians," she said.

The lady from The New Yorker suggested they try sailing around the horn of Africa and somebody else mentioned Alaska.

"No thanks," Lee Ann said. "It's air travel for me from now on."

After awhile they went downstairs and she walked a queen's walk through the ballroom and was seated in a long row of bright party dresses and pointed tuxedo collars. The band swelled the music and the emcee came on and told the jokes and everybody, plied now with champagne and whiskey and rum, rolled back their heads with laughter, and all around her was the reckless sound of success.

Then the nominations came.

"In the category of best short feature, the Manhattan Press Club awards Mary Dallas Page!"

"For best feature, Mary Dallas Page. . ."

"In the field of best series, ..."

The applause quaked through the audience. Again and again Lee Ann Pickler rose and gave a surprised and slightly embarrassed look and then bowed her head modestly and then threw back her head and laughed as though this could not be happening to her and she floated under the tapering red dress up the stairs to the lectern, the enormous screen behind her projecting her accomplishments in large print for all to see.

Stanley Goldberg stood in the corner burning with anger. He finished pouring wine into a woman's glass then slammed down the bottle and started to pace in his little booth. He picked up the bottle and turned it up himself. He felt like exploding in a string of powerful bursts like a Roman candle. He honestly could not remember having ever been this angry. His eyes burned like coals and he walked back and forth and back and forth and thought about the swan dancing before him and the phoniness of her feathers.

She rose a total of seven times that night. When Stanley Goldberg watched her grab her first three Press Club awards, he already suspected a fraud was underway. And now he thought maybe he could prove it.

Spending nights at his room at the Y, he poured through the books. He studied every line on every ledger and eventually discovered discrepancies in expense payments and found instances where payments seemed to cover other payments. He was not a financial wizard and the crunching of numbers pounded into his skull and throbbed his brain. But he knew what looked suspicious and he loomed and stared over the numbers with a pen and doodled in the margins and made photo copies and called some sources he had who were financial wizards.

Stanley Goldberg sensed mischief in the distribution of the awards and falsity in the cheap smile of the big winner. Having access to the books as the Press Club treasurer, Stanley scrutinized every line item. He investigated every mark, every column, every number. He added them up again and again.

Things didn't quite add up. There was a five thousand dollar hotel charge from the Mandarin Oriental in San Francisco and a seven thousand dollar charge from Saks Fifth Avenue and there were numerous smaller purchases. There were spa payments, an expensive health club membership, dinners and drinks at restaurants both famous and obscure. A charge for a single movie ticket at the Lincoln Center multiplex.

Stanley Goldberg asked Lee Ann Pickler for a list of the judges for the awards and she promised him that it would be forthcoming. Then nothing. Then she stopped taking his calls.

—⊰⊱—

When Stanley had assembled his case, he went before the board.

"Mary Dallas Page is a liar and a thief," he said.

The board stood there. No eyes moved.

"I'm not kidding," he said.

"What evidence do you have?" a man said.

"Good question," Stanley Goldberg said.

"These are serious accusations, you know?"

Stanley laid out his case before them and passed around statements and stuttered as he tried to explain it all.

Lee Ann Pickler just stood there smiling with her arms crossed.

"Everything's balanced," she said. "Look, if I paid for something out of the wrong account, I checked on it and got it right then paid it back from the right account. There's nothing to these allegations. And Stanley, I really don't appreciate this."

"I agree," said one of the board members. "There's nothing to these allegations."

Stanley Goldberg went home dejected but determined to nail Mary Dallas Page to the wall. After drinking seven beers at Muggs Ale House, Stanley told the waitress that he would get her if it was the last thing he did on this earth. A spoiled debutante brat. Goddamn her. He would get her.

"I know she's a damn liar," he said.

CHAPTER SIXTY-TWO

Stanley Goldberg picked up the phone and called the registrar at the University of North Carolina at Chapel Hill. The assistant registrar answered on the fourth ring.

"I'm looking to confirm that a former student in fact graduated from UNC," Stanley told the registrar.

"What's the name?"

"Mary Dallas Page."

There was a pause.

"Nothing's coming up," the registrar said.

"It would have been ten years ago at the most."

"I don't see anything. I'm sorry."

"Thanks for your help."

———

"I got Mary Dallas Page's number," Stanley Goldberg said. "She's nothing but a god damn grifter."

"What?" the editor said.

"She's phony as hell. I got her dead to rights."

"You sure about this?"

"A hundred percent."

"How do you know?"

"Her resume says she went to Chapel Hill but that's news to the school. They never heard of her."

"Maybe her last name's different."

"Nope. She's a stone cold liar. Her resume also says she won a European scholarship. They never heard of her either."

"Are you serious?"

"Hell yes, I'm serious."

"Jesus Christ."

"She says she started out writing for the Ravenel Reporter. That's true. But she told them she started earlier with the Carthage Weekly, some little rag out in some nowhere town in the middle of South Carolina."

"Did you check with the editor there?"

"Yeah."

"They ever heard of her?"

"They heard of her all right. I showed them photographs and everything."

"They recognize her?"

"Oh yes."

"So that part checks out then. So she lied about some school info? So what?"

"I'm not finished. They recognized her as someone else."

"Who?"

"A girl named Lee Ann Pickler."

"What?"

"Lee Ann Pickler. That's her name."

"You sure?"

"Yeah, I'm sure. She's a total fake."

"Jesus, Stanley."

"She grew up there in town. Her father used to run the press at the newspaper but he's dead now. Been dead for years. Her mom died several years ago. Nobody's seen her since then, apparently."

"You have any idea where she might have gone to school?"

"There's no record of her graduating from high school or college."

"She's a goddamn columnist for the World. She has to have a degree from somewhere."

"Chief, this woman is a high school dropout."

"Bullshit."

"I'm not kidding."

The editor shook his head.

"There's more. Chief, I'm telling you. She is a con artist. She's really pulled one over on the New York World. She's a criminal even."

"What?"

Stanley Goldberg opened up his manila folder. Inside was a stack of pictures. They showed Mary Dallas Page standing under a tray of florescent lights in front of a police station wall. She had an angry, defiant look on her face and held a plate with numbers under her chin. The plate said Florence, S.C. The white letters said Lee Ann Pickler. Prostitution. There was another one from Santee. It said Larceny.

"That's her all right," the editor said. "Jesus God."

"I told you. She pled guilty to the larceny charge."

"Jesus."

"That's not all. I went through the Press Club's financial records and found thousands of dollars in highly questionable purchases. The Press Club paid almost ninety grand to a marketing firm called Exordium Marketing LLC. I checked with the Secretary of State and found that the company's registered agent is a woman named Hannah Rosen. But a reverse search on the company phone shows it as being registered to Mary Dallas Page.

Other purchases include trips to San Francisco and Charleston, spa visits in the desert, and meals at expensive restaurants all over Manhattan."

"I don't know what to say," said the editor, crossing his arms. "I just don't know what to say."

"Say let's run with it. Chief, we got this girl. Got the World too for that matter. Got em by the balls. The biggest newspaper in the world is publishing a complete fraud and pushing her fiction off as fact. How reckless were they in hiring this damn woman?"

"You talked to her yet?"

"No. I'm saving the best for last."

"Get her on the phone. Her editor too."

The editor stepped out into the newsroom and shouted for the layout editor to hurry.

"I want you two to work together," he said, sticking his head back into the office. "I'm going down to talk to the boys in graphics. You boys got the cover with this one. I'll have them redo it and that'll piss them off but so what. That's their job. Now you boys earn it. This is a huge story. It's a tabloid scandal, an institutional scandal, you name it. This one has legs."

"You got it chief."

＝≒＋ ＋≒＝

Lee Ann Pickler's telephone rang at her desk.

"Mary Dallas Page," she said.

"I'm sorry," said Stanley Goldberg. "I was looking for Lee Ann Pickler."

She froze.

"I know who you are."

"Who is this?"

"This is Stanley Goldberg with the Gotham City News. Remember me? I'm calling you for comment. You want to tell me about perpetrating the biggest fraud in the history of American journalism?"

She felt herself exploding inside.

"I don't know what. . ."

"Save it, Pickler," he said. "I got you dead to rights. I got your mug shots from Florence and Santee. I know who you are."

"Please," she said. Her voice broke and her words began wavering. "Please. . . please, you don't understand. . . ."

"Stop it."

"Please. . ."

"There's nothing you can say, Pickler. I'm not gonna be another one of your suckers. It ends here. I just want to know why."

"But. . . I can't. . ."

"How did you fool the World for so long?"

"I. . ."

"Yeah?"

Lee Ann looked into the pane of glass facing outward onto Water Street. She saw herself in its dark reflection. It didn't matter anymore.

She slammed down the phone and began sobbing into her hands. Around the newsroom, people watched as she sat there and cried.

CHAPTER SIXTY-THREE

The darkness of the room and the random nature of things scattered within it were things that occurred to her when she was lying there mourning her own death. She lay on the bed hugging her pillow. The glow of the TV in blue lamplight shone against the distant wall.

"It wasn't negligence on our part," said Amy Diamond. "We believed in her. We did. We just weren't as careful as we should have been. But we've instituted new hiring protocols and measures to check up on past stories. So this is a mistake we won't be making again."

She cried as she watched the TV.

Then they went to Stanley Goldberg. He was clean shaven and wearing a blue starched shirt and a red tie. He had an easy look about him.

"Stanley Goldberg," the man said. "You're the one who broke this story open wide. Tell us, what does the Mary Dallas Page scandal mean to the future of the American news media?"

Stanley adjusted himself in his seat and smiled.

"Well it's clear what it means, but I'll leave that for the public to figure out for themselves."

"What does this scandal mean to you?"

"Well. It just means that a bad apple got weeded out. That's all it means. People will forget Mary Dallas Page as quickly as they learned about her."

The host turned to Amy Diamond.

"Do you agree with that?"

She nodded gravely.

"I do," she said. "I sure do."

Lee Ann Pickler fell onto her bed and bit hard into the pillow and screamed her lungs out.

She lay in bed with no lights for two days, tears welling and drying in her eyes and no one to care about her or offer her any compassion. She stayed bundled up, the windows shuttered and dark, no music or television or anything. The phone was broken in shards in the street below.

She lay there with the notebook next to her and the last living words of her mother and it was the last thing in her life that would ever be hers really and truly. She read them over and over again. The purple notebook was her only comfort and her only mercy and the knowledge that below lay the words and her connection to the words and their connection to those who had loved her and might love her again someday in heaven.

She took out a knife from the kitchen and took a long look at the whiteness of her wrist. She studied the route of the big blue vein. She placed the serrated edge of the knife to her wrist then took it away then put it back on there again. She decided she should be in the tub.

She set the knife aside and went to draw a bath. She turned on the faucet and listened to water begin to run. She sat on the edge of the tub with the knife in her hand. There was a knock on the door. She put down the knife and opened the door and saw two large police officers standing in the doorway. One of them held up a pink piece of paper.

"Lee Ann Pickler," he said.

She nodded.

It was good to hear her name, to be able to answer to her name, and for a moment she forgot her despair and felt almost a sense of exhilaration, like she was being greeted by a long lost brother.

"Yes," she said. "I'm Lee Ann Pickler."

"Got a warrant for your arrest," the cop said. "Turn around and put your hands behind your back."

She did as they said. She heard the clicking of handcuffs and felt the steel plates cutting into her wrists.

"Got a search warrant too," the cop said.

While one cop held her at the door, the other cop began searching through the apartment. He ransacked her things and made a mess of the place. When he picked up the purple notebook, she cried out in pain.

"No," she said. "No. Please God no. Not that. Don't take that."

"This is evidence, ma'am," the cop said. He opened it up and began thumbing through. When he was done, he tossed the notebook onto the floor along with the rest of the trash and walked back over to where the other cop was holding her.

After awhile they turned her around and led her away. The second cop followed with a bagful of her things. Tears rolled down her cheeks. They marched her down the stairs and into the street toward the waiting prowler. People in black winter jackets had massed on the walk and the photographers leaned in and crowded in on her to take her picture and she walked through the whirring and flashing and tried to make herself numb to it all.

It was cold and windy in the brownstone shadows of Brooklyn, New York, and they were taking from her her life and they were taking it quicker than she had put it together, taking it away one piece at a time.

She felt a hand on her head and she closed her eyes and sat down in the prowler and hung her head and cried against herself. The prowler door was slammed shut and the car pulled away from the curb.

They booked her into a jail in the Brooklyn North precinct. They took away her clothes and inspected her as she stood there shivering like an animal. They suited her in an orange jumpsuit and brown flip flops. She lay on a bench in a filthy cell and listened to the buzzing of the light and the slamming of heavy metal doors. The doors clanged and clanged and the place labored on like a machine.

Days went by and food trays moved through the narrow passageways in the cell doors and then there was the clanging noise again. Lee Ann told herself that in the Land of Reckoning, the clanging was the only sound you'd hear.

CHAPTER SIXTY-FOUR

One day the doors clanged and she heard a sound familiar yet known to her alone: the clumsy shuffling of vagabond feet in Italian loafers without socks. The creaking of the leather and the tip-tap of the heel to toe was like music to her. She knew the steps. She had heard them so many times on the hardwoods, on the steps. She now heard them on the jailblock.

She looked up and saw his ragged face behind the bars. He was looking down like a man being led to a cell of his own. Then he looked up and saw her and looked into her eyes. He looked very tired. She looked at him up and down. Her eyes wetted up and her voice broke.

"You look like you've lost weight," she said.

He nodded. "You too," he said.

His skin was drawn tight against his face and his gray hair was starting to thin out a little, showing the pinkness of his scalp. He started to speak but she silenced him by reaching out for him. He took her tiny hand in his and held her palm against his cheek. She could see that he was crying too. He held his head down as if in shame and dried his eyes with his sleeves. Then he looked up at her and smiled.

⊨⊰⊹⊱⊨

"My life's over," she said.

"Ain't nothin over."

"Yes it is."

"Your life is just getting started. Trust me. This coming from a man who sees death's long shadow darkening onto him. I can see life and death clearly, darlin, because I can see with my own eyes the gulf dividing them. And the green valley below on both sides and the rocks and the river running through its center. Crossing it, now that's the son of a bitch."

"Stop it. Don't say that."

"Believe me darlin. I am saying goodbye to this world. I'm making the crossing. Just as sure as you're making the arrival. But I'm looking forward to the next world, whatever that is. Maybe somehow I can be a part of both of them at the same time. Maybe I already am. See that's the way things are ordered, darlin. Different flowers bloom and die in different seasons and that's just the way it is. I had my blooming time, now you have yours. There's not nothing you could do about it anyway. Whether you like it or not. But this is only the beginning for you. Really. I mean it."

"I don't think so."

"What did I say about the world rewarding the biggest liars?"

"I don't remember."

"You will remember before it's over and you will say that I was right."

"How do you know?"

"It's just something I know"

"You think so?"

"Yep."

"Based on what?"

"Faith."

"Faith? In what?"

"In God or whatever you want to call it."

"God?"

"Yeah."

"You don't really believe in all that, do you?"

"Are you surprised? I used to talk about God all the time."

"I thought it was just because you were sick. I thought it was part of the whole act. I thought you were just staring at the reality of death and hoping there was something more. Your books seem to mock any notion of God."

"My books just describe things. I trust God knows what he's doing. All my books stand for is that I don't know what he's doing and the results of his efforts are sometimes funny to me. That's all. Don't get me wrong. I don't know him. I don't pretend to know him. But I think he's out there. Somewhere, anyway."

"You don't go to church or anything."

"But I pray."

"You pray?"

"I pray, yes. I pray everyday. I say: Please God, let there be a God."

"I'm surprised, really," she said. "I thought you were a little too cynical for that. And I mean that in a good way."

"I didn't use to. When I was younger I rebelled against God. But I changed my mind after doing a month in a Spanish hospital for liver poisoning. I prayed a lot and it worked. So yes, I think a man can pray. Even if he isn't even sure exactly who or what it is he's praying to. You will see, darlin, but it'll be a long time till then. And that's alright."

"You're going to be okay," she said.

"No I'm not. But that's alright too. This ole body and mind have had plenty of life. What's a little death mixed in?"

"Stop saying that. You're going to be just fine. When I get out I'm going to stay with you and take care of you. Then you'll get better. I'll cook for you and pick up after you and make you live civilized again. I love you so much. . . . You'll see."

He looked away and blinked. Lee Ann could see the wetness in his eyes. He wiped them dry.

"The time I spent with you," he said.

His voice broke.

"I'd give back everything I ever wrote, everything I ever did. To have that time again. I go back there in my mind everyday. You see, I live there most of the time now. And I'll live there till the end. You will always be there with me. Whether you're there or not, darlin."

He looked at her.

"You see, darlin, your life happens in spells and flashes. I told you once. It's like looking at individual film slides under a light. The light shines on only one part of the film at a time, but the other parts are still there, even though they round into the darkness. But once, each frame shines brightly. Different friends, different places, different things. Like a maze of flytrap paper.

"And when it's almost over you think about things. You remember your favorite moments. The times you were good. When the world was an important place to be and you were one of the important people in it. When it just couldn't have gone on without you. That's what you remember and nothing else. The time in your life when you were most alive. All I remember now is the time I spent with you, darlin."

Lee Ann began crying again. She reached her arms out through the bars and touched Beau and held onto his hands.

"I'm so sorry I broke your heart," she said. "I'm so sorry. I'm so sorry."

Beau gave a sad smile. He winked at her.

"It's not right," he said. "Beautiful young girl like you stuck with a broken down old man."

"I love you," she said. "I love you so much."

"Oh stop it darlin. I'm not the lovable type."

"No, you're wrong. You are so wrong. . ."

"You're going to be a star again, darlin. There's going to be plenty of love for you. You just wait."

"I'm nothing without you."

"Yes you are."

"No, I'm not. I couldn't write a sentence without you. I'm nothing but an agent for your gift."

Beau reached through the bars and sealed her lips with his finger.

"I couldn't write a word until you showed up in my life. Not in ten years. It's been all drinking and moping around and looking out at the river and laying in front of the TV. There was nothing else for me. My life was over before you came into it."

"That's not true. You wrote five books. You won the Pulitzer."

"I ain't written nothin but my signature on royalties checks. Ain't done nothin but lay on the couch and drink whiskey. Listen to Mozart. That was before."

"Before what?"

"Before you, darlin."

"Before me?"

"Yeah. Before you."

"You started writing again because of me?"

"Every damn day."

"Really?"

"Really. The fire is back, darlin. It was gone for ten long years. I even forgot I ever had it. Forgot what it felt like when I had it. But then you showed up grifting on my back porch. I remember standing there and looking at the river and then turning back and seeing you there. The yellow sunlight on your pretty little face. Those little blue eyes lasering into me. You weren't nothing more than an abandoned little sawdrupe. So lost and alone and so full of love for the world.

"And when you kissed me and brought me into your heart, you recalled me to life. It came back to me that day. It came back for good, darlin. I even have me a new novel coming out in the fall."

Her eyes lit up.

"Really?"

"Yes ma'am."

"You're actually going to publish it and everything?"

"Yeah. How about that? My agent says it's going to be a big hit."

"I can't wait to read it."

"I think you'll like it."

"What's it about?"

"It's about this lost little diamond in a thicket of weeds."

"A diamond?"

"Yep. And all she wants is to be like the weeds. But she can't be like the weeds cause she ain't a weed. She's a diamond."

"That sounds so sweet."

"It's the best damned thing I've ever written."

"What's it called?"

"The Counterfeit Girl."

"The Counterfeit Girl?"

"Yeah. The Counterfeit Girl. It's dedicated to a friend of mine."

"Who?"

"Sweet little thing who reminded me that I won't no weed neither."

Lee Ann bent over and sobbed. Beau held onto her hand and lifted up her chin with a gentle touch of his fingers and looked into the watery lamps of her eyes. He spoke to her tenderly.

"First page says: Dedicated to Lee Ann Pickler, who carries with her my heart wherever she goes."

There was no sleep that night. There was only the darkness and the light coming in from the door slats and the pneumatic metal hiss and the rolling and closing of the gate.

She closed her eyes and felt it all roll through her body and she wondered what tomorrow might be like and the tomorrow after that and the tomorrow after that. After awhile it disappeared. The walls and the people guarding them. She closed her eyes and went on a journey to some eternal point far beyond dreams. What existed there flickered like lightning bugs in summertime.

South Carolina. A palmetto tree whose shape is illuminated by a silver moon. Home. Home.

All she could think of now were the words in the purple notebook. She had carried the words around with her from the hospital to the funeral home to the grave site and back home again. To Ravenel, to King Street, to Broadway. She had carried them over long spaces of open ground, traveling the land in search of a resting place, some seminal point of completeness where they could sleep forever in peaceful interment.

The words rode dusty gravel roads, climbed over the pedals and stems of bright funeral flora and appeared on the backs of eyelid screens as mismatched faces brightened by synapses crossing the unknowable horror and wonder of dream space.

They had passed through their own little part of time's endless channel and come to rest here on the floor of a Brooklyn jailhouse. They were no longer hers and hers alone. They belonged now to all of humanity that came before them and the present and future had no claim on them.

She held them in the darkness tightly against herself guarding their mystery. Writing them down meant that they were no longer just words. They were now part of some physical matter. They would be nothing but trembles in the historical record and every-one and everything that she had ever been or loved or dreamed would vanish from the earth and there would be nothing there from now on but her and her alone. One bright empty future, one solitary future, her future. The world spread out before her like a quilt.

She was no longer afraid of being alone or dying alone. Everyone died alone but in dying alone they all died together. Death itself was an illusion. It was nothing more than the gateway to what was to come.

The visions that haunted her were now divested of their pallor. They were now fading traces on a painted horizon outstretching the gray pasture of death. The dance was a dance, and she would dance in it like all the rest at the hour of her own appointed time.

They would be there waiting for her at the dance and would welcome her home. She would see them all again. They would all be there, standing around the firelight, waiting for her. Someday. She stared out into the space between that hour and this one.

When she left home, she wrote the words down and saw them there on the paper and it was clear to her that they were now a part of something else entirely. And who Lee Ann Pickler had been before was a person not capable of belonging to a world encom-passing the words and the physical matter now representing them.

She cried a long time that night and then she closed up the notebook and put it in her bag. The words were there to be carried with her from now until the end of time.

ACKNOWLEDGEMENTS

I'd like to thank my editor and friend, Jane Rosenman, for her tremendous assistance in helping to bring this book to life. I'd like to thank Wendy Sherman for her encouragement and for introducing me to Jane. I'd like to thank Clyde Edgerton, one of my literary heroes, for his advice and support. I'd like to thank Lee Lloyd for introducing me to Clyde. I'd like to thank my family, particularly my mom, for their unwavering belief in me. I'd like to thank my son, Jack, for being the light of my life and for inspiring me every day. Most of all, I'd like to thank Kelley for her help in conceiving and shaping this novel, and for her faith in its ultimate success.

ABOUT THE AUTHOR

Ryan McKaig is a novelist, short story writer, attorney, and former journalist. In addition to The Counterfeit Girl, he is also the author of Bull City Blues. He lives in Raleigh, North Carolina.